The tension between them had become unbearable

Involuntarily his gaze traveled over her. Her hair was in disarray. Her face ws devoid of makeup. Her jeans and blouse were worn and faded. For all practical purposes, she was the perfect image of an average housewife who'd put in a long day, but he knew there was nothing average about her.

"What do you want from me?" he asked, his voice half angry, half plaintive.

"No more than you want to give," she answered.

Sean sighed, leaned his head back against the chair and closed his eyes. A part of him wanted to yell at her. Not because she'd done anything wrong, he acknowledged, but because she simply was. Because she was a solution to all his problems when he shouldn't need a solution in the first place. Because she made him feel when he didn't want to feel.

ABOUT THE AUTHOR

Carin Rafferty was born and raised in Colorado and loves to write about the state that will always be her home. She claims she and her husband have gypsy feet, having lived on the West Coast and the East Coast and a few places in between. They currently reside in Tennessee with their four beloved cats.

FULL CIRCLE

CARIN
RAFFERTY

Harlequin Books

TORONTO • NEW YORK • LONDON
AMSTERDAM • PARIS • SYDNEY • HAMBURG
STOCKHOLM • ATHENS • TOKYO • MILAN

With love to DeeAnn Brewer,
for making dreams come true

Published November 1989

First printing September 1989

ISBN 0-373-16320-7

Prologue

An uncomfortable cramping sensation pulled Whitney Price from her restless slumber. She lay still, waiting for her heart to slow as she wondered if she'd just experienced a contraction.

If she had been awakened by a contraction, then it would eventually happen again. Nearly twenty minutes passed before it did, and she stared in consternation at the illuminated dial of her alarm clock. Her obstetrician, Dr. Sean Fitzgerald, had told her to call him at the first sign of labor, but she hated waking him in the middle of the night when the contractions were so far apart. Besides, it could be false labor. She wasn't due for another week. She decided to wait and see if the contractions continued before she disturbed him.

She sighed, closed her eyes and stroked her abdomen. The past nine months had been a living hell for her, and she had a feeling that even after she'd delivered this baby, things weren't going to get better. She blinked back tears as she thought about everything that had happened.

Nine months before, her father, Senator Thomas Price, and her fiancé, Duncan Wells, had been killed in an automobile accident. Less than a week later, she'd discovered that Duncan had embezzled a huge sum of money from her father's campaign funds. Thankfully she'd managed to borrow the money from her childhood friend, Simon Prescott, in time to cover up the scandal, and she'd had every intention of paying Simon back as soon as she put her father's affairs in order.

Then Whitney had learned that not only was everything her father owned mortgaged to the hilt, but his patio furniture company, Price Manufacturing, was on the brink of bankruptcy. She had no idea what Duncan had done with the embezzled funds, and even after selling everything but her home and the business, she hadn't been able to pay off all her father's debts, let alone her debt to Simon. She'd been convinced that she was as low as she could possibly go, that nothing else could happen to her. Then she'd discovered that she was pregnant.

Now she was about to give birth to Duncan's child—a child she would be giving up for adoption. She blinked frantically against another surge of tears. She didn't want to give up this baby that stirred with life within her womb, and she'd used financial problems as an excuse when those few people who knew about the pregnancy asked about her choice of adoption. But she knew her reasons ran much deeper and were far more elemental. They were based on her early childhood years before her mother's death.

She wanted this baby to have the best, and the happiest memories of Whitney's life had been when she'd belonged to a family unit. It was essential to her that this baby have both a father and a mother; that it have the sense of family that she'd lost as a child and had missed so desperately. Knowing she couldn't provide that, she would entrust it into the care of a couple who could. Thankfully Dr. Fitzgerald had referred her to an attorney to handle the legalities. It was a relief to know her unborn child's future was already secure, and she would always be indebted to her obstetrician for his help.

She suffered through a third contraction, but she still waited as she mulled over her feelings for the man. He'd always treated her with impeccable professionalism, but there was something about him that disturbed her. Whenever she went to see him, she sensed a leashed tension within him—a sense of expectancy—that she didn't understand, and which seemed to increase with each office visit. He was also constantly trying to tell her the names of the adoptive parents. Even the attorney was continually harping on the subject. But Whitney knew that she couldn't handle knowing the identity of her child's parents, and she'd signed a legal document stating that she refused to be apprised of their names. When she gave the baby away, it had to be a clean break. It would be the only way she could maintain her sanity.

Her thoughts were interrupted by the arrival of her fourth contraction. When it was over, she reached for the phone. She had promised to call at the first sign of labor, and four contractions in an hour had her convinced that this was not a false alarm.

1:00 a.m.

LONG YEARS OF PRACTICE had trained Sean Fitzgerald to wake instantly, and he had the telephone to his ear before it rang a second time. His pulse quickened as he listened to his answering service recite Whitney Price's name and number, and his hand was trembling when he put the receiver back into its cradle. He'd have to make two calls. One to Whitney ordering her to the hospital, and one to his partner, who'd agreed to take over his schedule when Whitney went into labor.

He glanced toward his wife, Margaret. Over the years she'd trained herself to sleep through his middle-of-the-night calls, and he was hesitant to disturb her. This was Whitney's first baby, and the labor would most likely be a long one. But this was very possibly the beginning of his and Margaret's dream. He gently shook her shoulder until she peered up at him sleepily.

"What is it?" she asked through a yawn.

"It's happening," he answered, grinning as he watched dawning realization widen her eyes.

"Oh, Sean, I can't believe it. We're finally going to have a baby!" She promptly burst into tears.

Sean laughed as he pulled her into his arms and held her close, knowing that her tears were of joy—an exhilarating joy he shared with her. Then he felt a pang of guilt for experiencing such elation over another woman's tragedy.

2:00 a.m.

"LOOK, LADY, you aren't going to have this baby in my cab, are you?"

"No," Whitney assured the worried-looking young man as he assisted her into the back seat of his taxi and closed the door.

"Well, I'll hold you to that promise," he muttered as he climbed into the front seat and gunned the engine. "I've had the classes, but I'm not eager to get any hands-on training. I look tough, but I assure you I'm faint at heart."

Whitney smiled wryly as he pulled away from the curb. She'd always considered herself fainthearted, too, but during the last nine months, she'd learned that she had an inner strength that would allow her to do whatever she had to.

She couldn't help the gasp that escaped when she experienced her worst contraction yet, and then she laughed when the cabdriver cast her a frantic look, swore under his breath and slammed his foot down on the gas pedal. They reached the hospital in record time.

3:00 a.m.

SEAN FORCED HIMSELF to smile before he walked into the labor room to see Whitney. He'd hoped to be able to admit her to one of the birthing rooms, knowing she'd be more relaxed in the informally furnished rooms than the conventional labor room. Unfortunately all three birthing rooms were occupied.

"The nurses tell me you're doing just fine," he said when she glanced toward the door.

She nodded and looked away from him, embarrassed by the fact that for the next several hours he'd be examining her body even more intimately than he had over the past several months. She also decided the man was far too attractive for his specialty, which only made her embarrassment worse.

"I still think you made me come to the hospital too early," she complained, knowing she sounded petulant, but right now she felt petulant.

He heard the accusation in her voice and shrugged. "It's better to be early than too late. Besides, I'm going to be acting as your coach, remember?"

She didn't respond, and Sean knew she was uncomfortable with his role as coach. But if everything went as planned, this was going to be his child, and he wasn't going to miss a moment of its birth. He only wished Margaret could be here to share it with him, but whenever he'd tried to tell Whitney that he and his wife would be adopting her baby, she'd refused to listen. He felt another pang of guilt as he wondered if he should have made her listen.

4:00 a.m.

"IS SOMETHING WRONG with the baby?" Whitney asked, unable to hide her fear as she watched Sean attach the fetal monitor to her abdomen.

"Absolutely not." He reached over and gave her hand a reassuring squeeze. "Trust me, Whitney. I'm not going to let anything happen to you or the baby. This is standard practice."

Whitney didn't know if he was telling her the truth, but she decided to take his words at face value. He was supposed to be the best, and she had to believe that.

5:00 a.m.

THE CONTRACTIONS were coming at ten-minute intervals, and had been that way since she'd arrived at the hospital. Whitney was already exhausted. She welcomed the cool cloth that Sean wiped across her forehead, and the chips of ice he placed against her parched lips. When another contraction hit, he gently stroked her abdomen and spoke soothingly to her as he coached her through the breathing techniques that were supposed to help her relax. She hadn't taken formal Lamaze classes, but Sean insisted that she meet with an instructor once a week so she'd know how to work with him. She'd resented his insistence at the time, but now she was thankful for it.

6:00 a.m.

WHITNEY MANAGED TO DOZE. Sean knew she wouldn't sleep long, and he took the opportunity to slip down to the waiting room to see Margaret. She looked up at him with an expression that was a mixture of excitement and fear.

"They're fine," he said before she could voice the question. "It's going to be a long labor, though. Why don't you go home and rest? I'll call you just before we go into the delivery room."

Margaret shook her head, tears welling in her dark eyes. "I have to stay. I feel I owe that girl this much."

"You owe her?" Sean asked with an indulgent smile. Margaret, at the age of twenty-six, was all of eighteen months older than Whitney, and he was amused at her constant reference to Whitney as "that girl."

"She's suffering through labor and will end up with nothing. I'm going to have a baby without suffering through anything. The least I can do is sit here and worry and wait and pray for her," she explained.

"Oh, Margaret," Sean whispered as he drew her up into his arms, wondering if there was a kinder, more unselfish woman in the world. When they'd discovered that she was sterile, it nearly destroyed her. He breathed deeply of the lemony scent that lingered in her dark brown hair. "I love you so very much, but you have to remember that I must try to convince Whitney to keep her baby. Legally, to avoid any conflict of interest I have to give Whitney every opportunity to change her mind, and morally, I could never take her child away if she really wants to keep it."

"I realize that," Margaret told him as she hugged him tight. "But no woman should have to go through this alone. So regardless of the outcome, I want you to get back into that labor room, treat that girl as if she were me, and I don't want to see you again until it's all over," she ordered, her determined expression unable to wipe out the innate sweetness of her features.

7:00 a.m.

THE CONTRACTIONS had slipped to every five minutes. Whitney stared at the clock, awaiting the arrival of each one. When Sean had first entered the labor room, she resented his presence; but now she welcomed his strong hands that massaged her legs, rubbed her back and stroked her brow and contracting abdomen. He'd also begun to ask her questions. Personal questions that she would never have answered, except that talking was preferable to staring at that damn clock waiting for the next wave of pain.

She told him about her mother's death when she was seven. She told him about her lonely life as Senator Price's daughter. She told him about meeting Duncan, and how he'd swept her off her feet. She confessed the terrible secret of the embezzlement and the monstrous debt she owed Simon. She sobbed over giving away her child, but kept insisting that it had to have a mother and a father, despite Sean's constant assurances that thousands of single parents raised their children quite successfully.

Through it all, Sean listened, and suddenly he saw Whitney's life as it had truly been. On the outside she appeared to be a princess. In reality she'd been more of a Cinderella, and he admired her even more for the courage that had brought her here. Many women caught in her position would have opted for abortion, but the one time he'd suggested it to her, she reacted vehemently.

"This child is not responsible for any of my problems, and I'm not going to deny it its life for my convenience," she'd said.

Now as he stroked her silken blond hair, gazed into her wide blue eyes and listened to her pour out her deepest secrets, fears and wishes for her child, his heart went out to her. A nagging voice of conscience said he should insist that she listen to him—that he should tell her that the baby would be his so she'd be reassured about its future. However, he knew that the emotional trauma of such an announcement at this stage of the game would not only be cruel, but dangerous. So instead of confessing the truth, he silently vowed that if she did go through with the adoption, he would give the child everything she dreamed it would have.

As the hours progressed, he found himself feeling Whitney's pain as if it were his own, and like Margaret, he felt he at least owed her this much.

Noon to 3:00 p.m.

WHITNEY'S CONTRACTIONS remained at five minutes apart. The pediatrician Sean had standing by confirmed that the baby was in no distress. His partner agreed to examine

Whitney and confirmed that, unfortunately, she was just undergoing a long labor. They gave her medication that provided her with a measure of relief, but the only true relief would be when she finally delivered the baby that was so reluctant to come out and face the world.

Sean continued to make her talk as a distraction from the pain, and he learned that she hated shoes—that she kicked them off and ran barefoot whenever she could. He learned that her favorite color was blue. That her favorite meal was pepperoni pizza. He listened to her confession of how she hated to work in an office; how she felt confined and smothered inside four walls. He learned that she loved to work in her prize-winning rose gardens and dreamed of someday owning a greenhouse where she could grow specialty roses.

By late afternoon, Sean knew everything there was to know about Whitney Price, and he admired her even more.

3:00 p.m. to 6:00 p.m.

WHITNEY WAS HOARSE from talking, and Sean filled the gap by talking about himself. He felt compelled to reveal himself as intimately to her as she'd done to him. He told her about the first baby he delivered as an intern, and how he was so awed by the experience that he changed his specialty from general surgery to obstetrics. He, too, confessed his favorite color, which was green; his favorite meal, which was lasagna; that he loved to ride horses and go on picnics; and hated to shave, but looked atrocious in a mustache and beard.

Despite the fact that she'd been in labor for eighteen hours, Whitney managed to laugh at his last confession as she mentally applied a bushy dark brown beard to his square jawline. His features were strong and rugged, but his tawny brown eyes were too soft—the melodic baritone rasp of his voice too compassionate. She decided that he wouldn't look atrocious, but more like a lovable teddy bear.

6:00 p.m. to 9:00 p.m.

WHITNEY'S CONTRACTIONS were now three minutes apart, but her cervix was still not fully dilated. Sean examined her frequently, and called both the pediatrician and his partner back in. They confirmed that everything was fine, but he wanted Whitney's labor to be over. He wanted her suffering to stop. Yet after getting to know her, he suspected that even when the physical pain was over, her emotional pain would continue for several years. He did what he could to provide her with a small measure of comfort.

9:00 p.m. to 11:00 p.m.

WHEN SEAN TALKED to Whitney about his wife, he was unaware that his face glowed. He didn't know how his eyes softened with his feelings for Margaret. He didn't hear the vibration of love in his voice, and he didn't realize that as he talked, Whitney stared at him with an expression that bordered on adulation.

When she began to cry, he didn't know it was because Whitney suddenly realized that the love she once shared with Duncan could not compare with Sean's love for his wife. That knowledge only increased the guilt she carried about this baby. A guilt that had been eating at her from the time she'd learned about her pregnancy, for only she knew the truth behind the child's conception. Only she knew how she'd manipulated events instead of letting them move forward naturally. Now she was paying for that duplicity, and would pay for the remainder of her life.

11:00 p.m.

"IT'S ALMOST OVER," Sean assured Whitney, holding her hand as the nursing staff wheeled her into the delivery room.

Whitney could barely open her eyes. She was so tired. Her throat hurt and her body felt as if it were being ripped apart. But Sean's voice crept through the haze of pain, and gave her the stamina she needed. It was almost over. All she had to do was hold on a little longer, and then she could sleep. God, she wanted to sleep.

Midnight

"COME ON, WHITNEY, one more push and we're through!" Sean encouraged as he caught sight of the head of the babe he'd been waiting for.

"I can't!" she cried out in exhaustion.

"Sure you can," he encouraged, unable to give her a reassuring touch and knowing he had to coax her through this with words. "Come on, Whitney. We've come this far together. Let's bring this baby into the world. Just one more push, and it'll be over. Do it for me. Give a push for me."

He'd asked her to do it for him. Right now, she'd do anything to please him. They'd shared so much; been through so much together in the past twenty-four hours. Except for her father, she'd never felt as close to another human being as she did to Sean Fitzgerald. She gathered her remaining strength and pushed.

"It's a girl!" he exclaimed moments later. "A beautiful, baby girl!"

Whitney wanted to collapse. Her mind and body begged for sleep, but she fought against the darkness as she pushed herself up higher to see her daughter. "Is she all right?"

"She's perfect!" Sean yelled with a laugh as the baby let out a lusty squall. "Absolutely perfect!"

Whitney extended a trembling hand toward the babe, but she didn't know if it was trembling because she was weak from her ordeal, or the emotional upheaval of seeing her daughter, the child who, from this moment on, would never belong to her again. Tears welled in her eyes. She *was* doing the right thing, even if it was tearing her heart out. She tried, but she couldn't contain her tears when Sean placed the baby into her arms.

"She's yours," he told her solemnly. "She's yours until the moment you sign those papers giving her up for adoption. Give yourself a couple of days to think about the consequences, Whitney, because once those papers are signed, she's going to be lost to you forever."

Whitney caressed her daughter's head, which was covered with a silken layer of baby-fine blond hair, and peered down into the tiny, screwed up face that was looking up at her through unfocused blue eyes. She counted all the child's fingers and toes, needing to reassure herself that everything was as it should be. Then she pressed the baby back into Sean's arms.

"She has to have the best," she whispered hoarsely. "She has to have the very best, and I can't give it to her."

Sean cuddled the child to his chest and blinked against the tears stinging his eyes as he gazed at Whitney's face. He'd never seen an expression that reflected so much grief, nor so much love, and he felt honored to have been given the opportunity to know this woman.

"She will have the best," he said hoarsely. "I promise you that. But you mustn't make your decision now. You've been through too much and you're too tired. You have to give yourself a few days to think about this."

Whitney nodded weakly, knowing that if she had a few days or a few weeks or a few years, she wouldn't change her mind. She'd made her decision, and it was the toughest decision she'd ever made in her life. She also knew it was her just punishment, for she'd challenged fate, and fate had picked up the gauntlet. It had given her what she wanted with one hand, and snatched it away with the other.

Sean, the pediatrician and the nurses were all gathered around the baby, and they didn't hear her whisper softly, tearfully, "I love you, Amy. Please have a happy life."

Then she collapsed and closed her eyes. It was finally over. But was it the end of the beginning or the beginning of the end of the nightmarish chain of events that had begun so many months ago? She prayed it was the latter as she let sleep overwhelm her, because she didn't think she was strong enough to handle anything more.

Chapter One

Sean hung up the telephone, muttered a low curse and sank wearily onto the sofa in the doctor's lounge.

"Something's wrong?" Bill Hughes asked.

"Everything's wrong," Sean replied as he closed his eyes and massaged the bridge of his nose with his thumb and forefinger. "You're a psychiatrist. Tell me how to make a three-year-old understand that I can't take her out for hot dogs as I promised, because I have to deliver a baby."

"Since a three-year-old has no concept of childbirth, you can't," Bill answered. "Why do you make promises you might not be able to keep?"

Sean glared at his longtime friend. Bill looked like an absentminded professor with his unruly salt-and-pepper hair and half glasses until Sean met his green eyes, which were studiously alert. "That was a low blow."

Bill shrugged. "Maybe. But it was a truthful one."

"Maybe," Sean muttered as he tapped his fingers impatiently against the worn leather cushion beside him. "I hate it when I have to disappoint Amy, but it seems as if every time I turn around I'm doing just that."

"So stop making promises."

"You make it sound so damn easy!"

"It is easy when you stop trying to be both a mother and a father, and that's exactly what you've been doing since you lost Margaret. Why don't you concentrate on being a father?''

''Because she also needs a mother,'' Sean said as he rose from the sofa and began to pace.

''So give her one.''

Sean stopped in the center of the room and raked his hand through his hair. ''I can't do that.''

''Why not?''

''Because mother equates with wife.''

''And you don't want a wife?''

He frowned at Bill. ''You know how it was between me and Margaret. It was so special. So perfect. She was a once in a lifetime love. Anyone else would be a disappointment.''

Bill's eyes narrowed in concern. ''Your wife has been gone for a year, Sean. You're still a young man, and you have a young daughter. You can't stop living simply because you lost Margaret.''

''I haven't stopped living.''

''Oh?'' Bill challenged. ''How many women have you dated in the past three months? When was the last time you did something just for yourself? Something that didn't revolve around Amy?''

''That's not fair, Bill,'' Sean defended. ''I haven't dated because it's only been a year since Margaret died, and I have a right to mourn. As far as Amy's concerned, I have very little free time, so I spend as much of it as I can with her. There's nothing wrong with that.''

''Normally I'd agree with you. But I'm your friend, and I see a pattern forming that worries me. You're trying to be all things to Amy, and it's humanly impossible. It's a vicious circle, and not a very healthy one for you or your daughter.''

''How in hell did we get into this conversation?'' Sean grumbled as he dropped back down on the sofa.

''I think it had to do with a little girl bursting into tears.'' Bill leaned toward him, his expression serious. ''You're a doctor with a busy obstetrical practice. Outside of giving up medicine, nothing is going to change that. So stop trying to be a superparent. Amy will survive, Sean.''

Sean gave a vehement shake of his head. ''I want more than survival for her. Amy is my life, and I'll do anything to make her happy.''

Bill leaned back and eyed him for a long, thoughtful moment. ''Even give up your memories of Margaret and find her a mother?''

Thankfully Sean was paged so he wouldn't have to provide an answer.

SEAN GASPED and nearly spilled his coffee when he turned to the business section of the newspaper and Whitney Price's photograph jumped out at him. The caption declared her to be ''Denver's Businesswoman of the Year,'' and he quickly set his cup aside and smoothed the newspaper against the top of the kitchen table so he could see her picture better beneath the light centered overhead.

The black-and-white image didn't do her justice, he decided. It had captured her beauty, but there was no way it could show the texture of her alabaster skin that stretched over her delicate, aristocratic features. There was no way it could reflect the silken highlights of her silver-blond hair. Nor could it display her quiet dignity and inner strength.

A remembered feeling of admiration for her welled up inside him. Outside of Margaret, he'd never known a braver woman. In the past three years he had often wondered what happened to her; after she walked out of the hospital, she'd changed doctors. A part of him was relieved that she had. Seeing her and knowing she was unaware that he had adopted her daughter would have been uncomfortable. But another part of him felt connected to her, almost responsible for her, which, he supposed, was normal after all they'd been through together during Amy's birth.

He scanned the newspaper article, which gave an accounting of her achievements within the business community, and Sean gave an impressed nod, deciding that for a woman who hated to work in an office, she'd certainly done a laudable job in turning around her father's failing company. He wasn't surprised. After all, he'd seen her indomitable determination and was convinced it would allow her to accomplish just about anything she set out to do.

He leaned back in his chair and sipped his coffee. It was after midnight and he was exhausted after his sixteen-hour day, but during the past year he'd found that he liked to sit in the kitchen late at night when the house was eerily silent. He glanced around the room, finding it comforting. His late wife's personality was displayed everywhere he looked. Margaret had loved this old Victorian monstrosity that had been her childhood home, and it showed from the cheerful yellow curtains at the window to the frilly place mats on the old oak table.

He cocked his head, suddenly alert and listening to a childish murmur echo through the intercom system. It connected every room in the house to Amy's bedroom. She couldn't even breathe loudly without being heard, and he smiled and relaxed as he listened to another murmur, realizing that his daughter was dreaming. He could visualize her small hands and feet twitching as she romped in her dreams. What did three-year-olds dream about?

Margaret would have said parks and zoos and puppy dogs and kittens. What would Whitney Price say? he wondered as he returned his gaze to the picture.

He finished off the remainder of his coffee, carefully folded the paper so he wouldn't crease Whitney's picture and tucked it beneath his arm. Then he walked upstairs to Amy's room.

As he'd imagined, her tiny hands and feet were twitching, and he lovingly pulled the covers she'd kicked away back over her before gently brushing the baby-fine strands of her silvery blond hair away from her rosy cheek. Though he knew he was prejudiced, he was convinced that she was the most beautiful little girl in the world. And now that

Margaret was gone, she was also the most important thing in his life.

He sat down in the rocking chair beside her bed and released a weary sigh. Until a year ago, his life had been perfect. He'd had a wife he loved to distraction and a daughter that they both adored. They'd had such wonderful dreams and plans for the future. Then Margaret died. The pain of her loss was almost as sharp now as it had been then, and Sean blinked against the sting of tears as his gaze drifted back to Amy.

When he'd first lost Margaret, he convinced himself that he could go on alone—that he could be both a father and a mother—but as Bill had pointed out just last week, it wasn't working. Though he'd brought in another partner and cut back on his patients, he still had a busy practice. His partners were carrying more than their share of the load, and that made him feel guilty. More often than not, Amy was in bed by the time he came home, and that made him feel even guiltier.

His housekeeper, Mrs. Wilkens, was a godsend, but she was not a replacement for a mother's love. Amy was becoming fretful and more demanding of both his and the housekeeper's time. Recently she'd started coming into his room in the middle of the night and crawling into bed with him just to be near him, and Sean knew she was lonely. He also knew she needed a mother who would be a constant stabilizing influence, but how could he possibly provide a mother, since he didn't want a wife?

He laid the newspaper on his lap and studied Whitney's photograph in the dim glow of the night-light, recalling how she'd sobbed about giving up her baby, but insisted that it was essential that her child have a set of parents, and suddenly he saw the solution to his dilemma. Who would be a better mother to Amy than her natural mother?

"It's crazy," he whispered, but his idea didn't feel crazy. It felt right.

Sean shook his head, still trying to convince himself that the idea wasn't viable, but for every objection his mind provided, his heart kept countering with the same answer: Whitney had wanted her child to have both a father and a mother. Would she agree to a marriage of convenience if it meant fulfilling that dream? There was only one way to find out. He'd just have to see her, but first he'd have to come up with a plan—a proposal that she couldn't refuse.

"With any luck, you're going to have a new mama very soon, sweetheart," he murmured as he stood and bent down to press a kiss to Amy's temple.

But when Sean finally had his plan developed and turned his car onto the wide circular driveway that led to Whitney's front door, he was flooded with doubts. The sprawling red brick mansion with towering white Grecian columns looked impregnable, and the grounds and formal gardens were so impeccably groomed that they didn't seem real. When he came to a stop, he slipped the gearshift into neutral and left the engine idling while he studied the formidable structure.

Once again he decided his idea was crazy. She'd been raised as a famous Senator's daughter and spent most of her life socializing with the crème de la crème of the nation's capital. She was president of a patio manufacturing company, whose stock was rising at a phenomenal rate, and had just been named Denver's Businesswoman of the Year. Why in the world would Whitney Price ever consider moving into his old Victorian house to play mother when she had all of this at her disposal?

He slipped the gearshift back into first, determined to drive away, but as he rested his foot on the gas pedal, his mind flew back in time. He could almost hear Whitney's voice as she'd confessed her loneliness as a child, and all the other confessions that had made him understand that her fairy-tale-like existence hadn't been a true reflection of her life at all.

He glanced back at the house and knew that if he'd come this far he had to take a chance. The worst that could happen would be that he wasted an hour of his time. The assertion didn't stop his hands from becoming clammy as he climbed from his car and approached her front door. It took him several minutes to dredge up enough courage to ring the bell.

THERE WERE DAYS, and then there were days. For Whitney, today had been one of *those* days. There had been no major disasters at the office for her to sink her teeth into, just a series of minor disturbances that were more mentally exhausting than any crisis. Who would ever believe that running a manufacturing company could be such a pain in the neck? She sighed wearily as she entered her back door, kicked off her shoes and wiggled her cramped toes, wishing it was already Friday instead of Wednesday.

She hated working in an office and always had. A structured schedule was in direct opposition to her impulsive nature. Go with the flow had always been her motto, but unfortunately she'd also been cursed with a deep sense of obligation that tied her to her father's company. She couldn't wait to sell it but it would be at least three more years before she had paid off Simon's loan. She wondered if those three years were going to drag by as slowly as the past three had.

Her secretary had handed her a copy of the newspaper article that declared her "Denver's Businesswoman of the Year" just before she left the office, and she felt a mixture of feelings as she laid the article on the breakfast counter next to her purse and scanned it.

She was proud of what she had accomplished since assuming the presidency of Price Manufacturing. Yet she couldn't help but feel that if the reporter, who'd written about her in such glowing terms, knew the truth behind why she'd taken over the business, she'd probably be run out of town on a rail.

It still amazed her that she'd been able to avoid a scandal. If the public ever discovered that her father's right arm and future son-in-law had embezzled nearly half a million dollars in campaign funds, all hell would break loose. So far, with Simon's help, she'd managed to keep the secret and she would forever owe him her gratitude. She sighed again as she sorted through her mail.

She'd just finished the chore and slipped out of her beige linen suit jacket when her doorbell rang. After hanging it on the back of the kitchen chair, she hit the intercom switch that serviced the front door.

"Who is it?" she asked.

"Dr. Sean Fitzgerald."

Whitney paled at the familiar name that echoed through the tinny speaker. For a moment, she was thrust back in time. The memory of pain wasn't as intangible as the sense of loss and despair that had never really gone away, and which, she suspected, never would.

"Whitney?" he said with concern, and she realized that several seconds must have passed.

She cleared her throat, but the nervous lump remained. "Yes, I'm sorry, Dr. Fitzgerald, but you caught me off guard. What can I do for you?"

"I'd like to speak with you if you have a few minutes."

Whitney's mind was filled with a myriad of responses, the major one of which was to tell him to go away. But if he was here, it must be important. Was it about the baby? She shook her head. It couldn't be about the baby, not after three years. He was probably involved in some fund-raising project at the hospital and wanted to use her father's name. Even though he'd been dead nearly four years, her father's reputation as a statesman lived on. In fact, Whitney did everything in her power to ensure that it did so. But if that was why Sean was here, why hadn't he called first?

"I, uh, just got home, and I'm in the middle of changing clothes," she told Sean as she frantically eyed the refrigerator, trying to think of something she could possibly offer as a refreshment. "Why don't you meet me on the south patio, right across from the garage? It's such a beautiful day that we can indulge ourselves in some fresh air while we talk."

"That's fine. Take your time. I'm not in any hurry."

"Good. I'll join you in a few minutes."

She released the intercom switch and raced to the refrigerator. There was, as she expected, nothing in it but an almost empty can of coffee and two dill pickles floating in brine—definitely no substitution for hors d'oeuvres. So coffee it was, she decided as she filled the pot with water.

To save money, most of the rooms in the mansion were closed off, and Whitney had moved her bedroom to what had formerly been the cook's room off the kitchen. Now, after plugging in the pot, she headed there, stripping off her clothes as she ran. Thank heavens the weather was good and she could entertain him on the patio. Otherwise she would have had to do some fast talking to get rid of him. Only Simon Prescott had been granted entrance into her home during the past three years, and only Simon knew how frugally she lived.

She donned slacks and a sweater and ran her brush quickly through her hair. Back in the kitchen, she realized that the doctor might not drink his coffee black, and she went into another panic because she didn't have a drop of milk or a grain of sugar in the house.

She grabbed the pot and started to dump it down the sink so she could make tea, but realized that he still might require milk and sugar. With a resolved sigh, she decided to take a chance on the coffee as she transferred it into the silver pot and placed the pot on a silver tray. The service was among the few items she'd held on to to uphold her image in just such an emergency.

Nearly ten minutes had passed by the time she walked to the French doors that led out onto the patio. Balancing the tray on her hip, she opened them.

"Here, let me help you," Sean said, turning toward her as he heard the door open.

"No, don't bother. I'm fine." She carried the tray to the low, white wrought-iron table that sat between two deep-cushioned redwood chairs that faced each other—all of them courtesy of Price Manufacturing. After setting down her burden, she turned to him, extending her hand. "It's been a long time, Dr. Fitzgerald."

"Yes, it has, and please call me Sean," he said as he accepted her hand. He held it longer than necessary as he studied her face. There was fear in her Nordic blue eyes, and he felt a twinge of guilt. By the time he was through, there was going to be more than fear reflected in their depths—there was going to be anger, confusion and God only knew what else. For a moment—a very brief moment—he almost turned and walked away, but Amy's image swam before him. "You changed doctors."

He hadn't meant for the words to come out as an accusation, but they had.

Whitney pulled her hand from his and glanced away in embarrassment. "I needed to forget." Before he could respond, she gestured toward the chair behind him and carefully lowered herself into the other.

He hadn't changed much, she thought, as she allowed herself to study him. There were a few, almost invisible, strands of gray mixed with the dark brown hair at his temples, and the laugh lines around his eyes and mouth had deepened. His body was as strong and lean and muscular as she remembered, and his navy-blue suit complemented the nut-dark richness of his complexion.

"Do you still drink your coffee black?" she asked, deciding to take the offensive as she leaned forward and lifted the pot.

"Yes," he answered with a frown, trying to remember when they'd ever discussed his coffee preferences. He couldn't recall the event, but decided it wasn't worth mentioning. "Thank you," he said instead as he accepted the cup she handed him.

She nodded, poured herself a cup and leaned back in the chair. After taking a sip, she said, "I read about your wife's death last year. I'm very sorry."

"Me, too."

She didn't miss the flicker of pain in his eyes and silently chided herself for bringing up the subject.

"So what brings you here?" she asked with forced cheerfulness. "Don't tell me that after all these years you've decided to take me up on the offer to tour my rose gardens."

His smile was slow in coming.

"Not exactly, but I wouldn't be averse to a tour. If," he said, his eyes following the line of her legs to the flagstones, "you think you can keep your shoes on long enough to handle the walk."

She knew he could see her bare feet wrapped around the legs of the chair, and she blushed. "I've always preferred to go barefoot."

"I know."

It was an acknowledgement of the intimate confessions she'd made to him in the labor room as he'd tried to distract her from the pain. Her blush deepened.

"How have you been?" Sean asked, wondering how he was going to bring up the subject of Amy. On the way over, he'd rehearsed several different ways to open the conversation, but now that he was here and actually facing Whitney, all of them seemed inadequate.

"Better than could be expected," she answered. "And you?"

"Under the circumstances, better than can be expected."

"Of course," she murmured, knowing that he was referring to the loss of his wife. She remembered him talking about her during that long labor and the love that had lit up his face. As she'd listened to him, she'd woven a fantasy about someday finding a man who would care that much for her. She took another sip of coffee in an effort to distract herself from such thoughts.

"How have you managed with your loan from Simon Prescott?"

She glanced up in surprise. She'd forgotten that she told him about the embezzlement and the loan. And suddenly her mind was filled with all the other confessions she'd made to him. He knew everything about her, she realized. With anyone else, she might have felt threatened by his knowledge, but she knew that she could never feel threatened by Sean Fitzgerald. Her secrets were safe with him.

"I've paid back half of it."

He arched a brow. "I'm impressed, but what did you have to give up to pay back that much money in such a short time?"

"Everything," she said with a rueful smile. "I'd give my front teeth to bite into a steak."

His laughter was spontaneous, rich and deep. "If you did that, you wouldn't be able to bite into a steak."

"I suppose I wouldn't." She leaned forward and set her cup on the table. Then she sat back and eyed him curiously. "So why *are* you here?"

Sean shifted uncomfortably. When he'd seen her picture in the paper, she'd looked professional and in control. Just like a businesswoman of the year. But right now she looked vulnerable. Just as vulnerable as she'd looked in the labor room, and as he took note of the wariness reflected in the depths of her eyes, he realized he was going to hurt her.

He hated it, but he hated the thought of Amy being alone more. She needed a mother. A mother who'd love her as completely as Margaret had. He told himself that Whitney would give Amy that kind of love. After all, he'd heard the despair in her voice and felt her tears against his chest when she cried about giving up her daughter. He also knew that the woman sitting in front of him was not happy. That she would never be happy behind a desk or confined to an office, despite the accolades in the newspaper. He could give her back her daughter and the money to pay off her debt to Simon Prescott. He'd even finance the greenhouse she said she'd like to open. In return, Amy would have a mother, and he wouldn't have to live in a state of constant worry and guilt.

Instead of answering her question, he asked, "Have you ever wondered what happened to your daughter?"

It hurt. Really hurt. But Whitney managed a soft, "No."

"Liar," he chastised just as softly. Before she could reply, he reached into his breast pocket, pulled out a Polaroid snapshot he'd taken only hours before and tossed it onto the table.

Whitney stared down at the photograph, wondering if she'd ever be able to breathe again. He didn't have to tell her who the child was; she could see her own face peering out at her. A modern-day replica of her own baby pictures. Tears welled in her eyes, but she blinked them back. She'd written the last line to this chapter of her life three years ago. It was over. Finished. She wasn't going to cry.

"Why are you doing this to me?"

He grimaced inwardly at the raw pain in her voice and gently said, "Because she needs you."

"Oh, God." Whitney had promised herself that she wouldn't cry, but the tears came anyway. They hurt as badly as they had the day she'd walked out of the hospital, leaving her baby behind.

"Whitney, don't," Sean said as he rounded the table, knelt beside her and touched her arm. He'd expected anger and confusion. He'd prepared himself for them. He hadn't expected the tears, and they tore him apart. "Don't," he repeated.

"What's wrong with her?" she asked, clutching his lapels as every nightmare she'd ever had surfaced. Every day for the past three years she'd prayed that her daughter was healthy and happy, and now Sean was saying she needed her. Was she ill?

At first Sean didn't understand her question, but realization came as he saw the terror in her eyes and his mind replayed his words. Inwardly he cursed himself as a fool. He wasn't handling this well at all.

"She's fine," he assured. "There's nothing wrong with her."

Whitney's grip relaxed as she searched his face. He wasn't lying to her. She dropped her hands back into her lap and returned her gaze to the picture.

"Then why are you here?" she whispered hoarsely as she swiped at her tearstained cheeks. "I don't understand."

"Because Margaret and I adopted Amy," he said as he sat back on his heels. "Now I've lost Margaret, and Amy needs a mother. Her real mother, and only you fit the bill."

A shuddering sob passed through Whitney that emphasized her shock, and her head began to spin. Sean had adopted her baby? Why? But did she want to know why he'd adopted her child, or why he hadn't told her?

"Whitney," Sean said in concern when she became so pale that even her lips were chalk white.

"Don't!" she exclaimed harshly when he touched her arm again, and she jerked away from his hand. "Just don't touch me."

Sean withdrew his hand, but his eyes were still centered on her face. She dragged her hands across her eyes and shook her head in denial, but though her mouth opened and closed several times, she didn't utter a word.

The minutes ticked by, minutes in which every breath she heaved into her lungs, Sean repeated involuntarily. He could feel the pain emanating from her, battering against his own senses. His mind raced, seeking words to help her, but if he'd felt inadequate before, he now felt helpless.

He shouldn't have come here, he acknowledged. But what choice did he have? He'd promised himself that he'd give Whitney's child everything she wanted it to have, and without Margaret he simply couldn't do that. In order to fulfill Whitney's dreams, he had to have her help.

When she drew in still another labored breath, he said, "Whitney, I'm sorry. I know this has been a shock, but there wasn't any simple way to tell you."

Dear God in Heaven, was he right about the hurt! she thought as she rested her head against the back of the chair and gazed up at the clear blue sky. Her body felt numb, but her mind was on fire. Sean had her baby, but why? And what was all this talk about needing a mother, and why...?

She couldn't deal with the questions, and she closed her eyes, trying to gain control of her emotions, to regain her equilibrium, but her mind was refusing to cooperate. It insisted on providing her with the image of the first and last time she'd seen her daughter. It had been in the delivery room, and Sean was hovering over them. He must have known then that he was going adopt her daughter. He must have known, but she shook her head, refusing to accept that. He wouldn't have hidden the truth from her like that— he *couldn't* have. Not after all they'd been through together!

But if that was true, then how had it happened? Too frightened to voice the question, she opened her eyes and let them stray back to the picture. She could feel Sean's eyes on her and knew she had to say something. Finally she asked, "You kept the name I gave her?"

"Yes." He wished she'd look at him. He wanted to see her expression, and the look in her eyes. "Margaret looked it up in a book of baby names. Amy means beloved, and she was to us. She was the child we could never conceive together. Margaret couldn't have loved Amy more if she'd been her own daughter."

When she didn't respond, he continued with, "You're going to love Amy. She's beautiful, and bright, and spoiled rotten. But it's a nice kind of spoiled. The kind of spoiled that makes you want to hug instead of scold."

His voice was wrapping around her. His description of her daughter was wrapping around her. Whitney forced herself to shake her head, and thus, break the spell he was weaving. She'd given up her child three years ago and reconciled herself to that fact. That never took away the emotional pain she'd carry around for the rest of her life, but it helped her keep her sanity.

She rose from her chair and walked over to the edge of the patio, staring at the blooming rose gardens in the distance. She maintained the rolling lawns and gardens to perfection. On the outside, Senator Price's home was as beautiful as ever. Only she and Simon knew that it was dead on the inside. As dead as she felt at this moment.

She wanted to ignore Sean's words—wanted to send him away and tell him never to come back. But he'd brought her word of her daughter and said she needed a mother—her real mother, and only she, Whitney, fit the bill.

She rested her hand against her abdomen as she remembered the first time she'd felt her child stirring with life. In the weeks and months that followed, whenever the baby was extremely active, she'd sat in a rocking chair stroking her abdomen, reciting children's stories and singing lullabies. On those days she used to pretend that she was a mother, but she knew it wasn't true.

You didn't become a mother by giving birth. You earned the title by stumbling out of bed for middle-of-the night feedings. By walking the floors when a bout of colic struck. A mother changed diapers, and washed clothes, and listened to her daughter laugh her first laugh—watched her take her first step. She'd missed all of that and so much more. Another tear rolled down her cheek, and the pain that gripped her heart was almost crippling in its intensity.

Sean rose to his feet when Whitney walked across the patio, and he watched her intently as she stared off into the distance. His gaze followed her hand as it splayed across her abdomen. He knew instinctively that she was remembering her pregnancy, and his own memories stirred. From the moment he'd learned there was a possibility that her child was going to be his, he'd followed her pregnancy with the eagerness of any expectant father. He'd never forget the thrill he felt when he first heard Amy's heartbeat, nor the exquisite sensation of that first kick against his hand during a routine office visit.

He raised his eyes to Whitney's face, and his heart skipped a beat as he watched a bittersweet smile curve her lips and a tear roll down her cheek. He could feel her sadness, and it touched him in a place deep inside that he'd never known existed. He walked toward her, desperately needing to take that sadness away, but when he reached her he didn't know what to say.

"Marry me." The words came out impulsively, and though marriage had been his long-range goal, he'd meant to ease her toward it gradually, subtly. He'd planned it all so carefully, and now he'd blown it.

"What did you say?" Whitney gasped as she slowly turned her head and discovered Sean standing directly behind her.

He gripped her upper arms, turned her toward him and shook her lightly, as if trying to gain her complete attention. He needn't have bothered. He already had it. "I want you to marry me."

Marriage? To Dr. Sean Fitzgerald? The man who knew everything about her there was to know? Impossible!

"If you'll marry me, I'll pay off whatever you owe Simon Prescott," he said in a rush, fearing that if he paused, she'd never let him get the rest of his words out. "In return, you'll be Amy's mother. You'll have your daughter and your freedom. I'll even finance the greenhouse you've always dreamed of. I'll give you anything within my power if you'll just say yes."

Whitney was amazed at the calm that washed over her instead of the fury she should have felt. The man had just arrived on her doorstep and informed her that he'd adopted her daughter, and now he was offering to buy her hand in marriage. Did he really think she was that shallow after all they'd shared in the labor and delivery rooms? The realization that he must or he wouldn't have offered the money hurt her badly.

She regarded him for a long moment before saying, "Let me get this straight. If I marry you, you'll pay off my debt?" He nodded. "All of it?" He nodded again. "Are you that rich?"

"You've heard of Fitzgerald Chemical?"

Heard of it? Oh, yes, she'd heard of it. The Fitzgerald Chemical fortune rivaled Simon Prescott's. "You're them?"

"A part of them," he admitted. "My father's president, my mother's vice president and I have a handful of brothers and sisters who hold numerous other titles. I guess you could say that I'm a silent partner."

She should have such a silent partner, she thought as she pulled away from his hands. Her legs felt rubbery, out of control and she returned to her chair and sat down.

Dreams stirred as her gaze returned to the picture of her daughter. Dreams in which she'd wake up and find out that everything was different. Dreams where her father was alive and laughing, where she and Duncan were happily married, and where they all shared a baby girl named Amy. But they were only dreams, and Sean Fitzgerald didn't fit into any of them.

She picked up her coffee cup and drained it before saying, "No."

"No, what?" Sean asked as he moved back to her side, even though he knew she was turning down his proposal.

"I'm not going to marry you."

"Why not?"

"Because that chapter of my life is over, and there is no way I'm going to reopen it."

The determination in her voice and her closed expression told Sean that it would be fruitless to argue. He had expected this reaction and had come prepared for it.

"Well, I guess that's that." He withdrew a heavy, cream-colored envelope from his pocket and dropped it in front of her.

Whitney eyed the envelope warily, but when she glanced up to ask him what it was, Sean was gone. Her gaze drifted toward the picture of the silver-haired cherub that had come from her womb, and at that moment, she hated Sean Fitzgerald. She hated him for his kindness and support three years before. She hated him for adopting her baby. And most of all, she hated him for offering her money when all he would have had to do was offer her her daughter.

With a trembling hand, she lifted the photo and dropped it onto the silver salver that held the coffeepot before she opened the envelope. Inside was an invitation to Saturday afternoon tea. Below the boldly scrawled words was the childish block-printed signature of a toddler named Amy.

Whitney drew her feet up into the chair, buried her face against her knees and began to sob three years' worth of guilt and anguish.

Chapter Two

Whitney turned onto the street where Sean lived. Considering the doctor's connection with Fitzgerald Chemical, and the fact that half of his office practice was composed of the very wealthy, she had expected him to live in an exclusive neighborhood. To her surprise, his address wasn't even a moderately expensive one. The houses that lined the street were a good hundred years old, and the towering elms that shaded them had to be at least as old. If she'd been asked to assess the economic standing of the community, she would have said mid-middle income.

When she parked at the curb in front of his house, she allowed herself a moment to study it. It was a huge Victorian structure with a wraparound front porch. It was painted white and trimmed in bright yellow. She often saw houses with character, but she'd never seen one that seemed to smile before.

My daughter is in there! she thought, but then shook her head. *Sean's* daughter was in there. She had to remember that distinction at all costs.

She still wasn't certain why she'd accepted the invitation to tea. The R.S.V.P. requested regrets only, and she'd spent the past three days telling herself that she was going to decline. But the days and hours had slipped by, and before she knew it, it was time to go. Since the invitation specifically stated casual—with jeans in parentheses, her normal Saturday attire—she had to do nothing more than sling her purse over her shoulder. She refused to curl her hair or put on makeup. If Sean Fitzgerald wanted casual, he was going to get it.

She hadn't understood the directions that instructed her to follow a yellow brick road until she neared the front porch. A brightly painted yellow brick path joined the sidewalk and disappeared down the side of the house. Enchanted, she followed it, stopping in stunned surprise when she reached the backyard and discovered that the bricks led to a small Victorian replica of the main house. It was evidently a child's playhouse, but it was large enough for an adult to stand in. She shook her head in disbelief before approaching it.

As she stepped onto the porch, a childish giggle sounded behind the door. Whitney almost panicked and ran. The child who'd stirred with life in her abdomen for so many months was in there. The baby who'd been so reluctant to come out and meet the world that she had fought for twenty-four hours to make her do so. Her hand was trembling, but she managed to rap her knuckles against the door.

She didn't even have time to pull her hand away before the door flew open and a tiny, silver-haired girl dressed in dungarees and a T-shirt with a bright blue teddy bear on the front yelled, "Hi!"

Whitney caught her lower lip between her teeth as she fought against tears. She'd promised herself that if she came, she wouldn't cry, and she had to curl her hands around her purse strap to keep from reaching out for Amy with the desperation she felt inside. She released her lip and murmured, "Hi, yourself."

The little girl placed a hand over her mouth as she giggled. Then she said, "My name is Amy, and I'm three years old."

It took Amy a minute to figure out how to hold down her little finger with her thumb, but she finally mastered the trick and stretched her hand toward Whitney.

"Dear me, you're really a grown-up young lady, aren't you?" Whitney asked as she stared at the small hand that was covered with something that looked suspiciously like jam.

"Amy, remember your manners, and invite Miss Price in," Sean drawled from inside the playhouse, and Whitney's head shot up in surprise.

She'd been so entranced with the child that she hadn't even noticed him until now. Gone was the professional, white-coated doctor she'd come to know so well. In his place was a well-muscled, chambray-and-denim-clad man.

She switched her attention to Amy who was gazing up at her with a puzzled frown.

"I'm sorry, Amy," she said, realizing the child had been speaking. "What did you say?"

"Would you please come in and have tea with us, Miss Price?"

Her concentrated expression told Whitney that the line had been carefully rehearsed, and she wanted to bend down and hug the child to her chest. She actually bent her knees to do so before she managed to stop herself. If she touched her daughter, she might not be able to let her go.

She forced herself to stand upright and said, "I would love to have tea with you, however, I want you to call me Whitney, not Miss Price, okay?"

Amy glanced toward her father, as if seeking approval. When he nodded, she grinned. "'Kay. Let's eat."

Sean chuckled as he watched her race toward the table that sat in the playhouse. "As you can see, her manners extend as far as the cookie jar."

"She talks so well," Whitney said when he stepped aside and gestured her inside.

"Margaret spent a lot of time working with her." He closed the door. "Amy was talking in complete sentences by the time she was two. She's very bright, and I expect her to do wonderful things with her life."

Whitney knew it was dangerous, but she couldn't help the feeling of pride that swelled within her. This adorable, precocious toddler was a part of her. She'd never felt the loss as completely as she felt it at that moment.

"I hope you like chocolate chip-cookies smothered with strawberry jam. I'm afraid that's Amy choice for today's menu," Sean muttered good-humoredly.

Whitney was about to tell him she was allergic to strawberries, but when her gaze drifted toward Amy, the confession wouldn't come out. Instead she returned his grin. "Well, as I've always said, when in Rome."

He chuckled as he took her arm and led her to the table.

Whitney sat in the chair he pulled out for her. Since it was child-sized, her knees rose above the tabletop, and she watched Sean curiously, wondering how he was going to manage with his much longer legs. Evidently he was an old hand at tea parties, she decided, as she watched him lift a pillow from the corner and drop it to the floor. He sat down on it, folding his legs Indian fashion and shaking his head as he watched his daughter run her finger through the jam on top of one of the cookies and then lick it off.

"Amy, we're using proper manners today, remember?"

"Oops," the little girl said, clapping her hand to her mouth and looking toward Whitney.

Whitney, after looking out of the corner of her eye to assure herself that Sean wasn't watching, wrinkled her nose and gave Amy a long, slow wink that made the child giggle.

She accepted the unmarked cookie that Amy handed her on plastic china, and then the miniature cup of tea that the child expertly poured. When she glanced toward Sean, he was regarding her with challenging amusement as he raised his eyes from the cookie to her face. She took a healthy bite of the cookie, praying that her allergic reaction wouldn't hit until she got back home.

"Mmm. Delicious," she sighed dramatically as she washed down the deadly jam with a sip of highly sugared tea. "Do you have tea parties often?"

"Every Saturday," Amy answered as she passed her father his cookie and tea before serving herself. "Daddy says it's a tra...tra..."

"Tradition," Sean finished for her.

She grinned happily. "Yeah, it's that. That means we do it all the time."

She gulped her cookie down in two bites, and reached for another one.

"Find out if your guest wants more first," Sean chided.

"Oh, yeah," Amy said, turning her bright blue eyes on Whitney. "Want some more?"

One strawberry jam-covered cookie would have Whitney popping antihistamines and sneezing all weekend. She shook her head. "I'll finish my tea first."

"Coward," Sean mumbled as he accepted another haphazardly prepared cookie.

"A guest's privilege," she mumbled back, feeling inordinately pleased when he gave her a conspiratorial grin.

Amy said, "When we have a tea party, we're supposed to share con...con..."

"Conversation," Sean provided again.

"Yeah," Amy agreed with another happy grin. "Do you do that, Whit...Whit..."

"Whitney," Whitney finished this time.

She expected another "yeah," and was surprised when Amy screwed up her face and carefully tried the name. "Whit-nee." Then she giggled and stretched out her leg. "It's like knee," she said, patting her dungarees.

"Yeah, it sure is," Whitney said in a voice clogged with emotion. Once again, she had to remind herself that she wasn't going to cry, but holding back her tears was getting harder by the minute. Was there anything in the world that hurt worse than this? She didn't think so, and she let her gaze pore over her daughter's face, drinking in the sight of every curve and hollow. "And yes, I do share conversation. What would you like to talk about?"

Amy shrugged and stuffed another cookie into her mouth. "Don't know."

"Don't know your manners," Sean grumbled. "You aren't supposed to talk with your mouth full."

"Sorry," she muttered before glancing back at Whitney.

It took Whitney a moment to realize that she was trying to mimic her wink when she wrinkled her nose and closed both of her eyes. Whitney's laughter warred with her tears, but the laughter won out.

"You're not supposed to encourage her," Sean said.

"I can't help myself," Whitney replied as she wiped at the tears of laughter on her lashes. "She's adorable."

"She's spoiled rotten," he muttered, casting his daughter a mock glare that sent her into infectious giggles that soon had them all laughing.

"Do you have any little girls like me?" Amy asked Whitney as she propped her elbow on the table and rested her head in her palm.

Whitney cringed at the thought of the strawberry jam that would have to be washed out of her hair, and then found herself longing to perform the chore. "No, I don't have any little girls."

"How come?"

"Because I'm not married, so I don't have a daddy to share them with," she answered.

She was unaware of Sean's scrutiny as he half listened to them exchange dialogue. They were talking about dolls, one of Amy's favorite topics, and if the gleam in Whitney's beautiful blue eyes wasn't a trick of the light, he'd guess she'd never outgrown dolls herself.

As he had so many years ago, he sensed innocence within her, and wondered how she managed to hold on to it. He'd been surprised when a twenty-four-year-old Whitney informed him that her only lover had been her fiancé. He'd been surprised because he knew that she'd lived with her father in Washington, D.C., for several years. Somehow the fast-moving world of politics and virginity didn't mesh in his mind, but he had believed her confession.

And now, three years later, he had a feeling that twenty-seven-year-old Whitney was still as sweetly innocent as the young woman he'd come to know so well during her pregnancy. It only convinced him that he was right in trying to reunite her with her daughter.

"Daddy!" Amy exclaimed as she threw herself into his arms, her small hands burrowing into his hair. "You aren't hearing me!"

He ignored the squishy, uncomfortable feeling of strawberry jam against his scalp, and hugged his daughter's sturdy body close. "Guilty as charged. Does this mean you're going to replace me with a better host?"

"I don't like ghosts," Amy whispered seriously, as she leaned back in his arms and peered up at him wide-eyed.

"Not ghost, honey," he said, hugging her close again. "Host. A host is a person who entertains your guests, and I haven't been very entertaining, have I?"

"No," she answered, even though he could tell from her expression that she wasn't quite certain what entertaining meant. He chuckled, deciding he liked her style. When in doubt, accept the worst. A man had no choice but to climb up from there.

"What were you saying that I wasn't hearing?"

"Whit-nee says she has to go, and she wants me to walk her to her car. Can I?"

Sean glanced toward Whitney in confusion. She was leaving this soon? Why? He searched her face, and was concerned to see that her eyes looked swollen, as if she'd cried for hours and hadn't quite recovered. He was certain the swelling hadn't been there when she arrived, but he'd been so glad to see her that he had to honestly admit that he hadn't looked at her that closely.

"Why don't we both walk her to her car?" he suggested.

"'Kay," Amy agreed.

Whitney retrieved her purse as Sean pushed himself to his feet and gathered Amy into his arms. They were silent as they walked to the curb.

When they reached her car, Whitney turned toward father and daughter, and Sean definitely saw the shimmer of tears in her eyes as she said, "I had a wonderful time, Amy. I hope you'll invite me back again."

"Sure," Amy said, ingenuously opening her arms for a hug.

Sean felt Whitney's hesitation, but then she stepped forward and wrapped her arms around her daughter, heedless of the strawberry jam that transferred to her T-shirt and into her hair.

"I want a kiss," Amy demanded, and Sean smiled when Whitney complied, knowing from personal experience that one of Amy's sloppy sticky kisses was often less than desirable.

But Whitney didn't wipe her lips when she pulled away. Instead she tugged on Amy's hair and said, "You be a good girl, and I'll see you soon."

"'Kay," Amy said as she wrapped her arms securely around her father's neck. "Next time, bring me a present."

"Amy!" Sean exclaimed in horror.

Whitney just laughed. "Next time, I'll bring you a present."

"A big one," Amy ordered.

"Gigantic," Whitney agreed with a smile. "You take care of your daddy, okay?"

Amy leaned back in her father's arms and peered at him as if trying to decide if he needed taking care of. Then she nodded. "'Kay."

Before Sean could speak, Whitney climbed into her car, started it and pulled away from the curb. As he watched her drive down the street, he frowned. She was upset, and he'd caused her distress. This visit had to have been one of the hardest things she'd ever done in her life, and Sean had a feeling that she would be in tears before she got home. He also knew he had to check on her.

"Did you like Whitney?" he asked his daughter as he carried her toward the house.

"Uh-huh," Amy said as she yawned and rested her head against his shoulder. "She's nice."

Sean smoothed his hand over her hair. "Yes, she is. She's very nice."

WHITNEY SNEEZED, cursed and sneezed again. The strawberry jam had taken its toll. With a groan, she popped another antihistamine into her mouth, telling herself that the jam had been worth it. Seeing Amy had been worth it.

"'Kay,'" seemed to be Amy's standard response, and Whitney swiped at the tears that welled in her eyes. Right now, she needed one of those "'Kays." In fact, she needed a lot of them. She also needed those sturdy little arms around her neck, and one of those wet kisses that tasted of jam and fresh little girl.

"Damn you, Dr. Sean Fitzgerald," she muttered as she washed the antihistamine down with water. "Damn you to hell."

And yet, despite the ache in her soul, she wasn't angry with Sean. Today he'd given her a piece of life that she'd never dreamed she'd be able to experience. He'd let her meet Amy, and let her look at that smiling house that said, "Come in and be happy like we are."

Happy. God, was she ever going to be happy again? she wondered as she rolled her eyes plaintively toward the ceiling in her bathroom. Here she was, the president of a corporation, drawing a top executive's salary, and she lived like a bum searching for his last meal. Outside of the few hundred dollars she absolutely had to keep in order to survive, every penny of her monthly check went to Simon, despite his objections. He kept telling her that she could take the rest of her life to pay back his loan.

But she didn't want to spend the rest of her life paying it back. She had it all worked out in her mind. In another three or four years, she'd have the loan paid off and she could sell the business and start a new life. But now Sean Fitzgerald had entered the picture. He was offering her her daughter, and the chance to pay off the loan. She'd never accept his money, but regaining Amy was enticing. In fact, it was more than enticing—it was a dream come true.

"Oh, God, what am I going to do?" she moaned as she sneezed, pulled a tissue from the pocket of her robe and blew her nose.

Marriage to her meant commitment. It meant living together, loving together and sharing together. Could she commit herself to a marriage of convenience just to have her daughter?

She shook her head in despair. She'd always dreamed that she'd marry for love, but look what love had gotten her. Duncan's betrayal had almost destroyed her. She'd believed that he was loyal to her father and devoted to her. When she learned about the embezzlement, her first reaction was denial. But proof was proof, and no denial would change that.

If she could have found a reason why he took the money, she might have been able to accept it. But the private investigator she'd hired came up with nothing. There was no hint that Duncan had been involved in gambling or drugs. There was no indication of involvement with other women, or even something as sordid as blackmail. The private investigator concluded that it had simply been greed, and he told her that the money was probably sitting in a Swiss bank account and would never be recovered. Then he'd handed her his bill.

She went into the kitchen to fix herself a cup of tea. As she sneezed several times in rapid succession, she decided that if she ever joined Amy Fitzgerald for another tea party, she'd bring along the dessert. And yet, she felt that this physical suffering was appropriate when her mind was in such pain.

She'd made her choice about adoption clearly and logically, and never regretted it in the true sense of the word. She'd given birth to a child and chosen the best life for it. It wasn't her fault that Sean's wife had died. It wasn't her fault that Amy was being raised without a mother. And, she admitted as she poured the boiling water into her cup, Sean did appear to be a good father.

How many fathers shared a traditional Saturday afternoon tea party with their daughters? Certainly not hers. She'd adored her father, and he'd adored her, but she was lucky if she saw him two or three times a week. He'd always told her that quality time was better than quantity time, and even though she basically agreed with him, it hadn't stopped the loneliness—the loneliness that Amy would soon be feeling and wouldn't have a mother to buffer it. She gripped her teacup until her knuckles were white.

The ringing of her doorbell broke into her thoughts, and she decided to ignore it. It was only early evening, but she was dressed for bed. The antihistamine was already making her drowsy, and if she could just stop sneezing for five minutes, she'd be fast asleep.

When the doorbell rang a second time, she shivered with an ominous premonition. Outside of the paperboy and an occasional solicitor, no one ever came to her door. Only Sean had dared invade her domain, and she knew it was he as certainly as she knew she was about to sneeze again.

Her temper flared. Why wouldn't the man leave her alone? She had enough problems in her life without dredging up the past. The third ring of the doorbell made her temper explode, and she strode through the house determined to send him away.

"My word, Whitney, what happened to you?" he exclaimed when she flung open the door. He stared at her swollen eyes with concern.

"Strawberry jam," she automatically answered as she glared at him. "I'm not entertaining this evening, so stop leaning on my doorbell. In fact, I want you to leave and never come back," she said as she tried to slam the door.

But Sean wasn't that easily thwarted, and he pushed his way inside. "Strawberry jam?"

"I'm allergic to strawberries. Now please get out of here."

"Dammit, why didn't you say something?" he asked, ignoring her order to leave and closing the door behind him.

"And ruin Amy's tea party?" she shot back.

Sean felt a giddy sense of accomplishment. She had to have known the consequences if she ate that cookie, but she ate it anyway. Such maternal sacrifice had Margaret written all over it. She, too, would have eaten the strawberry jam without blinking an eye just to see Amy smile. His heart did a little jig when he realized he hadn't been wrong about Whitney. She was going to be a wonderful mother.

But as he glanced around the living room, his elation gave way to disbelief. The only piece of furniture in the room was a baby grand piano.

"What happened to your furniture?" he asked.

"What do you think happened to it? I sold it," Whitney replied sullenly.

"Sold it? Why?"

"Because I needed the money," she snapped. "How else was I supposed to pay my ridiculously high medical bills?"

Sean's temper flared. "I told you that the adoptive parents would pay your expenses, but you said they were covered."

"And they were," she said, waving her arm around the barren room. "Had I known that you and your wife were going to become the proud parents of my daughter, I might have had a change of heart, but you didn't see fit to tell me that, did you?" Before he could respond, she drew her frayed robe around her and said, "As you can see, I'm ready for bed. Lock the door behind you when you leave."

She spun on her heel and walked toward the kitchen.

Sean followed, pleased at her show of anger. He knew she had to resent the fact that he'd adopted Amy and not told her. He also knew she had to air those feelings, and the sooner the better. Once she released all her anger, she'd be more receptive to his proposal.

"Why did you keep the piano?" he inquired curiously.

She came to a stop in the kitchen doorway, her spine suddenly stiff. For a moment Sean didn't think she was going to answer. Then she drew in a deep breath and said, "It's the only thing I have left that belonged to my mother."

Her kitchen was nearly as empty as the living room. She had one kitchen chair and a card table. He watched her sip a cup of tea and then quickly set it aside in order to press a tissue to her nose as she began to sneeze.

When the sneezing fit ceased, he asked, "Are you taking any medication?"

Whitney glared at him again, but provided him with the name of her prescription.

"And is it helping?"

"I'll be fine after a good night's sleep," she stated pointedly.

He nodded and leaned against the doorjamb. "What did you think of Amy?"

The color drained from her face. "Damn you."

She turned away from him, but not before he'd seen the shimmer of tears in her eyes. "Whitney—"

"Please, go away," she interrupted, unable to control the catch in her voice. He must have known how seeing Amy would affect her. He must have known that it would make her want to accept his proposal. She wanted her daughter back, and she'd do almost anything to have her. But she wasn't ready to admit that to Sean. She was too confused, and she needed time to think. "Just go away and leave me alone."

"I can't," he responded wearily. "I don't want to upset you, and I know you feel betrayed because I never told you that I was going to adopt Amy, but in all fairness to me, you never let me. You even signed a legal document stating that you refused to be apprised of the parents' names."

"And that justifies your deceit?" she asked as she spun around to face him, her anger renewed. She wanted to pick up something and throw it at him, but the tops of her cupboards were as bare as her living room. "I came to you as a patient, told you I planned to give my child up for adoption and you referred me to an attorney, instead of one of the many adoption agencies around town. You planned on stealing my daughter from the beginning!"

Sean rose to his full height at the accusation, and his eyes were blazing with fury as he said, "That's not true, Whitney, and you know it. You were the one who wanted to handle the adoption privately, so I sent you to a reputable attorney, whom I knew specialized in private adoptions. And I had no intention of adopting Amy at the time."

Whitney's expression said she didn't believe him, and Sean released a heavy sigh and leaned back against the doorjamb. Yelling at her wasn't going to make this any easier. He had to explain calmly and patiently, until he made her understand what had happened.

"Your attorney had two sets of parents in line to adopt Amy," he informed her, "but one couple adopted through other channels within days after you visited his office. The wife of the second couple became pregnant shortly after you went into your second trimester, and they withdrew their application. He happened to know that Margaret and I were considering adoption, and since he had no other clients at that point, he contacted me to see if we'd be interested.

"We were interested," he continued when she didn't respond, "but I was on shaky ground because of the possible conflict of interest. As your doctor, I was obligated to keep your welfare uppermost in my mind, and there was the question of whether I could do that if you decided to keep the baby. I tried to refer you to my partner, but you refused to see him, stating that you wanted me and only me. Then I tried to tell you that I wanted to adopt Amy, but you refused to listen. Finally my attorney conferred with yours, and they decided that as long as I did everything I could to try to convince you to keep the baby, and if I did it in front of witnesses, you wouldn't have grounds to sue me.''

There was a hint of righteous indignation in his voice, as he concluded with, ''I followed the law to the letter, right up to the moment you signed the adoption papers. And, if you'll recall, I did everything I could to make you keep Amy. I even had a psychiatrist spend some time with you in the hospital to make sure you were making your decision clearly and logically. *You* made the choice of adoption, so don't you even dare to try to accuse me of stealing her from you.''

Whitney pushed her fingers through her hair in frustration. Heaven help her, she hated the sincerity in his voice almost as much as she wanted to hate him. During all those hours of labor she'd told him everything about herself. She'd told him things she'd never told anyone. She bared her soul to him, and she felt that he'd bared his to her. He'd shared so many intimate details with her, but he never shared the most important one of all. He was right. She felt betrayed, even if everything he just told her was true.

''I hate you!'' she whispered as she struggled against a new surge of tears. ''I hate you for not telling me about Amy then, and I hate you for telling me now.''

''Oh, Whitney.'' Sean's heart went out to her as he heard the pain in her voice, and he walked across the room and drew her into his arms, feeling her distress as deeply as if it were his own.

Whitney raised her hands to his chest to push him away, but instead her fingers curled desperately around his shoulders, seeking comfort from his touch and his strength. If she could just feel for one minute that she didn't carry the weight of the world on her shoulders, she might be able to handle Sean and his wild proposal. Every ounce of her common sense told her she couldn't marry him, but he was offering her Amy. She'd already missed three years of her daughter's life. Could she really deny herself the rest of it when he was so willing to let her share it?

Sean sighed as he continued to hold her, wondering if he could have sprung all of this on her differently. Could he have handled it better? Approached her in a different manner? He was certain he could have, but at the moment he couldn't think of how.

"I'm sorry I've had to put you through this," he said as he threaded his fingers through her tangled hair and forced her to look at him. "But I'm doing it for Amy. She's my world, Whitney, and I want to give her the best of everything, just as I promised you I would."

"You can do that without me!" she exclaimed in agitation. It wasn't fair for him to throw her words of so many years back at her. It just wasn't fair!

"No, I can't do it without you," he disagreed with a firm shake of his head. "At first I thought I could, but I can't. I have a busy and demanding practice, and that means I have to spend a good deal of time away from home. I don't want Amy raised by housekeepers and nannies. I want her to have a mother who loves her as much as I do. I want her to have a mother she can confide in as she grows up—someone she can tell all those girl things that she'd be too embarrassed to share with her father."

Memories from Whitney's own childhood and adolescence welled up inside her. How many times had she longed to talk to her mother for just that very reason? Panic raced through her. Her daughter needed her, and she had to help her, but there was the complication of Sean. He didn't love her, and what would she do if, somewhere down the road, he left her? She'd lose Amy again, and this time it would surely kill her.

"I'm sure there are a million women out there who can fulfill that role. Why are you picking on me?"

She was having great difficulty holding back her tears, and she had to control them until he was gone. She blinked and swallowed hard, sending the tears back to her aching chest.

"Because you're her mother," he answered as he tucked a lock of hair behind her ear. "Because I remember your pride and your strength and your innate dignity when you first walked into my office."

"Some dignity," she muttered. "I was an unwed mother."

"You were an unwed widow," he said as he clasped her face in his hands and stared deeply into her eyes. "You were engaged to be married, and your fiancé was killed."

"And if I'd saved myself for my wedding night, none of this would have happened!" she yelled in bitter frustration. "I allowed myself to be weak, and I paid for it. I'm still paying for it."

Sean heard the self-disgust in her voice and was surprised by it. It was the one confession she hadn't made to him during those long hours of labor.

"You allowed yourself to be human," he corrected. "You were in love, and love makes us all do things that we wouldn't dream of doing in other circumstances. And if you hadn't allowed yourself to be human, Amy wouldn't be here. Can you honestly say that you regret that after meeting her?"

"No." It came out as a half sob, and the tears were back. Blinking and swallowing wasn't helping this time.

She closed her eyes tightly and wished Sean away. She wanted him to go so she could cry, and wail, and grieve. After she relieved herself of her tears, maybe she'd be strong enough to stand up to him. Strong enough to refuse his offer that was too tempting and made everything look much too easy.

She had learned the hard way that when things came too easy, they were usually covered with nettles. And the nettle in this case would be that to regain her daughter, she'd be caught in a loveless marriage.

"It's all right to cry," Sean murmured as he drew her close and cradled her head against his chest. "It's all right, Whitney."

And the tears came. Hot, and heavy, and filled with hopelessness. When they were over, she pulled away from Sean, and he reluctantly released her.

"I need some time to think," she told him.

Sean's concerned gaze traveled over her tear-ravaged face, and that perennial guilt resurfaced. He had hurt her. Really hurt her. Knowing that he had done it for all the right reasons didn't assuage his conscience. He also knew he had to give her the time she was asking for, because he was asking her to make choices that would affect the rest of her life.

"I understand," he said as he withdrew a card from his pocket and laid it on the edge of the counter. "My office and home phone numbers are on this card. Call me when you're ready to talk."

Whitney nodded as she wiped her cheeks with the back of her hand. It was only when Sean reached the doorway that she said, "Sean? Why did you really decide to pick on me?"

He turned to look at her, stuffed his hands into his pockets and shrugged. "I kept remembering how important it was to you that your child have both parents, and I'd made myself a vow that I'd give Amy everything you wanted her to have."

His eyes darkened then, reflecting his own inner turmoil as he confessed, "But I can't do that without Margaret, and what woman but you would be willing to take on a daughter without taking on a husband? I don't want a wife, but I do want Amy to have a mother."

"So our marriage would be..."

"... strictly platonic," he finished for her.

Considering the events leading up to her pregnancy, Whitney found the irony of his words somehow appropriate. She couldn't help but release a bitter laugh after he was gone.

Chapter Three

It was long before dawn when Whitney, clad in a pair of shorts and a baggy sweatshirt, wandered barefoot through her house. It wasn't the empty rooms she saw, but times past. Memories that haunted. Family scenes that brought tears to her eyes.

As she stood in the center of her old bedroom, she recalled the nights when she sat on the edge of her bed while her mother brushed her hair. One hundred strokes a night, her mother had insisted. It was a habit Whitney still carried out to this very day. In the master bedroom, she recalled the Sunday mornings when she was allowed to scramble into bed between her parents. They'd tickle and tease her, and the maid would serve them all breakfast in bed.

But it was in the living room, as she sat down at the piano, that she allowed her tears to fall. It was here that the memories were the most poignant. She could still see her mother sitting behind the piano, light from the candelabra encircling her, and the remainder of the room dark. Her hair had glistened like silver, and her long slender fingers had created musical magic. All her life, Whitney had wanted to play that way, but though she was an excellent technical pianist, she'd never been blessed with her mother's artistry. She stroked the keys, summoning up a childish piece her mother had taught her.

It was those sacred memories of her mother—so few, but so terribly vivid—that made her decide to marry Sean. When she'd given Amy up for adoption, she did it in the belief that her daughter would have both parents. That she'd build a lifetime of memories based on a complete family. But now Sean was alone, and as busy in his practice as her own father had been in his political career.

Amy had barely been two when Margaret Fitzgerald died. She hadn't had time to fill a small treasure chest of memories to keep her company on the long, lonely days when her father was simply too busy to even notice her. Whitney knew she could never let Amy be consigned to days without motherly memories to warm her; days when even the tea parties with her father would fail to bridge the gap.

Amy needed her, and fate was offering her daughter back to her. Not only would she be crazy to turn her back on fate, but she simply couldn't do it.

Her tears had dried by the time she'd played the last notes and she rose and walked out to her rose gardens to greet the day. Soon the crimson sky had lightened to blue, and she released a sigh as she broke off a yellow rose blossom and held it beneath her nose, inhaling its fragrance as she eyed the small contingent of billowing clouds that played chase around the blue-shadowed peaks of the Rocky Mountains.

For almost four years, she'd been living in a world turned upside down. Now she was prepared to embark on a new life with Sean and Amy, provided, of course, that she could find a way to enter the marriage financially unencumbered, for no matter how much she wanted her daughter, Sean's offer to buy her hand in marriage still rankled, and she knew that she could never accept it. If she was to regain her daughter, she had to do it on her terms.

Twirling the rose between her fingers, she went back into the house. She needed to call Simon, because he was the solution to her financial problems.

SEAN'S EYES SNAPPED OPEN as the mattress dipped. The pale light filtering through the window informed him that it was near dawn.

"Daddy?" Amy said plaintively.

"What is it, pumpkin?" he questioned as he reached out and drew her small body close.

She sighed and snuggled against him. "I'm cold."

He curled protectively around her, his heart aching at that lonely, lost-little-girl tone in her voice. "I'll make you warm."

Her small feet came to rest against his thigh, and he reached down to rub his hand against them. "Have you been walking on ice cubes?"

Amy giggled. "No."

"You're sure?" he teased as he continued to rub her feet.

"Sure." She cuddled even closer.

"I'm sorry I didn't make it home in time to say good-night last night," he murmured against her hair.

"S'kay."

"No, it's not." He pressed a kiss to the top of her head. "Are you getting warm now?"

"Uh-huh."

"Love me?"

"Uh-huh."

"I love you, too. So much it makes my heart hurt."

Amy's response was a soft adenoidal snore, and as Sean frowned up at the ceiling, he wondered how long he'd have to wait before it would be prudent to call Whitney.

WHITNEY DRUMMED her fingers against the kitchen counter as she waited for Simon to come on the line. Thank heavens, he was at his ranch outside of Durango and not running around the world checking on his holdings.

"Hi, kid!" he greeted her heartily a few moments later. "What's up?"

"You wouldn't believe me if I told you," Whitney said with a heavy sigh. "I need to talk to you, Simon. Are you going to be at the ranch this week?"

"No. I'm leaving in the morning and won't be back until Wednesday or Thursday. Is it important?"

Important? It was critical. "Yes."

There was a long silence before he said, "Honey, are you all right?"

Whitney blinked against still another surge of tears. Simon's father had been her godfather, and both she and Simon had lost their mothers as children. Though Simon was nearly ten years her senior, he'd always treated her as a cherished friend, and for as long as she could remember she'd gone to him with her problems.

"No, but I'm going to survive. Is it all right if I come to the ranch on Thursday?"

"You know you're always welcome, but why don't I fly into Denver after I finish my business?"

She knew it was his way of telling her he knew she couldn't afford the airfare, and she felt both irritated and relieved. "I don't want you to go out of your way."

"You're never out of my way. Besides, I've been watching the stock market. If what I see is true, this might be a good time for me to make an offer on Price Manufacturing."

Whitney wrapped the telephone cord around her hand, wondering if the man was psychic. "That's what I want to talk to you about. I think I might be ready to sell."

There was another long silence before Simon said, "I'll be there Wednesday night, and I'll call you as soon as I check into my hotel."

After she hung up, Whitney found herself once again dashing away tears. In the old days, Simon would have stayed at the house, but in the old days, she would have had a furnished guest room to put him in.

SEAN SAT behind his office desk and glared at the blank wall in front of him. It had been four days since he'd left Whitney's house, and for the past two days, Amy had been running a slight fever and complaining of a sore throat. Though he was sure it was tonsillitis, Mrs. Wilkens would be taking her to the pediatrician later in the day to confirm it. This morning, Amy had begged him to stay home with her and burst into sobs when he walked out the door. He knew Mrs. Wilkens was qualified to look after the girl, but he also knew that a housekeeper's attention was not a substitute for a parent's love.

All morning he'd been fighting the urge to pick up the telephone and call Whitney to tell her Amy was ill. But that would be emotional blackmail of the worst kind. She had to decide to come to them because she wanted to, not because she felt guilty, or worried, or even obligated. The question was, how long would he have to wait for her answer? A week? A month? Two months? He rubbed his hand against the back of his neck in an effort to relieve the tension centered there.

The buzzer sounded in his office, informing him that his next patient was waiting, but he ignored it for the moment. He would give Whitney until Sunday to call, he decided. That would be a full week since he'd last seen her. If she hadn't made up her mind by then, he'd find a way to expose her to Amy again. He was sure that the more she was around her daughter, the more she'd realize how much the child needed her.

The buzzer sounded again, and with a weary sigh, he rose to his feet and headed for the examining room.

WHITNEY NERVOUSLY TOYED with the pen in her hand, watching Simon as he rose to his feet and walked to her office window, staring out at the gleaming high-rise buildings of downtown Denver. In the fifteen minutes she'd been talking, he hadn't interrupted her once, and though that wasn't unusual, it was unusual for him not to respond the moment she'd finished. The minutes dragged by while he continued to keep his own counsel.

She jumped in surprise when he finally asked, "Do you love him?"

Whitney coughed. There were a lot of things she'd expected Simon to ask, but this wasn't one of them.

"No, but how can I turn my back on my own daughter?" she answered honestly.

He turned to face her and shrugged, his expression serious, searching. "I want to buy Price Manufacturing. In fact, I wanted to buy it three years ago, but I knew you'd think I was making the offer out of pity. I also knew you'd eventually reach the point where you were willing to let it go, but I never thought it would be over something like this."

"Neither did I," she said as she leaned back in her chair and brushed her hand over her eyes. "When I gave up Amy I never thought I'd see her again."

"And that's what bothers me," he said. "Honey, I've always thought of you as a little sister, so I'm going to talk to you like a big brother. I know how guilty you felt about giving up the baby, and I've watched how hard you've struggled to put everything back together. You've done a wonderful job here, and you've accomplished more than I ever thought you could. Now this man pops into your life, says he wants to give you back your daughter and all you have to do is marry him and give up everything.

"Can you walk away from all this?" he asked, widening his arms in an encompassing gesture. "You've proved you're an astute businesswoman. Are you going to be satisfied just being a mother?"

Whitney once again began to toy with the pen in her hand. "The counterpoint to that question is: Am I satisfied here?"

"Okay," Simon said. "Are you?"

Whitney glanced around her utilitarian office. "No."

"So what this man is offering is what you want?"

Her chin rose a determined notch. "What I want is my daughter, and I'll do anything—give up anything—to have her."

Simon sighed and thrust his hands into his pockets. "Fine. I'll buy Price Manufacturing under one condition."

"What condition?" Whitney asked cautiously.

"That you agree to a one year option to buy it back. If, after you've married this guy, you suddenly find that you're not happy, you won't have lost anything."

"But I may not be able to afford to buy it back," she objected. "If the stock continues to rise at the current rate, in one year, it'll be worth—"

"I'll carry the difference," he interrupted with an impatient wave of his hand. "Just call your attorney so we can get started on the details."

She parted her lips to issue another protest, then realized that, despite his autocratic dismissal, he was simply giving her an option. It would be up to her to exercise it, so why should she waste her breath arguing over a moot point?

Because she'd had to train herself to move with caution, weighing each and every alternative and the possible consequences before making a decision. And yet, in considering Sean's marriage proposal, she'd made her decision with very little thought to the possible ramifications. Amy was her primary objective, and as she'd just told Simon, she was ready to give up anything to get her back.

Everything was falling into place too easily, and there was a nagging voice inside her predicting doom. Whitney forced herself to ignore the voice as she hit the intercom switch and asked her secretary to call her attorney. While she waited for him to come on the line, she decided that she had to find a way to protect herself and her hold on her daughter.

SEAN BRAKED TO A STOP in Whitney's driveway, turned off the ignition and looked at Amy. She had, indeed, been suffering from tonsillitis, and two days' worth of antibiotics had made her as good as new. He smoothed her hair into place and pressed a kiss against the top of her head before he released her seat belt.

"Do you remember what you're going to say?" he asked her.

She lifted her small face and grinned. "I get to yell s'prize."

"That's right." He caressed her cheek, realizing for the first time just how much she resembled Whitney. She had the same huge Nordic blue eyes, the same straight little nose and the same cupid-bow lips. He bent down to snuggle her against his chest. "I love you, pumpkin."

Amy giggled as she wrapped her arms securely around his neck, and Sean prayed that Whitney's call this afternoon was going to fulfill all their dreams.

But as he led Amy to the door, he drew her to a stop and listened. The dulcet tones of a piano were drifting through the open windows, and he tilted his head to the side, trying to identify the melancholy tune. He recognized it as classical, but the title and the name of the composer escaped him.

He was frowning when the music finally came to an end. Whitney had told him that the piano had been her mother's, but she hadn't told him she played it. Gut instinct told him the piano was an essential part of her life, and he knew that if he had convinced her to marry him—which, considering the sad tune, was still doubtful—he'd somehow have to find a place for the instrument.

He glanced down at Amy when she tugged on his hand and whispered, "When do I get to yell s'prize?"

"Right now," he said, smiling down at her, while wondering where in hell he was going to put a baby grand piano if Whitney's answer was yes.

WHITNEY HAD JUST SELECTED another piece of music, and she glanced toward the front door in confusion when the bell rang. It couldn't be Sean this time. She'd made arrangements to have lunch with him tomorrow, and he wouldn't dare disturb her.

She crossed over to the door and peered through the peephole, but she couldn't see anyone. With a frown, she opened the door.

"S'prize!" Amy exclaimed, clapping her hands in delight.

Whitney wanted to laugh and to cry as she watched the child perform a toddler jig. Love welled inside her and was so intense that it actually hurt. "What are you doing here?"

"We brought a picnic," Amy said, and Sean suddenly appeared, a picnic basket in his hand and a blanket draped over his shoulder.

Whitney released a sigh of resignation. If nothing else, the man was persistent.

"Amy and I voted, and we decided that we want to eat down by the rose gardens. What do you say?" he asked.

She knew she should send them both away, but as her gaze drifted to Amy, she knew she couldn't. She hungered for the company of her daughter. "I say that it sounds like I'm outvoted."

She stepped onto the porch and took Amy's hand, feeling a tug at her heart when the child's small fingers entwined with her own.

Sean led the way across the wide expanse of lawn. He came to a stop at the edge of the rose gardens, set the picnic basket on the ground and spread out the blanket.

"Miladies," he said with a courtly bow that sent Amy into giggles. "Imp," he muttered as he caught her up in his arms, spun her around and then tossed her high into the air, catching her easily.

Amy's giggles had turned into breathless laughter by the time he swung her down to the blanket.

"Let's eat," she said, prying open the lid of the picnic basket.

"I do believe the child thinks with her stomach," he said, casting Whitney a rueful smile.

"If she doesn't eat, she'll never grow up to be a big girl like me," Whitney said as she gazed fondly down at the girl.

"I suppose you're right."

She sat down on the blanket, assisting Amy in removing the basket's contents. There was a huge platter of fried chicken, a bowl of cole slaw, biscuits still warm from the oven and a tin of chocolate chip cookies sans strawberry jam. There was also a thermos of grape juice for Amy and a bottle of Chablis for her and Sean. She handed him the wine and the corkscrew as she removed plates, silverware and glasses.

Under Amy's supervision, she filled plates for all of them, laughing when Amy insisted that she pick the carrots out of her coleslaw.

"But carrots are good for you," Whitney protested in motherly concern.

Amy gazed up at her seriously and solemnly announced, "But they're orange."

"I see. You don't eat anything that's orange?"

"Nope."

Whitney glanced toward Sean, who was grinning indulgently at his daughter. "You agree with this?"

"When I was a kid, I hated anything green," he answered, his eyes dancing with laughter. "If she'll eat green, I won't fight her over orange."

It sounded like a logical compromise, so Whitney carefully picked out the carrots from Amy's coleslaw. When she was finished, Sean handed her a glass of wine.

Then he lifted his glass in a toast and said, "To the future."

Whitney hesitated, but decided it was an innocuous toast, and clinked her glass with his, repeating, "To the future."

They ate in a companionable silence, Amy periodically breaking it with chatter about her day. Both Sean and Whitney answered her sporadic bursts of conversation with murmurs of "Mm-hmm" and "how exciting."

By the time Amy finished the food on her plate and began chasing a butterfly across the lawn, Whitney was surprised to find that she'd eaten two helpings of everything.

She felt replete and comfortably lazy as she pulled her legs up to her chest and wrapped her arms around them. Resting her chin on her knees, she watched Amy romping, a smile curving her lips.

Sean sipped his wine and regarded Whitney with interest as he lay sprawled on the blanket, his head resting on his hand. He realized with a jolt that this was the first true smile he'd seen on her face in all the time he'd known her. Looking at her closely for the first time, he noted how terribly thin and pale she was. She was at least twenty pounds lighter than she should be, and there was a fine tremor in her hands that told him the past few years had not been kind to her.

He broke off a piece of grass and trailed it along her arm, smiling at her when she glanced toward him. "A penny for your thoughts."

She sighed and glanced back toward Amy. "I told you I'd have lunch with you tomorrow. Why did you come tonight?"

Sean considered lying, but decided against it. He knew that honesty was essential in any relationship, be it friendship or more, and their past was already shaded by too many half-truths and omissions.

"The suspense was killing me, and I guess I thought you needed to see your daughter." His smile faded, and he regarded her somberly. "I've asked you to make choices—and maybe they're unfair choices—but I felt you should act on them with your heart, instead of your head. I decided that the best way for you to do that was to see Amy again. Are you going to marry me?"

Whitney shrugged. This wasn't exactly the way she planned to give him her answer, but she could sense his nervous anticipation and knew it would be unfair to drag it out until tomorrow.

"I'm going to marry you if you'll agree to a few terms of my own."

"Which are?"

"Before I go into them, I'd like to say that I don't want or need your money. I'm selling Price Manufacturing to Simon Prescott. My stock isn't quite enough to pay off his loan, but he's accepting it as full payment since he believes that as soon as Prescott Industries takes over, the value of the stock will escalate."

She was too afraid to pause for breath as she continued with, "As far as my terms, I want a standard prenuptial agreement that states what's yours is yours and what's mine is mine, and should we get a divorce, I won't demand alimony. I also want to adopt Amy."

She risked a glance toward him, wondering what he was thinking, but his expression was neutral.

"Why do you want to adopt her?"

"Because if things don't work out between us, I don't want to lose her," she answered. He parted his lips to respond, and she held up her hand for silence, anticipating his objection. "I won't take her away from you, Sean. You've had her from the beginning, and as far as I'm concerned, she's more yours than mine. I will, however, insist on joint custody and visitation rights. I gave her up once, and I'll never give her up again. If I adopt her, the courts will consider her mine and accord me the rights of any parent."

He was quiet for several minutes, his gaze centered on Amy as she continued to race around the yard. Finally he asked, "Do you have any other terms?"

"No." When he didn't say anything, she said, "I don't expect you to give me an answer right now. I know you need time to think this over."

He leaned his head back and stared up at the sky. "I don't need time to think it over. I'll admit I'm a little confused, and even a little wary, particularly about the adoption. But if the prenuptial agreement specifically states that I'll maintain physical custody of Amy, I won't fight you. I'm just concerned that if you're already discussing joint custody and visitation rights, you haven't made a commitment."

He lowered his eyes to her, and their intensity locked her into his gaze. She couldn't move if she wanted to.

"I'll sign your prenuptial agreement," he said. "And I'll let you adopt Amy, but only if you swear to me that you will try—and I mean really try—to make this..." he struggled for the right words. "This situation work," he finally concluded. "Amy has already lost one mother, and I'm not about to let her lose a second one."

"I would never walk away from Amy," Whitney said while gazing down at her hands, nervously linked in her lap. "As I said, I gave her up once, I won't give her up again. But I also have to be realistic. There's no guarantee that you won't find someone you want to marry for all the right reasons, and if that happens, I could never stand in your way."

Sean almost laughed at her last statement, knowing that after Margaret, he'd never find someone he wanted to marry for all the right reasons. He'd heard the sincere vibration in Whitney's voice when she made her demands and her vow to hold on to her daughter. He reached out and folded his hand over hers. When she looked at him, he asked, "Do you want my lawyer to draw up the agreement, or yours?"

"Are you sure about this?" she questioned. "Maybe you should give yourself a few days to think it over."

His eyes shifted back to his daughter, who came running to the blanket and threw herself into his arms. He pressed a kiss against the top of her head, before raising his eyes to Whitney's.

"I don't need a few days," he said, "because I've never been more sure about anything in my entire life."

Chapter Four

This was not how Whitney had envisioned her wedding day. She'd always dreamed of white lace and satin. Music and joyful singing. A long walk down the aisle that would lead her into the arms of the man who loved her and was vowing to do so for the remainder of his life.

No, this wasn't how it was supposed to be, she thought sadly as she and Sean sat waiting outside the judge's chamber, the cacophony of a busy courthouse reverberating through the maze of corridors surrounding them. But then, during the past four years, none of her dreams had turned out the way they were supposed to. At least she'd be gaining something from this shattering illusion. Amy would be hers.

She risked a glance toward Sean. He looked handsome in a gray pin-striped suit that complemented her light pink linen one. He also appeared to be completely at ease, as if he didn't have a care in the world, and Whitney felt a spark of resentment toward him. It wasn't fair that he should be so calm while she was filled with a teeming mass of doubts, the major one of which was her ability to be a good mother.

Having been raised as an only child, she'd rarely been exposed to small children. Good heavens, she hadn't even had a baby-sitting job! Was she being naive to believe that all she had to do was give her love in order to fill the role? What if love wasn't enough? What if she botched everything and ruined Amy's life?

The questions continued to devil her, and she glanced back at Sean, wanting—needing—his reassurance, but she couldn't find the courage to ask for it, because motherhood wasn't the only issue tormenting her.

She frowned down at her hands, which were linked in her lap, chagrined by the fact that she'd spent last night tossing and turning, trying to define a "platonic" marriage. She knew, of course, that if she put it into strict dictionary terms, it was a marital union that did not involve sexual love, but what roles, if any, did Sean expect her to fill as his wife? Hostess, surely, but what about friendship and companionship? And what should she expect from him in return? Anything? Nothing?

She resisted the urge to thrust her hands through her professionally styled hair, her one feminine concession to this day. Why hadn't she discussed all of this with Sean earlier so that she would know exactly what he expected of her? Because she hadn't had a chance to think, let alone talk, during the past week, and her frown deepened as she thought about those seven harried days.

Sean had insisted that they marry immediately and called and reserved the first open spot on the judge's calendar. Then Simon Prescott had sent in a contingent of executives to learn the ins and outs at Price Manufacturing. Though the sale wouldn't be completed for several weeks, she and Simon agreed on an interim takeover, which would allow Whitney to devote her full attention to Amy from the beginning, something she felt was crucial. They needed a concentrated time together to begin bonding as mother and daughter, and the sooner that bonding happened, the better off they'd both be.

Unfortunately, between clearing up everything at the office, putting the mansion up for sale, getting a blood test, applying for a marriage license, and packing up her clothes and few personal belongings and moving them into Sean's house, her days had been inordinately long and she'd tumbled into bed each night exhausted. Thus, she simply hadn't had the opportunity nor the energy to contemplate her marriage to Sean in any detail. Now she wondered if he'd purposely rushed her into it so she wouldn't have time to think.

No, she decided as she looked at him again and he gave her a friendly smile. That accusation wasn't fair, because she knew that if she'd asked, Sean not only would have delayed their nuptials, but he would have gladly sat down with her and defined their relationship. The truth was, she'd ignored asking her questions because she'd feared that she might not like his answers, and what could she possibly do if she didn't? Not marry him and lose Amy? Of course not, so why fret now? Because it was out of character for her not to face a troubling situation head-on. The admission only increased her tension, and unable to sit still a moment longer, she rose to her feet, needing to move to counteract it.

Sean eyed Whitney with concern as she began to pace the width of the small hallway. He'd been aware of her growing agitation and had the feeling that it wouldn't take much to make her bolt. He silently cursed himself for bringing her here twenty minutes early. But he'd known she was nervous and thought that she would be more at ease waiting at the courthouse with him, than alone at home. Now, it looked as if he'd miscalculated, and he had no idea how to calm her, because he was damn nervous himself. Even though he was still convinced that Whitney was the solution to his problems with Amy, the ramifications of marriage to her had begun hitting home.

When he'd first conceived the idea, it had sounded so simple. They'd get married and she'd move in and take care of Amy. He had never considered how much she'd be sacrificing to do that. That knowledge gradually evolved as he watched her put her affairs in order, and he suddenly realized that though they wouldn't be interacting on a physical level, he was going to have to deal with her on an emotional one. He was going to have to make her happy, and he wasn't sure he knew how to do it.

When she continued to pace, he asked, "Whitney, are you all right?"

Whitney stopped in the center of the hallway and straightened her skirt for at least the twelfth time as she said, "No, I'm not all right. I'm scared to death. I keep asking myself what qualifications I have to be a mother, and I keep coming up with zip. Nothing. Zero."

Sean released an inward sigh of relief. He'd expected her to announce that she'd changed her mind. But all that was wrong was motherhood jitters, and that he could handle. Hadn't he done it a thousand times with Margaret? He smiled confidently as he pushed himself out of the chair and walked to her. He caught her chin in his hand, and tilted her head upward, forcing her to look at him.

"Then someone gave you the wrong application form," he informed her. "Good parenting is based on a combination of about fifty percent love and common sense, and fifty percent luck. You have the first two qualifications down pat. As far as the luck goes, you'll just have to take your chances along with the rest of us. And I'm going to be there to help, Whitney. We're going to be a team, and I believe that we're going to be a damn good one."

Whitney agreed with what he was saying in principle, yet she couldn't help but wonder how he would characterize a team. To her, it was two or more people who were not only working toward a common goal, but were imbued with a spirit that made them willing to work for the group as a whole.

And that was what was wrong with this picture! she suddenly realized. Raising Amy was their common goal, but what would happen to them when the child grew up and left home? On the tail end of that question came a flood of others, and she knew that she couldn't marry him without some answers.

"Amy isn't my only concern," she said, forcing herself to look at him directly, though she would have preferred to study the toe of her shoe. "I'm also concerned about us."

"Us?" Sean repeated in confusion.

"Yes, us," she repeated. "When I gave Amy up for adoption, I did it because I wanted her to be part of a family, and a family is more than two parents and a child, Sean. It's a feeling—a type of spirituality, if you will, that binds people together. It's that sense of family that's missing here, and I'm not sure that we'll be doing Amy any favors by getting married if we can't provide it."

Sean wanted to object, to tell her she didn't know what she was talking about, but he'd be telling an outright lie and he knew it. Parents and family were not synonymous. Regrettably, when one of those parents was a physician, it only added to the difficulty of a harmonious family. If he was Joe Jones with a nine-to-five, weekends-and-holidays-off job, he wouldn't be standing here in the first place.

"What do you want me to say, Whitney?" he asked wearily. "That you're right? If that's what you want, then I'll concede that you've outlined the normal definition of a family. However, you've been privy to my life this past week. I'm forever running late, or having to cancel out, and believe me, this was a good week compared to most. Considering that fact, can you honestly say that you think Amy would have a better sense of family without you?"

Whitney spun away from him and walked a short distance down the hallway as she tried to deal with the war raging inside her. He was right. The life Amy led right now was not a family life, but still . . .

She spun around to face him and boldly asked, "What's going to happen to us when she's all grown up and gone, Sean? Do we divorce and go our separate ways?"

"I have no intention of ever divorcing you," he said quietly, but insistently.

She frowned at his answer. "That could be even more cruel. There has to be something more substantial between

us than Amy. There has to be a sense of friendship, of..."
She bit her lip when she realized that the word love was
trembling on the tip of her tongue. He'd already made it
clear that he wasn't looking for that type of commitment.
What was it he'd said? *I don't want a wife, but I do want
Amy to have a mother.*

Heaven help her, she wanted that too! But the two roles
went hand in hand, and how could she ever separate one
from the other?

You did it with your father, an inner voice provided, and
she reluctantly admitted that it was true. Her father had
never remarried, and as the years passed, Whitney became
her mother's substitute everywhere but in the bedroom. She
was his homemaker, hostess and confidante. Yet she'd always had his love and devotion, his understanding and respect. They were more than father and daughter; they were
the best of friends.

She widened her eyes at the sudden realization that,
though her father's love and devotion had been there from
the beginning, she had to earn the rest. In Amy, she and
Sean had a common bond—a foundation to begin building
on. There was no reason why they couldn't build a close and
binding friendship, and who knew... As time passed, they
might be able to build even more.

She jumped in startled surprise when the judge's clerk
opened the door and called for them. Her eyes flew to Sean's
face, only to discover that he was watching her through a
screen of lashes that hid his thoughts.

"Well, Whitney, the choice is yours," he said in a neutral tone. "Do we go inside, or do I drive you home?"

Her hesitation was so momentary that if Sean hadn't been
watching for it, he wouldn't have seen it.

"Can't we be found in contempt of court if we keep a
judge waiting?" she asked as she walked over to him and
slid her arm through his. Before he could reply, she gave him
a cheeky grin and said, "I don't know about you, but I have
a feeling that we'd never be able to live it down if Amy dis-

covered in her teenage years that her parents were ex-jailbirds.''

Sean didn't know whether to sag in relief or laugh, so he did a little of both. Then he sobered as he looked down into her eyes, noting that behind her smile was a twinge of something that suspiciously resembled fear.

"I promise that you won't regret this," he told her.

Whitney knew that it was the type of vow that no man or woman should ever make, because it was just tempting fate. She also knew that his words had come from his heart, so she forgave him for the infraction.

"I'm sure I won't," she said sincerely.

Five minutes later, she was Mrs. Sean Fitzgerald, and it didn't really matter if she still had doubts, because it was now a fait accompli, and she'd just have to make the best of it.

SEAN HAD NO SOONER PULLED into the driveway than Amy burst out the front door, and she ran to him, throwing herself into his arms as he climbed out of the car.

"Hi, pumpkin," he said, lifting her into the air and kissing her cheek.

"Did you and Whit-nee get married?" she asked him.

"We sure did."

Amy squirmed to be released. When Sean placed her on the ground, she ran over to Whitney, who'd gotten out of the car and was standing close by in nervous anticipation. Though she and Amy had been together several times during the past few days, Whitney didn't know how the child felt about her sudden new role in her life. Was Amy ready to accept her as her mother? Did she even want to?

Whitney squatted down so that she would be at Amy's eye level. "Hi," she said with a tentative smile.

"Hi," Amy repeated. She reached out and stroked Whitney's cheek with childlike curiosity, as if she were observing a new toy that she didn't quite understand. "Daddy says you're my new mama."

"That's right," Whitney said, unable to control the husky waver in her voice. "Is that okay with you?"

"Uh-huh."

"In that case, do you think I could have a hug?"

"Sure."

Whitney had to blink against tears as Amy's sturdy little arms wound around her neck, and her equally sturdy little body pressed up against her. She buried her nose in her daughter's hair, reveling in the scent of fresh little girl. When Amy darted away Whitney gazed after her, feeling oddly empty. That moment of closeness had been far too short, and she yearned for more. But soon those short moments would begin to build up into a stockpile of memories. She had to take everything one step at a time, she told herself, as she stood upright.

"Let's get you settled in," Sean said.

"I know my way," Whitney responded absently. "Up the stairs and the second door on my left."

"Whitney."

She glanced toward him automatically. "Yes?"

"She's just a little girl. Her attention span is short."

She had no idea how he'd known what she was thinking, but she was grateful he did. "I know that, Sean. It's just that..."

"That you want more," he provided when her voice trailed off and she glanced away from him. "You'll eventually have it. It'll just take some time and..."

"...a lot of patience," she finished for him, following up the words with a sigh. "I think I'd better go change."

Sean watched her walk up the sidewalk and enter the front door, her posture proud and straight. He found himself struggling for a way to deal with her. If she'd laughed or cried, he'd have been able to give her the words, but what was he supposed to say when he didn't really know what she was feeling or thinking?

He glanced at his watch, stuffed his hands into his pockets and followed after her. He was due at the office in less

than two hours, and he wondered if the decision to treat today as if it were any other day had been the right one. Perhaps he should have taken the day off. Perhaps he should
have... But it was too late for "perhaps he should haves."
It was also too late for second thoughts about their marriage, though that declaration didn't stop them from inun-
dating him.

WHITNEY WALKED OUT of her room and down the stair-
case, trailing her hand along the highly polished mahogany
railing. Though she'd initially felt a cheerfulness about the
house, the image was quickly fading. The colors were too
bright for her taste, and it seemed that every available space
was filled with organized clutter.

There was a thimble and a bell collection that dominated
the upstairs hallway. The living room had a carved bird
collection that was so immense it was difficult to distinguish one replica from another. There were collages of
photographs everywhere she looked, and if there wasn't a
photograph, there was a needlepoint picture with some
prosaic saying stitched on it.

Whitney preferred mellow blues and greens, rather than
the yellows and oranges that dominated the house. She also
preferred spartan order to the jumble that surrounded her.
But this was the home that Sean's first wife had created for
him and Amy. Right now she was an intruder. It would take
months before she could make it her own, and each change
would have to be made slowly and subtly, so that neither
Sean nor Amy felt threatened in any way.

As she came to a stop in the living room, she saw two
areas that she could attack at once. She could replace the
bowl of cinnamon candies with lemon drops. She could also
replace the silk plants with real ones. She might even be able
to replace the mountain landscape on the far wall with a
large mirror to give the room an appearance of more space.
Then she could probably...

"Whitney, are you ready for lunch?"

Whitney jerked her head around, startled by the sound of Sean's voice. Her cheeks flushed crimson in embarrassment, though she knew on a rational level that Sean couldn't possibly know that she'd been mentally redecorating.

"Of course," she said, giving him a forced, but cheerful smile. "I was just getting acquainted with my surroundings."

He glanced around the room fondly. "It is an inviting room, isn't it?"

"It's very...nice," she agreed, wondering if her nose was going to grow. But it wasn't exactly a lie, she thought as she followed his gaze. To someone else the room would be inviting. It just wasn't to her.

Thankfully she was saved from having to say anything more when Sean stated, "Mrs. Wilkens has lunch ready."

"Then by all means, let's go eat."

Though Mrs. Wilkens, Sean's housekeeper, was as pleasant today as she'd been on the other occasions they'd met, Whitney sensed an air of censure from the middle-aged, stocky woman as they all sat down at the table. Though Whitney wasn't particularly pleased by the woman's attitude, she did understand it. After all, she'd come to work for Sean right after Margaret had died. Not only would her allegiance lie with her employer, but she had to be wondering about Whitney's and Sean's sleeping arrangements. Whitney knew Sean well enough to understand that he hadn't offered any explanations, and she wondered if she should tell the housekeeper the truth about their marriage, or simply ignore the situation. Ignoring it seemed the better part of valor at this point in time.

Sean, sensing the undercurrent between the two women, glanced uneasily from one to the other, deciding that he definitely should have made plans to stay at home today. When he'd made the decision to spend the afternoon at the office, he'd figured that Whitney would prefer being alone as she settled in and became familiar with her new home. He hadn't even anticipated that Mrs. Wilkens might present a problem, because the woman was one of the most placid people he'd ever met.

As he cut Amy's sandwich into bite-size squares, he wondered if he should take the housekeeper aside and talk to her, but by the time he handed Amy her plate, he'd decided to give them a chance to get to know each other. If the situation hadn't resolved itself in a few days, then he'd step in.

Amy, however, appeared to think a more direct approach was in order, and Sean could only gape at his daughter in abject horror when she blithely asked Whitney, "How come you're going to fire Mrs. Wilkens?"

Sean didn't have time to see Whitney's reaction, because Mrs. Wilkens, who'd just taken a bite of her sandwich, began to choke, and he leaped to his feet and raced around the table, ready to perform the Heimlich maneuver. The housekeeper, however, had recovered by the time he reached her side, and he suspected that her bright red coloring was due more to embarrassment than her choking.

"Are you okay?" he asked her as he placed his hand on her shoulder and gave it a reassuring squeeze.

"Fine," she whispered, casting her eyes downward.

Sean turned toward Amy, ready to scold her severely for her rudeness, but before he could even part his lips, Whitney said, "Out of the mouths of babes. Or is that, little pitchers have big ears?"

He shifted his gaze to her, and she gave him a wry smile. Then she looked at Amy and said, "I'm not going to fire Mrs. Wilkens, Amy, and if she's worried about that, she shouldn't be. Not only do I want her to stay, but I need her here to help me, because housekeeping is not my forte."

"What's that mean?" Amy inquired curiously.

"That means that I'm not very good at cleaning house."

"Oh." The child then grinned widely as she announced, "Mrs. Wilkens is good at that."

"I know," Whitney replied with a chuckle. Then she looked at the housekeeper and said, "Mrs. Wilkens, I really would like you to stay on, provided, of course, that you want to. I should also warn you that I love to cook, but I hate doing the dishes. Do you think you can live with that?''

Sean's gaze flew back and forth between the two women as they eyed each other. He wasn't aware that he was holding his breath until Mrs. Wilkens finally nodded and said, ''I can live with that, but I also love to cook.''

Sean released his breath and returned to his chair when Whitney responded with, ''I think we can work out a compromise that will let us both indulge ourselves. I'll even do the dishes when you cook.''

Mrs. Wilkens's laughter was almost girlish. ''Don't be silly. I get paid to do the dishes.''

Sean relaxed back in his chair, and he grinned when he met Whitney's eyes. She grinned back and then winked at him. Crisis number one had been faced, and she'd handled it beautifully. He didn't know why, but he suddenly felt as if everything was going to be all right.

But Whitney wasn't sharing his sentiment when, an hour later, she roamed around the perimeter of the backyard, feeling at loose ends. Sean had gone to the office. Amy was taking her nap, and Mrs. Wilkens had everything else under control.

When she told the housekeeper she wanted her to stay on, she meant it, though she hadn't been quite truthful about her reasons. She wasn't particularly fond of housework, but she was very proficient at it. Despite the fact that she was raised in a houseful of servants, her father had insisted that she be trained in all homemaking skills, because, as he'd said, there might come a day when she'd need them.

Boy, had he been right about that, she thought as she came to a stop and peered up at the second floor, locating Amy's room. She could cook, clean and mend with the best of them, and her decision to keep Mrs. Wilkens on had been strictly selfish.

Well, not strictly selfish, she amended. She'd figured that if she wasn't tied down with housework, she'd be able to spend more time with Amy. She'd also realized that for the past year the woman had been Amy's mother figure. Though she knew that that fact alone could create a problem between her and Mrs. Wilkens as she assumed more and more of the role, she also felt that it would be better for Amy if, while she was adjusting to Whitney, she had someone familiar to hang on to.

Even though her justification felt right, it didn't alleviate her restlessness, and she resumed her prowl around the yard. She'd always been able to keep herself busy. If nothing else, she'd been able to putter in her rose gardens, but Sean didn't have a rose on the place. He'd informed her that Margaret had been allergic to them. An ironic laugh escaped her as she stopped at the edge of the small strawberry patch. She couldn't eat the fruit ripening in the sun, but she could weed the patch. She dropped to her knees and proceeded to do just that.

She'd nearly completed the task when a small voice asked, "What's you doing?"

Whitney glanced up in surprise and smiled at Amy, whose eyes were still heavy with sleep. "Pulling weeds," she answered.

Amy squatted down beside her. "How come?"

Whitney sat back on her heels and frowned as she tried to decide how to answer the girl's question in terms she'd understand. Finally she decided to keep it simple. "Because weeds will make the strawberry plants sick."

"Oh. Can I pull one?"

"Sure, but you have to pull it out just right," Whitney told her. She smiled when Amy stood and watched avidly as Whitney put her hand at the base of the stalk. "You have to keep your hand close to the ground so it won't break off. Then you just give it a pull, and it comes right out."

"I'll pull this one," Amy said as she approached a large weed on the edge of the patch.

The plant was almost as tall as Amy, and Whitney said, "Okay, but I think you'll have to use both hands to pull that one up. It's pretty big, so its roots go way down into the ground."

She smiled again as she watched Amy chew on her bottom lip in concentration as she bent and placed both hands around the stalk.

"It won't come up," the child complained.

"You'll have to pull really hard," Whitney told her. "Give it a big tug."

Amy did as instructed, and as the weed suddenly gave way, she lost her balance and fell on her rump. "It made me fall down!" she exclaimed with an exuberant laugh.

"It sure did," Whitney said, laughing herself. "Are you okay? You didn't hurt yourself, did you?"

"No," Amy answered. She tossed the weed aside and said, "So what can we do now?"

Whitney gave an amused shake of her head. It was apparent that weeding wasn't going to become one of Amy's favorite pastimes. So what should they do now? she wondered as she glanced around the yard. What did she and her mother do when she was Amy's age?

"I think we should make mud pies," she announced.

Amy's eyes widened in hesitant excitement. "But we'll get all dirty."

"Well, I certainly hope we will," Whitney stated solemnly. Then she ran her muddy finger down Amy's small, pert nose. "I want to take a bubble bath, and how can I take one if I'm all clean?"

Amy squealed in delight. "Can I take one, too?"

"Only if you get real dirty," Whitney said with a laugh as she grabbed the child and hugged her to her chest.

They spent a messy afternoon making mud pies, something Whitney had frequently done with her own mother. Knowing that this would be the first mother-daughter event for Amy to tuck into her treasure chest of memories made Whitney's long ago memories even more special.

SEAN WALKED OUT of the labor room and over to the nurses' station. Mrs. Barnett's labor was progressing much more slowly than he'd anticipated. Since he was on call, that meant that he was going to have to stay at the hospital until the woman delivered.

"So go the best laid plans of mice and men," he muttered as he scrawled his notes on the woman's chart. He'd planned on being home in time for dinner. Now he'd be lucky to make it by midnight, and he hated leaving Whitney with the responsibility of Amy on her first night at the house. "May I use the phone?" he asked one of the duty nurses.

"Sure." She handed it to him.

Sean sighed as he punched out the number and waited for a ring at the other end. When Whitney answered, he said "I'm sorry, Whitney, but I'm stuck at the hospital waiting for a baby to arrive. I don't have any idea what time I'll make it home, but it's going to be late."

"I understand." Whitney twisted the telephone cord around her hand, feeling guilty that her prayers had been answered. The closer the time came when Sean was due home, the more nervous she'd become. So far she and Amy were hitting it off famously, but Amy had an early bedtime. She'd been wondering what she was supposed to do with herself between the time that she put Amy to bed and went to bed herself. How was one supposed to behave around a platonic husband?

"I really am sorry to leave you alone on your first night," Sean said as he leaned against the counter surrounding the nurses. "You haven't even had a chance to learn Amy's nighttime routine, but Mrs. Wilkens will help. How are you and Amy doing?"

"We're doing fine." She smiled at Amy, who'd already had her promised bubble bath and was dressed in her pajamas. The child was sprawled on the floor in front of the television watching a Disney movie on the VCR. Whitney had been stunned by the collection of tapes that Sean had built up for his daughter. "We've been spending most of the day getting acquainted, but Amy's watching a movie right now."

"Good. I'm glad everything is going all right. Give her a good-night kiss for me."

"Of course."

An awkward silence stretched between them as they each tried to come up with an appropriate sign-off. Finally Sean said, "I've got to go. Mrs. Barnett needs me."

"Does she want a girl or a boy?" Whitney asked, finding herself oddly reluctant to let him go.

Sean laughed. "She's isn't my patient, so I don't know."

"Well, ask," Whitney said. "And then try to give the woman what she wants."

"I'll do my best," he replied with a laugh. It was the same kind of nonsensical order Margaret would have given him, and it made him feel warm inside. It also made him realize how much he'd missed that verbal camaraderie that could only be shared between husband and wife. But Whitney wasn't actually a wife; she was Amy's mother, and an inexperienced one at that. He had no doubt about her competence, but he couldn't help recalling her fears earlier in the day, and he wasn't sure he'd allayed them. "Whitney, if you need anything, just call the hospital and have me paged."

"I will, but I'm sure we'll be fine. Amy's movie is almost over. I promised to read her a story, so I'd better go. Good night, Sean."

"Good night." When he hung up, he found himself feeling thrust aside, and for the life of him, he couldn't figure out why.

He was still contemplating that strange, elusive feeling when, after checking on Mrs. Barnett, he decided to go to the doctors' lounge for a cup of coffee. He regretted the decision the moment he opened the door and discovered Bill Hughes sitting there, thumbing through a magazine.

His first impulse was to leave before Bill noticed him because Sean knew that the news of his marriage had already spread through the hospital. He also knew instinctively that Bill would not approve of what he'd done. Finally it was the odor of freshly brewed coffee that made him decide he might as well get the confrontation over with and be done with it.

"Isn't it a little late for you to be here, Bill?" he asked as he walked into the room.

Bill glanced up in surprise, and then smiled. "I have a patient who's terrified of hospitals, and her husband has been in surgery for the past three hours. I thought I'd hang around in case she needs me." He leaned back against the sofa as Sean crossed over to the coffee pot. "I'm surprised to see you here. Rumor has it that you got married this morning."

Sean purposely took his time filling the disposable plastic cup, and then took a sip before saying. "Rumor's right."

"So come on, Sean," Bill said. "Tell me about your new wife."

Sean settled into a chair across from the man and shrugged. "There isn't much to tell."

Bill leaned forward, bracing his elbows on his knees as he eyed Sean critically. "Of course there is. Where did you meet her? *When* did you meet her? The last time we talked, the only woman in your life was Amy. Now in less than a month, you've remarried."

"All you need to know is that I took your advice and found my daughter a mother. And a damn good one, if I say so myself," Sean responded impatiently.

Bill stroked his chin. "I wish my patients would take my advice so readily. Where did you find her?"

"In the yellow pages, of course."

"Sarcasm doesn't suit you, Sean. Why are you being so evasive?"

Sean sighed and shook his head in defeat, knowing from experience that when Bill was in this mood, he was like a dog with a bone. He wasn't going to let go until he had a satisfactory answer. Sean decided to save himself the hassle and give it to him.

"Because I'm sure you'll disapprove. So why don't we just change the subject?"

"Why would I disapprove?" Bill countered quickly.

"Because she's an ex-patient of yours."

"Now I am intrigued. Where did you meet an ex-patient of mine?"

"Actually she's an ex-patient of mine, whom you consulted on."

Bill's brows drew together in a thoughtful frown. "I've only consulted on one patient of yours, and she's Amy's..." His voice died and he stared at Sean in shock. "You didn't! Not that poor woman. My God, Sean, what do you think you're doing?"

"Giving my daughter a mother who will love her as completely as I do."

"And what about Whitney Price? Have you thought about what this could do to her? You're asking her to relive the past. A past that will be very painful for her, and one that I doubt she's been able to resolve."

Sean's eyes turned cold. "I am not asking her to relive the past. I'm asking her to share her daughter's future. I've given her back what was taken away from her."

Sean had never seen Bill angry, and he leaned backward in surprise when his friend leaped up off the sofa and advanced on him, his small frame shaking and his fists clenched at his sides.

"You were right when you said I wouldn't approve, and I can't believe that you're playing on that woman's emotions. You're as bad as her fiancé. He used her for money. You're using her for your convenience."

"I'm using her for my daughter!" Sean shot back. "I'm giving Amy the love she deserves."

"And what about the love Whitney deserves? Did you ever stop to think about that? Of course, you didn't," Bill snapped before Sean could respond. "You can't even say *our* daughter. You keep saying *my*. You selfishly looked at yours and Amy's needs and didn't even bother to examine Whitney's. She loved a man who was in love with her father's money and prestige. He was killed, and she bore his daughter. She cared about that child so much that she gave her up for adoption."

"So what do you want me to do?" Sean asked in disgust. "Go home and tell her that I made a mistake? That I want a divorce because she deserves more than what I can offer?"

"Why didn't you talk to me about this?" Bill inquired plaintively. "I could have shown you that this choice was not viable for you and Amy, and especially not for Whitney."

Sean raked his hands through his hair, more shaken by Bill's response than he wanted to admit. Why hadn't he talked to his friend about it? Because he had known what Bill's reaction would be, and he simply hadn't wanted to hear it.

"I didn't talk to you because I thought I was doing what was best for Amy, and I'm still not convinced I was wrong. And you don't need to worry about Whitney. I've already decided that I'll do everything I can to make her happy."

"Everything but what she really needs," Bill replied, shaking his head wearily. "After what she's been through, she needs a man who will love her unconditionally, despite her past. She needs understanding and respect."

"I can give her understanding and respect. I already have."

"But don't you see that it won't be enough?" Bill asked. "What is her life worth if it isn't balanced with love? How can she possibly cope when she's never been anything but a pawn? And that's what she's always been, Sean. Even her father used her, though she'll probably never be able to face that fact. Now you've stolen her only chance to find peace with herself."

"I think she can find peace with Amy."

"I hope you're right," Bill said, though he sounded doubtful. "I *pray* that you're right."

"I am right," Sean whispered as he watched his friend walk away. "I *am*."

But that avowal didn't stop a shiver from crawling up his spine, or the underlying feeling that his friend had just predicted doom.

Chapter Five

"Read me another story," Amy demanded, and Whitney reached for another book, even though she knew she should tuck the child into bed and order her to go to sleep. But ever since Amy joined her after her nap, Whitney had been unable to keep her hands off of her.

She rocked the rocking chair they sat in, loving the feeling of Amy cuddled against her. She'd already missed three years of this, and soon Amy wouldn't want to be held. The words of the book blurred as her eyes filled with tears at the realization of just how much she had lost.

By the time she finished the book, Amy had fallen asleep, but Whitney continued to hold her, each rock of the rocking chair healing another small wound inside her. She had her baby back, and she'd never let her go again. After shifting her daughter into a more comfortable position, Whitney leaned her head against the chair and closed her eyes. She'd hold her just a little longer, and then tuck her into bed for the night.

SEAN WAS EXHAUSTED when he let himself into the house. It had been a long day, and all he wanted to do was sleep. He wearily climbed the stairs, automatically turning toward Amy's room. He'd kiss her good-night, and then fall into bed. He pushed open her bedroom door and froze.

Whitney was asleep in the rocking chair beside the bed with Amy curled in her arms. Emotion clogged his throat, and his eyes moistened, despite his frantic blinking. How many times had he found Margaret like this? More times than he wanted to remember, because then he would have to recall all the long hours he'd been away from home.

He crossed over to them, and brushed his hand against Amy's silken head, resisting the urge to do the same to Whitney. They looked right together. Even more right than Margaret had, and he had to blink even harder. It wasn't fair, he thought, as he experienced a surge of anger, though he didn't know if he was angry at Whitney for looking as if she belonged, or at Margaret for dying.

He carefully retrieved Amy from Whitney's arms and held her against his chest for a long moment. She was his, by damn, so why did he feel like an intruder? He put Amy to bed and covered her.

"Whitney?" he whispered softly as he squatted beside the rocking chair and gently shook her shoulder.

"Where's Amy?" she asked as her eyes opened and she peered groggily at him.

"In bed. She's asleep," he replied. She looked just like Amy with her face soft from sleep, and he smiled at her fondly. "Come on, let's get you into bed."

"What time is it?" she asked with a yawn, leaning against him and releasing a contented sigh as he helped her to her feet and held her against his side when she stumbled.

Sean tightened his hold around her, surprised at how easily she fit against him. "It's way past your bedtime."

"Was it a girl or a boy?" she asked next as he led her into her bedroom.

"One of each. Mrs. Barnett surprised us with twins."

She smiled up at him sleepily. "That's wonderful. My grandmother was a twin, and I've always wanted to have twins."

"They're just double trouble." He sat her down on her bed and pulled off her shoes.

"But they're such nice trouble." She fell back on the mattress and yawned widely. "Just imagine. Two sets of memories to hold on to in your old age."

"And two sets of worries to make you turn prematurely gray," he said with a chuckle as he pulled the covers from beneath her and tossed them over her, clothes and all. "Sleep tight."

Sean thought she'd drifted off to sleep and he turned back toward her in surprise when she said, "Sean?"

"Yes?"

"Thank you for giving Amy back to me. I finally feel as if I'm whole again."

"You're welcome," he said huskily.

As he closed the door behind him, he couldn't help but wonder if he would ever be able to feel whole again, and he veered away from his bedroom and the lonely expanse of his bed. Instead he reentered Amy's room.

He sat in the rocking chair Whitney had just vacated and lifted a book that rested beside it. It was Amy's favorite, *Goldilocks and the Three Bears*. He'd read it to her so many times he could nearly recite it by heart, and he knew Amy could do exactly that because if he improvised, she always corrected him.

He held the book against his chest, finding it oddly comforting, and as his eyes drifted around her room, they came to rest on a photograph of Amy and Margaret that sat on the child's dresser. Dear God, he missed Margaret, but she was gone, and for Amy's sake, he had no choice but to get on with his life.

"I just wish," he whispered to Margaret's image, "that you could come back for one moment and tell me that I've done the right thing."

But it was a wish that would never come true, and with a sigh he rose to his feet, knowing that only time would give him the answer. He could only pray that it would be the one he wanted.

WHITNEY NODDED and murmured appropriate sounds of agreement as she dressed for dinner and listened to Amy, who was sitting in the middle of Whitney's bed, chattering away. Except during her nap, Amy hadn't stopped talking, but Whitney didn't find her constant dialogue irritating. She found it pleasant and comforting, a lot like a radio playing in the background.

"What's you doing?" Amy asked when Whitney sat down on the edge of the bed and began to pull on her nylons.

"Putting on stockings," Whitney answered.

"Oh," Amy said, coming up on her knees. "What's this?" she asked as she curiously touched Whitney's bra.

"It's a brassiere. It's underwear that grown-up women wear, and when you're grown-up, you'll wear one, too."

"Why?"

Whitney smiled, having already learned that the child's questions rarely required more than simple answers. "Because all grown-up women wear them."

"Oh. What's this?" Amy asked then as she touched the strap of Whitney's garter belt that she'd just fastened to her stocking.

"It's called a garter, and it holds up my socks." She tapped her finger against Amy's nose. "I'd look pretty silly if my stockings fell down, wouldn't I?"

Amy giggled. "Uh-huh." She sat down beside Whitney and watched as she fastened her other nylon. "I like my slippers," she said, wiggling her feet.

"I'm glad," Whitney replied as she grinned at the bright pink rabbit-faced slippers they'd bought that afternoon. "Do you like your new nightgown?"

Amy pulled at the neck of her matching pink nightgown that had rows of white eyelet lace from the neckline to the waist. "Uh-huh. Can I have a puppy?"

Whitney blinked in surprise at the question that had come from nowhere. "I don't know. Maybe we should talk to your daddy about it."

"My daddy loves me."

"He sure does," Whitney agreed.

"Do you love me?"

Whitney's eyes flooded with tears, and she hugged her close. "I sure do."

Amy squirmed out of her embrace and scrambled off the bed. "I'm going to get my dolly."

After Amy had raced out of the room, Whitney pulled her slip over her head, and sat down at the small vanity in her bedroom to apply her makeup. She'd just put on the last of it, when she heard Amy burst into hysterical laughter.

Deciding she'd better check on her, she slipped into her robe and crossed the hallway. She smiled when she discovered Sean kneeling on the floor, tickling Amy unmercifully. He'd already left by the time she awakened that morning, and she wondered if she should say something about his having tucked her into bed last night.

"Hi," she said as she leaned against the doorjamb and watched them, deciding she'd just play it by ear.

He glanced up at her and smiled. "Hello. How was your day?"

"Mine was fine. You'll have to ask Amy how hers was."

He glanced down at his daughter. "Did you have fun today?"

"Uh-huh." She stuck her foot into his face. "Whit-nee bought me Mr. Rabbit shoes."

Sean caught her foot and eyed the slipper. "Well, I'll be. They're gorgeous."

"And we got a new nightgown," Amy said as she sat up and pulled out the front of the garment under discussion.

Sean touched the ruffled lace. "You look just like a princess."

Amy nodded, before announcing, "When I grow up I get to wear a bazzear."

"Oh, yeah?" Sean questioned, glancing toward Whitney with a brow arched in question.

Whitney blushed, realizing he was waiting for an interpretation. "She was helping me dress, and she was fascinated with my bra."

"Oh," Sean said, grinning in understanding as he returned his gaze to his daughter. "Well, you're right. When you grow up, you'll wear a brassiere."

"Whit-nee's socks don't fall down," Amy then informed him.

"They don't?" he responded with a laugh. "How come?"

"'Cause she . . . she . . ."

Amy glanced toward Whitney for help.

"Holds them up with a garter belt," Whitney supplied, her blush deepening.

"Yeah," Amy said, clapping her hands.

Sean sat up, one knee raised. He wrapped his arms around it and grinned at Whitney devilishly. "I can see it's been a very interesting day."

"Yeah," Whitney said, nervously twirling the tie of her robe. "I'll go finish dressing."

She'd started to walk out of the room, when Amy said, "Whit-nee said I could have a puppy."

"No," Whitney corrected, turning back to face Amy. "I said we'd ask your father."

Amy's head lowered and she stuck out her lower lip. "I want a puppy."

Sean glanced from his daughter to her mother. "We'll talk about it tomorrow."

"But I want a puppy," Amy said as she wrapped her arms around her father's neck. "Please."

"We'll talk about it tomorrow," Sean repeated as he tapped his fingers against her nose. "Now I'd better go get cleaned up for dinner. Have you eaten?"

Amy nodded. "Zanya and scaregus."

"Lasagna and asparagus," Whitney interpreted again, when Sean gave her another questioning look.

"What a great meal," he said, tousling Amy's hair. "You be a good girl and stay in here and play, okay?"

Amy nodded.

In the hallway, Sean stopped Whitney before she could enter her room. "How *was* your day?" he questioned.

"Fine," she repeated, smiling up at him.

He returned her smile. "I hope her interest in your underwear didn't bother you."

Whitney shook her head. "It was natural curiosity."

"How do you feel about a puppy?" he asked as he absently brushed a stray lock of hair away from her cheek, a habit he'd developed with Amy. The softness of her skin caught him by surprise, as did the strange tingling warmth that shot through his fingers. He rubbed his hand against his thigh in confusion.

Whitney shrugged, feeling oddly off balance. Sean's unexpected touch and his closeness were doing wild things to her nerves. "I'm game if you are."

"A puppy is a lot of work."

"Maybe we should consult with Mrs. Wilkens."

"Probably so."

As it had last night on the telephone, an awkward silence stretched between them as they each searched for an appropriate parting comment. Whitney lowered her eyes and discovered that Sean had pulled the knot of his tie down several inches and opened the top two buttons of his shirt. For some reason, his dishabille after a long day's work reeked of intimacy, especially when she realized she wore nothing but her old robe over white lace and satin.

She took a quick step backward and self-consciously clutched the lapels of her robe tight around her neck. "Well, I guess I'd better finish dressing for dinner."

"Me, too," Sean said, his voice low and gruff as her eyes rose to meet his. They were inordinately wide, making her look soft and vulnerable and ultimately feminine. A wave of tenderness flowed through him, and he had to resist the urge to pull her into his arms and reassure her, because he had no idea what he was supposed to reassure her about. "I'll be down shortly," he said instead.

Whitney nodded as he entered his bedroom. She felt as if something significant had just happened between them, but she didn't have the vaguest notion what it was.

"I THINK HAVING A PUPPY around would be fun," Mrs. Wilkens said as she helped Whitney put the finishing touches on the table.

"Yes, but a puppy's a lot of work."

"I think the two of us can handle it."

"Handle what?" Sean asked from the doorway, and Whitney spun around in surprise.

He'd changed into a pair of chinos and a white shirt that was open halfway down his chest, revealing a thick mat of hair that she stared at in fascination. Both her father and Duncan had had chests as smooth and hairless as a baby's.

The hair on his head was tousled and slightly damp from his quick shower, and the shading of his evening beard gave him that rough-and-tumble look she'd seen the day of Amy's tea party. Though Whitney had always thought him attractive, this was the first time she'd realized just how handsome he truly was.

"Handle a puppy," she said in answer to his question.

"Oh." He gave a sage nod as he strolled into the dining room. "If the two of you agree on a puppy, I won't object. However, let's get a small dog. One that we'll feel comfortable about letting into the house. After all, what's the purpose of having a pet if we can't make it a full-fledged member of the family?"

He pulled out Whitney's chair, and then sat down in his, rubbing his hands together as he eyed the warming plate of lasagna. "I'm starved."

Mrs. Wilkens chuckled. "You two enjoy your meal. I'll go keep Amy entertained."

"I knew there was a reason for you to decide to keep her on," Sean said when Mrs. Wilkens left. "Dining takes on an entirely new meaning when it involves Amy."

"Eating with Amy is fun," Whitney said in the girl's defense.

"Spoken like a true mother," Sean said with a laugh. As he waited for her to fill her plate, he studied the soft denim dress she wore. It was sleeveless, with a fitted bodice that had bright red snaps closing it down the front, and a flowing skirt that hit her at midcalf. She looked young and more relaxed than he'd ever seen her. Even the tremor was gone from her hands. All she needed was to gain about twenty pounds and she'd look as healthy as the proverbial horse. As he lifted the spoon and dug into the lasagna, he said, "Thanks for remembering."

"Remembering what?" she asked in surprise.

"That lasagna's my favorite meal."

She smiled shyly. "I also remember that your favorite color is green, that you love to ride horses, go on picnics and that you hate to shave."

He laughed again and rubbed his hand against his jaw. "We know so much about each other, and yet there's so much we don't know. For instance, I don't know what kind of music you like, or what your politics are."

She chuckled. "I think you should have an idea about the latter considering who my father was."

"Mmm, I suppose you're right." He finished filling his plate before saying, "We need to take care of some mundane chores like getting your name on the checking account, credit cards, et cetera. Is it okay with you if we do it tomorrow morning?"

"Yes."

"Then it's a date." His eyes sparkled with mischief as he said, "As Amy would say so eloquently, let's eat."

They talked as they ate, and Whitney was pleased to learn that they both liked pop music, old movies and a good mystery novel. It appeared that they would have enough in common to at least be able to communicate.

As they neared the end of their meal, Sean said, "Why don't you tell me about your years at Price Manufacturing?"

Whitney was slightly startled by the request, but she shrugged and said, "There isn't much to tell. Simon Prescott helped me hire a highly trained staff that put the company back on its feet.

"And, of course, you didn't have anything to do with that success."

She released a self-conscious laugh. "Well, I suppose I had something to do with it."

"You should be proud of yourself, Whitney."

"I am," she stated matter-of-factly. "I also know that I was only as good as the team working with me. What about you? I looked in the phone book and saw that you've taken on another partner. Has your practice grown that much?"

"Yes," Sean answered, "but I didn't take on a second partner until Margaret died. I wanted to spend more time with Amy, and that was the only way I could possibly do it. I'm also indebted to both of them. They've tried to make my life easier by doing little things for me, such as covering for me for a few hours on the Saturdays I was on call so I could always have Saturday afternoon tea with Amy."

Though Whitney knew Sean's wife had died, the papers hadn't given any details on her death. This was her first opportunity to ask.

"How did Margaret die?" she asked, immediately regretting the question when his smile faded and pain flickered in his eyes as he clenched his napkin against the tabletop. She automatically reached across the table and laid her hand on his. "You don't have to tell me."

"It's all right." He leaned his head back, stared up at the ceiling, and released a heartfelt sigh. "She had appendicitis and had to have surgery. She had a rare allergic reaction to the anesthesia and never came out of it."

"I'm very sorry," Whitney said. "I know how it feels to lose someone you love so unexpectedly."

He glanced back down at her. "Yes, you do." Then he laid his napkin aside and said, "I also think that's enough serious conversation for this evening. Why don't we go tuck Amy in for the night, and then have our dessert in the living room?"

"Okay."

When they entered Amy's room, Mrs. Wilkens climbed out of the rocking chair and left Sean and Whitney alone with their daughter. Amy was already half asleep when they kissed her good-night.

"It's evident Amy had fun today," Sean told Whitney as he led her back downstairs, "and you don't look as if she drove you crazy."

"She didn't. She talks a lot, but I just nod my head and go on about my business."

"You mean you've already mastered the trick of shutting her out?" he teased.

"Not quite, but I'm working on it," she teased back.

Mrs. Wilkens stuck her head through the kitchen doorway. "I'll serve dessert. You just get settled."

"You don't have to bother," Whitney objected.

"No bother," Mrs. Wilkens said cheerfully as she disappeared back into the kitchen.

"As I said, I knew there was a reason for you to keep her on," Sean told her as he steered her into the living room. "Besides, this'll give me a chance to give you your present."

"My present?"

"That's what I said." He settled her on the sofa, and walked out of the room. He reappeared a moment later, sat down beside her and handed her a long manila envelope.

Curious, Whitney opened it and pulled out a sheaf of papers. With a puzzled frown, she studied six artistic sketches of what appeared to be small houses. They were built out of wood and had glass fronts that created a greenhouse effect. Scrawled at the bottom of each sketch was the signature of a prominent local architect.

When Whitney looked up at Sean in confusion, he asked, "Don't you like them?"

"They're beautiful, but I don't understand what they are."

"They're possible designs for a conservatory. Since there isn't room for your mother's piano in the house, I decided we should build a home for it in the backyard. Don said that if you didn't like any of these designs, he'd be glad to meet with you and come up with something you do like."

Whitney could only stare at him. The fact that he'd understood how important the piano was to her caused a lump of emotion to form in her throat. Unable to speak around it, she shuffled the pictures again.

Finally she managed to find her voice. "I love them all, but this is much too expensive to build just for a piano."

"No, it's not. Besides, I figured we could include a couple of small bedrooms and a bath on the second floor so we'll have a guest house. You haven't met my family yet, but when you do, you'll realize that we're going to have lots of company. The entire clan has a habit of showing up on the doorstep for unannounced visits." He grinned at her. "Sometimes I feel as if I'm being invaded, but they're all so much fun that I can't get mad at them. I hope you'll feel the same way."

"I'm sure I will. Exactly how big is your family?"

"I have two brothers, four sisters, a half dozen nieces and nephews, and of course, my parents." He released a fond chuckle. "Mom and Dad are like a conquering army all by themselves, and Amy is in seventh heaven when Granny and Gramps come to visit. By the time they leave, it takes a month to get her back on schedule."

"It must be nice to be from a big family," Whitney said wistfully.

He laughed. "Those words could only be spoken by an only child. But as exasperated as I get with them, I guess it is nice."

Mrs. Wilkens came bustling into the room and placed a tray with cherry pie and coffee on the table in front of them. "Thanks, Mrs. Wilkens," Whitney said.

"Sure. I'm going to my room now. Just leave the dishes, and I'll take care of them in the morning."

When she was gone, Sean handed Whitney her dessert, leaned back on the sofa with his, and asked, "Now where were we?"

"Talking about a combination conservatory and guest house." She cut off a piece of pie, but instead of eating it, she eyed Sean in concern. "It really is an expensive-looking project, and it isn't necessary. I've already decided to sell the piano."

"The hell you will!" Sean exclaimed as he bolted up from his relaxed position and slammed his pie plate down on the coffee table.

Whitney was so startled by his reaction, she almost dropped her plate.

Sean took it from her and placed it on the table. Then he leaned toward her and took both of her hands into his. His face was so close she could feel his breath, and his eyes were positively blazing.

"Sean," she began in an effort to soothe him, but he interrupted.

"You are not going to sell that piano, Whitney. You told me yourself that it's the only thing you have left that belonged to your mother."

"Yes, but—"

He interrupted again. "I heard you play, Whitney, and I know that it isn't there just because it belonged to your mother. You use it to help yourself work your way through your problems, don't you?"

"In a way, but—"

He didn't let her finish, because he needed to do this for her. Had to do it for her. She'd given up so much for Amy and him, and he couldn't stand the thought of her giving up one item more, particularly one that not only had sentimental value, but, he was convinced, therapeutic value as well.

"We are going to build a conservatory in the backyard," he stated firmly. "All you have to do is decide which design you want."

Whitney frowned at him in frustration. "If you feel that strongly about it, okay. But at least let me pay for half of it. As soon as the mansion sells, I'll have plenty of money, and . . ."

"You still don't understand, do you?" Sean muttered with an irritated shake of his head. "This is something I have to do for you. You've given up so much for this family, and what have you gained? Nothing."

"I see," Whitney said, jerking her hands away from his as her temper flared. She picked up the designs and waved them at him. "This is to be my reward for giving up so much and gaining nothing?" He parted his lips to respond, but she shook her head in a manner that demanded his silence. "Don't make me out to be some type of martyr. What I gained was my daughter. Nothing is more important than that, Sean. Not even my mother's piano.

"If you want to build a conservatory, fine," she concluded, "but don't do it because you have some farfetched notion that I deserve some kind of reward. You've given me the most precious gift that I could ever receive, namely Amy. Because of that, I owe you, and will for the remainder of my life. I don't want or need anything else from you, Sean. Your debt is paid."

Knowing she was close to tears, and determined not to shed them in front of him, she said, "I've had a long day, and I'd better call it a night. I'll see you in the morning."

Sean remained on the sofa, his gaze wandering around the room, but seeing nothing. His emotions were in a jumble that he wasn't quite able to sort through. He'd expected Whitney to be excited about his gift, and the fact that she wasn't confused him. And what was all this business about the conservatory being a reward? He wasn't trying to reward her, but to show her how grateful he was. Maybe that was the problem. Maybe he was trying too hard. But what choice did he have?

He'd known from the moment he saw her picture in the newspaper that she'd agree to marry him. He'd learned that much about her in the labor room. And now, he realized, he'd just committed the one sin that he'd fought so hard to avoid when she was his patient; he'd involved himself in a conflict of interest.

If he hadn't convinced her to marry him, Whitney would have eventually found a loving husband. Perhaps even had more children. But, as Bill had pointed out, not once had he thought about her welfare. Amy's had been uppermost in his mind, and Amy's welfare directly affected his own peace of mind.

Yes, he'd been selfish, and Whitney's reaction tonight made that evident. She said she owed him, but he knew his debt far outweighed hers. He also knew he'd be spending the remainder of his life trying to pay it off, whether she liked it or not.

He levered himself up off the sofa and headed up the stairs, deciding that he should offer Whitney an apology. But when he reached the top of the stairs, the light beneath her door went out. He frowned, wondering if he should knock on her door anyway, but he decided against it. She'd been upset. He'd let her rest and apologize to her in the morning.

But Whitney wasn't resting. She was prowling her bedroom, feeling more angry than she had in years. First, the man had tried to buy her hand in marriage. Now he was trying to reward her! For two cents she'd grab him and shake him until he finally got some sense into his thick head, because she was convinced that he didn't even realize he was insulting her.

She stopped at her window and looked out into the starless night. The weatherman had predicted rain, and she watched a bolt of lightning flash in the distance. She began to count, waiting for the resulting boom of thunder, but it never came. The storm was still a long distance away. Too bad. She would have liked to match her inner storm with it.

"Somehow, some way, I'm going to set you straight, Sean Fitzgerald," she muttered. "Even if it means bopping you over the head to get my point across. I'm warning you now that your day is coming."

Chapter Six

Whitney shot straight up in bed from a sound sleep. She didn't know exactly what had awakened her, but she knew something was wrong with Amy. She leaped out of bed and ran across the hallway, barreling right into Sean's back. He was already at the door and flinging it open.

Sean reached out to steady her, but she pushed his arm away, exclaiming impatiently, "Check on Amy!"

"Right." He switched on the overhead light and hurried into the child's room. Amy was sitting up in bed, tears streaming down her face as she gasped for breath.

"What is it, sweetheart?" Sean asked as he gathered her into his arms.

"Ghosts," Amy sobbed as she clung to her father and buried her face against his chest.

"Oh, pumpkin, there's no such thing as ghosts," Sean crooned as he stroked her hair. "All you had was a nightmare."

"No," Amy disagreed with a violent shake of her head. "There's ghosts, and they want to eat me."

"Sweetheart, even if there were ghosts they couldn't eat people. They wouldn't have any teeth." He sat down in the rocking chair and gave Whitney a resolved smile. "When my sister came to visit a couple of months ago, her six-year-old son decided to tell Amy ghost stories. She's had this nightmare ever since."

Whitney brushed her hair back from her eyes, so relieved that she had to lean against the bedpost in order to keep standing.

"I have the perfect cure for ghosts," she told him hoarsely. "Do you have any colored tape in the house?"

"I have white bandage tape in my doctor's bag."

"That'll work," Whitney said as she glanced down at the bright pink-and-blue shag carpeting. "Where's the bag?"

"In my bedroom beside the bed."

She nodded. "I'll be right back."

It was the first time Whitney had been in Sean's bedroom, but she didn't spare much more than a cursory look around the room. Like the rest of the house, it was decorated in bright, cheerful colors, and Whitney blinked against them.

She bent down to retrieve Sean's bag, and her gaze caught on the photograph beside the bed. She recognized the woman. It was Sean's Margaret. There were pictures of her, Sean and Amy scattered throughout the house. But this photograph was different. Margaret was standing in the front yard with an infant Amy clutched in her arms, the child swaddled in blankets, and her tiny newborn face screwed up against the sunlight.

There was so much emotion on the woman's face, that Whitney felt it pierce right through her soul. *It should have been me,* she thought. *She was my baby.* But she'd given up that right, she reminded herself, and she both hated and envied Margaret at that moment. Yet there was a part of her that was grateful to see that the woman had felt so deeply about the child in her arms. Whitney had wanted Amy to be blessed with love, and it was evident that she was. And now was not the time to contemplate the past. Whitney lifted Sean's doctor's bag and ran back to Amy's room.

"Okay, Amy," she said when she arrived. "We're going to put a magic circle around your bed that no ghosts can get across. Only me, your daddy and Mrs. Wilkens can get near you, okay?"

"'Kay," Amy said as she swiped childishly at her eyes and watched Whitney curiously.

Whitney pulled out the bandage tape and a pair of small scissors. Starting at the top of Amy's bed, she began to place strips of tape down on the carpet until they completely surrounded the bed.

Then she walked over to the rocking chair. "You have to help me say the magic spell that will keep the ghosts away, okay?"

"'Kay," Amy said again as she held out her arms.

Sean lifted her until Whitney could get her settled on her hip. His lips curved into a smile as Whitney told Amy, "You have to say: 'Ghosts go away. Only Whitney, Daddy and Mrs. Wilkens can stay.'"

Amy repeated the words after Whitney, who carried her completely around the bed, making her say it several times.

"Now," Whitney told her as she pressed a kiss against her cheek, "no ghost can come near you, because if they cross over the tape, they'll blow up and disappear. And if you see them, and you're scared, you just tell them to go away and that only me, your daddy and Mrs. Wilkens can stay."

She tucked the child back into bed and pulled her covers up to her chin. "Are you scared now?"

"No," Amy said with a sniff.

"Good," Whitney murmured as she dropped another kiss to her forehead. "You go back to sleep, and I promise you that no ghost can get you."

"'Night, pumpkin," Sean said as he, too, bent to give her a kiss. "You just yell if you need me."

Amy nodded. As they walked out of the room, she was chanting, "Ghost go away. Only Whit-nee, Daddy and Mrs. Wilkens can stay."

"Where in the world did you learn that?" Sean asked with a chuckle as he leaned against wall and shook his head. "It's marvelous!"

"My dad," Whitney answered. "I was terrified of ghosts, too, and he finally got tired of getting up with me. We made a magic circle that only special people could cross, and I never had the nightmare again.''

"I knew you were going to make a wonderful mother,'' Sean told her as he reached out and chucked her affectionately under the chin. "Would you like to slip into your robe and slippers and join me downstairs for some hot chocolate before we call it a night?''

"Sure,'' Whitney replied, feeling particularly pleased with herself that she'd solved the problem of Amy's nightmare. A cup of hot chocolate would be a great way to celebrate.

"Great. I'll meet you in the kitchen,'' Sean said.

When Whitney arrived in the kitchen, Sean was standing at the stove, and she paused in the doorway, watching him as he poured chocolate syrup into the pot of milk already on the burner, eyed it consideringly as he stirred it, and then added more.

Whitney couldn't help but smile. With his rumpled hair, haphazardly belted robe and bare feet, he would have looked boyish, except the dark shading of his beard made it apparent that he was all man. She was not only confused, but startled by the trembling sensation in the pit of her stomach.

"What can I do to help?'' she asked, deciding to ignore the physical aberration.

He glanced up from the pot and grinned. "Sit down, and when I finally bring this watched pot to a boil, rave about my culinary talents.''

"I think I can handle that.''

She sat down at the table, continuing to watch him watch the pot. The only light in the room was the light over the stove, giving a sense of intimacy to the scene that she found extremely comfortable and warming.

Finally the milk had warmed, and Sean poured it into two mugs. Then he dropped two fat marshmallows into one, before glancing toward Whitney while dangling two over the other mug.

She shook her head. "I don't need the marshmallows. They're fattening."

Sean's brows flew upward in comical disbelief. "In that case, you need three." He promptly dropped in the marshmallows and tossed in an extra.

When he deposited her mug in front of her a second later, Whitney frowned at him. "I really didn't want the marshmallows."

"You really need the calories," he replied as he settled into a chair across from her. When her frown deepened, he gave a frustrated shake of his head. "You're far too thin, Whitney. You need to gain at least twenty pounds."

"Twenty pounds!" she gasped. "I wouldn't be able to wear any of my clothes."

"Then I'll buy you a new wardrobe." When her lips tightened in a mutinous display, he said, "I'm not picking on you, Whitney, but I am a doctor, and I do know about these things. The body needs a good layer of subcutaneous fat to not only keep it warm, but to fall back on in times of illness. Right now, a good case of the flu would land you in the hospital, and I don't think you'd like that."

Whitney parted her lips to argue with him, but she found the words wouldn't come. She knew that she'd shed several pounds in the past few years, and it had been so darn long since anyone had really cared about her that she found his concern oddly touching.

"Maybe it wouldn't hurt me to gain a few pounds," she conceded.

Sean merely smiled his agreement. He took a sip of his hot chocolate before saying, "I owe you an apology for the conservatory. I only meant to do something nice for you, but I ended up insulting you. I am truly sorry, Whitney."

Whitney eyed him for a long, thoughtful moment. "You don't really know what you did wrong, do you?"

"No," Sean answered honestly.

Whitney stared down into her mug of chocolate as she circled its rim with a finger. A part of her said that she should just accept his apology and forget it, but another part insisted that she had to make him understand. Regardless of how convoluted their relationship was, they were still married. They had to develop a system of communication or they'd never make it.

"I was hurt," she explained. "I felt as if you were trying to buy me off."

"Buy you off?" he repeated, dumbfounded by the revelation. "I wasn't trying to buy you off. I was just trying to do something nice for you."

"But you were doing it in terms of a trade-off, Sean," she stated passionately, needing for him to understand. "When you first came to me about Amy, you didn't say, 'Your daughter needs a mother, are you interested?' You offered to pay off my loan from Simon and finance my greenhouse. Tonight you didn't say that the conservatory was something we could both enjoy, you said that I'd given up too much and . . ."

"You don't need to finish," Sean murmured softly as he reached across the table and caught her hand. Then he gave a miserable shake of his head. "I really am a bumbling fool, aren't I?"

"No," Whitney insisted as she automatically turned her hand and entwined her fingers with his. "I think that you don't know what motivates me any more than I know what motivates you. The only way we can make those discoveries is to talk, Sean. To be open and honest about our feelings."

Sean drew his hand away and cradled his mug in it. As he gazed down into its liquid depths, he said, "I know you're right, and I promise you that I'll really try. The problem is, I'm not very good at expressing my feelings. I have to think everything through, weigh the pros and cons, decide what will hurt and what won't, and then decide if the hurt is worth it.

"I also have a tendency to be impetuous—to do something because it feels right, even though I don't always understand why it feels that way." He raised his eyes to hers and confessed, "That's how I felt about the conservatory. It was just . . . right."

Whitney's smile was shaky when she said, "Then let's build it."

"You're sure?"

"Yes, I'm sure."

Sean reached across the table and took her hand again. When she gave it a squeeze, something deep inside him loosened, relaxed. He didn't know what it was, but it felt right. It took an effort to release his hold on her hand.

WHEN SEAN CAME DOWN for breakfast, he was surprised to find Whitney setting the table in the dining room, humming to herself. Since she was unaware of his presence, he leaned against the doorjamb and allowed himself the pleasure of watching her.

She was dressed in a simple peach-colored cotton sundress and low-heeled white sandals. Her hair was caught at her neck with a white ribbon, and he followed the shimmering fall that dropped down her back.

"Did we have a fire in the kitchen?" he finally asked.

Whitney jumped and let out a startled cry as she turned to face him. "I didn't hear you come downstairs," she said as she pressed a hand against her chest.

"I'm sorry. I didn't mean to scare you."

"It's all right."

"No, it's not. Next time I'll stomp my feet." He walked into the room, stopped beside her and let his eyes roam down her. "You look pretty."

"Thank you," she said, the color in her cheeks deepening beneath his appraisal.

He nodded and glanced at the table. "Why are we eating in here?"

"Because it's the dining room," she answered, as if it should be obvious. "Don't you like eating in here?"

He didn't like it, and he wasn't certain why. He supposed it was because Margaret had always saved the dining room for special occasions, and they'd taken most of their meals in the kitchen. But Whitney wasn't Margaret, he reminded himself, and he was going to have to get used to changes like this.

"I don't mind," he lied. "Where's Amy?"

"In her playhouse. I was just about ready to go get her."

"I'll get her. You finish what you're doing and sit down and rest. We have a lot to do this morning."

Whitney frowned at his back as he walked out of the room, sensing that he was upset. Was it something she'd done? She shrugged dismissively, deciding that she couldn't have possibly done anything wrong in the few seconds they'd been together.

By the time he and Amy joined her and Mrs. Wilkens for breakfast, she was relieved to see he was back in his normal good humor. The four of them chatted easily, and Amy kept the group highly entertained with her constant antics. Every other word out of her mouth was puppy, but Sean kept telling her he was still thinking about it.

Whitney gazed at him curiously, wondering why he was prolonging the girl's agony when they'd already decided she could have a puppy. But she didn't question him in front of the child. She waited until they'd left the house. On the drive to the bank she asked him, and he laughed.

"Because you and I are going to get her a puppy this afternoon. If I told her she could have one, she'd want to pick it out, and knowing Amy, she'd choose a Great Dane or some other huge monster." He gave her a lopsided grin. "I can't deny her anything she really wants, and do you want a dog in the house that's bigger than you are?"

"No," Whitney said with a laugh. "It is too bad, though, that she can't choose it herself. A puppy's pretty special."

"That's why you're going to do the picking," he said, reaching over to tap his finger against the tip of her nose as they sat at a stoplight. "You're going to have the major responsibility for the mutt, and I want you to have a puppy that you'll love, too.''

"What if I pick out a Great Dane?" she asked, her eyes dancing with laughter.

He grinned. "Well, if you bat those big baby blues of yours at me, I guess I'll be sunk."

They went through the tedious red tape at the bank to get her name put on all of Sean's accounts and major credit cards. When they walked outside, Whitney tilted her head toward the clear summer sky and drew in a deep breath. "This would be a perfect day for a walk in the woods, wouldn't it?"

"If that's what the lady wants, then that's what we'll do," Sean said as he took her elbow and led her toward the car.

"I thought we were going to pick out a puppy."

"The day's still young. We can do both."

He helped her into the car, and when he rounded it and climbed in beside her, she said, "I'd rather go puppy hunting than walking in the woods."

"Are you sure?" he questioned, his eyes searching her face. "We can do both, Whitney, or we can pick out a puppy on another day. It's not as if Amy's expecting us to come home with one."

"My sandals aren't exactly made for hiking, and I want to get her a puppy. Can you imagine the expression on her face when we give it to her?"

"Yes," he whispered huskily, knowing that Amy's expression would never rival Whitney's. There was a poignancy to her; a kind of happy sadness. It tugged at his heart. "What's wrong?" he asked as he automatically reached up to brush an errant strand of hair away from her cheek.

"Nothing," she said, as she unthinkingly rubbed her face against his hand. "It's just that I've missed so many of the special times with Amy, and I guess I feel that giving her the puppy will make up for some of them. It won't, of course, but if I try really hard, I can make myself believe that it will."

Sean's hand dropped limply into his lap, and he swallowed against the sudden lump in his throat. Over the years he'd grown so used to giving Amy presents that he was shocked to realize that he'd begun to take the special, heartwarming events in his daughter's life for granted. Seeing them through Whitney's eyes made him see how much he was missing.

"We'll make sure that you get a chance to make up for all those special times," he told her.

Puppy hunting with Whitney turned out to be an experience in itself. She dragged Sean through four pet stores, unable to make up her mind. Finally she instructed him to take her to the pet shelter, and Sean almost had heart failure when she went wild over a half-grown St. Bernard puppys that raced up to her and nearly knocked her off her feet.

But, to his relief, she didn't choose him. She chose a fluffy white puppy of dubious parentage who was so cute, even Sean was instantly in love. As they waited for the tiny dog to be brought out to them, Whitney wandered to the door that housed the cats. Sean knew he was in trouble when she called for him in excitement.

"A white puppy, and a black kitten," he muttered to himself as he carried the two cardboard pet carriers out to the car, put them into the back seat and headed back to the pet store to pick up all the pet paraphernalia they needed.

He enjoyed following Whitney as she flew through the store, picking out a cat box, beds for both animals, toys and food and vitamins. In record time, they were back in the car, and Sean was grinning as she leaned over the front seat and poked a finger into each of the cardboard pet carriers, crooning to both the animals, who were by this time howling and yowling to get out.

But it was the sight of her softly rounded bottom as she leaned over the seat, and the flash of one silken thigh that he enjoyed the most. He was quite content to sit and enjoy the view until she was ready to go.

On the drive home, she chattered with as much animation as Amy. Sean made all the appropriate sounds of agreement he did with his daughter whenever Whitney paused long enough to take a breath. When he turned onto their street, she was nearly bouncing up and down on the seat with excitement, and Sean couldn't help but chuckle when he pulled into the driveway.

"I'm being silly, aren't I?" she asked in embarrassment.

He turned off the ignition, and turned toward her. "You're being positively motherly. It's a good thing that tomorrow's Saturday, and I'm not on call, because between you and Amy and the screeching duo in the back seat, I don't think we're going to get much sleep tonight."

"You don't really mind about the kitten, do you?"

He shook his head. He would have brought the entire shelter home if it would have kept the glow of happiness on her face. "I don't mind. Now how about if we get these bereft animals inside and give them their freedom?"

She nodded, and then impulsively threw her arms around his neck. As she hugged him, she whispered, "Thank you."

"Oh, Whitney, you're very welcome," he said as he hugged her back, surprised at how much effort he had to exert to make himself release her.

Amy was predictably excited about her new pets.

"Oh!" she squealed as Sean helped her open the first carrier. "It's a puppy!"

"Are you sure?" Sean teased as he helped her lift the dog out. "I thought it was a mouse."

"Daddy!" Amy giggled as the dog wriggled in her arms, his tongue lapping at her face. "He's washing me!"

"That's what happens when you don't wash behind your ears," Sean responded, his lips twitching with laughter. "Dogs can't stand to be around dirty little girls, so you're going to have to do a better job of washing yourself."

When the dog managed to free himself from Amy's clutches, Sean said, "Whitney has another surprise for you."

Amy glanced toward Whitney, her eyes wide with excitement as she surveyed the box at Whitney's feet. "Is it another puppy?"

Whitney gave an eloquent shrug. "I don't have any idea. I suppose the only way we can find out is to open the box."

Amy ran to her, saying, "Open the box."

Whitney obediently complied.

"A kitty!" Amy screamed as her small hands dived inside.

"Careful," Whitney warned. "It's still a baby, and babies are hurt very easily. Also, kittens have claws that can scratch."

She reached down to help the child remove the kitten, and her eyes moistened as she saw the excitement that wreathed her daughter's face as she clutched the kitten in her arms. This was better than a thousand Christmases, Whitney decided, when Amy laughed and buried her nose in the kitten's fur. Well, maybe not better, but it was sure in the running.

She caught Amy's arms to hold her upright as the puppy raced up to her and nearly knocked her down. Amy laughed infectiously as she sat down on the floor and tried to hold both animals at the same time. The kitten and puppy exercised their natural dislike of each other, and Whitney and Sean both hurried in to stop the fray. Then Sean set the animals on the carpet, nose to nose, ordering Whitney and Amy to stay out of the way.

"They have to make friends," he informed them, "and they'll only do so after they've faced off a few times."

After several barks and hisses, accompanied by a couple of paw swipes from the kitten, they reached a truce and began to explore their new home. Within the hour, both animals had gotten into enough mischief to send Sean out to the garage in search of a large box that neither of them could escape. While he was gone, Whitney and Amy sat together on the sofa and contemplated names for the pets.

"How about Snowball for the puppy since he's as white as snow," Whitney suggested.

"Yeah!" Amy agreed clapping her hands in delight. "And the kitty?"

"Well, she's as black as night. We could call her Midnight."

"'Kay. Daddy, we picked names!" she squealed when he walked into the room. "Snowball and Midnight. Aren't they pretty?"

Sean felt as if Amy had just kicked him in the stomach, and his hold on the box tightened as he glanced from Amy to Whitney and back to Amy. He would have never believed it, but he actually felt jealous about being left out of the name selection.

Sean coughed to clear his throat, knowing he had to respond to his daughter's question. "Yes, Amy, they're very pretty names. Now let's get them into the box before Snowball eats the coffee table," he said, dropping the box to the floor and scooping up the dog, who was testing the table leg for gnawability.

Whitney corralled the cat and put it into the box with the dog. Then standing beside Sean, who was peering down into the box with a frown, she laid her hand on his arm.

"What is it?" she asked quietly so Amy wouldn't hear. "Are you sorry that we got the animals?"

Sean glanced toward her and shook his head. "No." Since the truth sounded childish, there was no way he was going to confess it. He gave Whitney's hand a reassuring pat. "Everything's fine, Whitney. Just fine. I think I'll go change for dinner."

Whitney stared after his retreating back, perplexed. It was evident that everything wasn't "just fine," but since Sean didn't want to discuss what was wrong, there wasn't much she could do about it. She shrugged resolutely and turned her attention to Amy.

The box sat on the floor between Whitney and Amy when they sat down for dinner, and despite Sean's firm order that the pets were not to be fed at the table, both mother and daughter sneaked them morsels of food when he wasn't looking, grinning at each other in guilty mischief.

Sean knew what was going on, but decided to ignore it, enjoying their secret language of winks and giggles. It had been so long since he'd seen Amy in such a happy mood, that he couldn't summon up enough disapproval to scold them.

He released a sigh of regret when one of his partners called, informing Sean that he had an emergency cesarean and needed him to assist.

"Under no circumstances are those animals to sleep in Amy's bed," he stated firmly as he slipped into a lightweight jacket.

"Whatever you say," Whitney responded, her eyes wide and innocent.

When he came home, however, he found that his order had been followed to the letter, but Whitney and Amy had found themselves a loophole. They'd made a bed on the floor and were curled up with the puppy and kitten between them.

Sean chuckled as he stood in the doorway and shook his head, trying to decide which of them looked more adorable. Amy with the puppy clutched in her arms, or Whitney with the kitten snuggled against her chest. He put the animals into the box, where they curled up sleepily together. Then he put Amy into bed, pressing a kiss to her forehead.

When he turned back toward Whitney, he was startled to find her sitting up and regarding him with an amused smile. He extended his hand, and she took it, rising easily to her feet. He didn't release her hand until they were in the hallway, and he tried to look stern when he said, "You're spoiling her rotten."

Whitney shrugged negligently as she grinned up at him. "Little girls are supposed to be spoiled rotten."

"But there's rotten, and then there's *rotten*."

Whitney reached up and patted his cheek. "When I've crossed over the line, you'll let me know."

Sean sighed as he caught her hand again and absently brushed his thumb across her knuckles. "Does this mean you're going to make me into the bad guy?"

Her laugh was low and husky with delight. Sean's toes curled in his shoes at the sound. "Of course not, Sean. You'd look awful in a black hat."

"Oh, lady, what am I going to do with you?" he asked with an exaggerated sigh.

The question was heavy with innuendo, but Whitney refrained from commenting on it. Instead she slid her hand from his and leaned against the wall. Peering up at him, she asked, "Why were you so upset about the animals this afternoon?"

Sean gave an uncomfortable shrug. "I wasn't upset."

"You're an even worse liar than I am. You were upset. Why?"

"It's silly," he muttered as he glanced away from her.

"Oh, now I understand. *The* Sean Fitzgerald, Obstetrician Extraordinare, isn't allowed to be silly, right?"

He scowled. "I'm as human as the next man."

Her smile softened with encouragement. "Then tell me how you were being human."

"All right," he said with a resigned sigh. "I was jealous because you and Amy picked out names for the animals and I wasn't a part of it."

Whitney blinked at him in surprise. "You were jealous?"

"That's what I said."

She tried to hold back, but even though she'd clapped her hand over her mouth, her laughter still escaped. When Sean looked as if he would like to strangle her, she impulsively reached out to hug him.

"Oh, Sean," she chuckled as she rested her forehead against his shoulder. "I know it's not funny, but you have to admit that it's very..."

"If you say childish, you're in trouble," he warned as his arms instinctively linked around her waist.

"I wasn't going to say that at all." She leaned her head back to look up at him. "I was going to say it was out of character."

"And how do you know what's in my character?" he asked, his eyes glued to her lips, which were so close and inviting. It would be so easy to close the distance between them and see if they were as soft as they looked.

Whitney's heart hesitated as she watched his head begin to move toward her. He was going to kiss her, she realized, and a tremor of longing raced through her. It would be so easy to wind her arms around his neck, lean against him and seal his lips with hers. He'd been so kind to her today, so patient, so indulgent. Would it be so wrong to take what he was offering?

Yes, it would be wrong, she acknowledged, because she knew in her heart that when it was over, Sean would regret it.

She began to ease away from him, whispering, "I don't think this is what you want."

Shocked back to reality, Sean released her abruptly. He took a step backward, and thrust his hands into his pockets. "I think it's time for us to go to bed."

Only when her lips curved in wry amusement did he realize his faux pas, and he frowned at her as he took another step backward.

"Good night, Sean," she said softly and turned away.

It was long after she'd closed her door behind her that Sean was able to convince his legs that they could make it across the hallway.

Chapter Seven

Sean cursed softly. It was five in the morning and he had a patient in labor. He should have been at the hospital fifteen minutes ago, but it was pouring rain and he couldn't find his damn umbrella. For years it had lain on the table right inside the back door, but he couldn't find the damn table, either. In fact, during the past two weeks he hadn't been able to find anything. Every time he turned around, Whitney had moved something. It was driving him crazy.

He looked out the window, trying to decide if he should make a dash for the car, but he knew he'd be drenched before he got a foot out the door. To make matters worse, he'd left his raincoat at the office. He closed his eyes and shook his head in frustration, knowing his only option was to wake Whitney. He hurried up the stairs and cursed again when she didn't answer his knock. He knocked more loudly and was finally rewarded with a call for entrance.

"Whitney, I can't find my..." he began only to feel the words die in his throat.

She was sitting up in bed, her covers clutched against her chest, her hair tangled and her face soft from sleep. The desirable picture she presented was like a blow to his solar plexus, and Sean had to grit his teeth to keep from groaning. Ever since that almost kiss, he'd become too aware of her on a physical level. It was bad enough that he had to watch her prancing around the house in shorts and clinging

T-shirts. It was bad enough that he had to put up with her lacy underwear draped over the towel rack in the bathroom they shared. Now, he had to...

"You can't find what, Sean?" Whitney asked, interrupting his grumbling thoughts.

"My umbrella," he muttered as he forced his eyes to focus on a point above her head. "I have to get to the hospital, and I can't find it. Do you have any idea where it is?"

"In the umbrella stand next to the front door."

Of course, Sean thought grimly. It was the logical place for an umbrella, and the fact that he hadn't thought to look there made him furious.

"I'm sorry I woke you," he stated, knowing his temper was vibrating in his voice but unable to control it. "In the future I would appreciate it if you'd tell me when you move something, so I don't have to tear the house apart looking for it."

"Of course," Whitney said. "I'm sorry if I inconvenienced you."

Sean lowered his gaze, and his temper turned inward at the contrite look on her face. It was obvious that he'd hurt her feelings, and he knew he owed her an apology. But he didn't feel apologetic. He felt angry and put upon and confused.

He nodded and said, "I'm on the way to the hospital, and from the sound of things, I'll be there all day and all night. If there's a change in that schedule, I'll let you know."

"What about Amy's tea party?" Whitney asked, reminding him that today was Saturday.

Sean's jaw tightened, and he felt a muscle twitch in his jaw. He'd forgotten about the tea party—a tradition he hadn't missed in more than a year. But he knew he had to get away from Whitney and stay away. If he didn't, he was going to end up either screaming at her or dragging her into his arms. He found both options untenable.

"I'm not going to be able to make the tea party. I'll call her later this morning and tell her."

"But..." Whitney began, only to have Sean shut the door.

She peered at it in distress. That he was upset with her was obvious, and she knew it was more than moving his umbrella. Ever since he'd almost kissed her he'd been emotionally distant, and she wished he'd talk to her about it so they could relegate it to the past and get on with their lives. But it was clear that he had no intention of talking about it, and that frustrated her.

She threw herself back down on the bed and punched her pillow. The man was driving her crazy, and if it wasn't for Amy, she'd walk right out the door.

WHITNEY GLANCED UP from the book she was reading when her bedroom door cracked open and Amy peered around it, her doll clutched tightly in her arms.

"Dolly can't sleep," the girl informed her.

"That's terrible," Whitney said. "Do you think she might be able to sleep if she was in bed with me?"

"Don't know," Amy answered hesitantly. "She likes me."

"Well, in that case, maybe you should both sleep with me."

"'Kay," Amy said as she ran across the room.

Whitney held up the covers so the child could scramble into bed. She knew Amy had been asleep an hour ago, because she'd checked on her, and she brushed the girl's hair off her forehead and studied her face, looking for a clue to this uncustomary insomnia. Her skin wasn't hot. Her eyes were clear. Her nose wasn't running. It didn't appear that she was ill.

"I bet Dolly ate too many hot dogs tonight and that's why she can't sleep," Whitney suggested.

Amy shook her head. "Dolly doesn't like hot dogs."

Whitney widened her eyes in mock-disbelief. "You're kidding me. I thought everybody liked hot dogs."

"Not Dolly," Amy insisted.

"Well, I'm sure glad you like hot dogs. Otherwise I'd have to eat them all by myself, and no one should have to eat hot dogs all alone," Whitney said as she searched her mind for questions that would get Amy to reveal whatever problem had her awake.

Before she managed to come up with any, Amy asked in a quavering voice, "Does Daddy love me?"

"Well, of course he does," Whitney responded, startled by the question.

Tears welled in the girl's eyes. "How come he didn't come home for my tea party?"

Whitney's heart wrenched at the sight of her daughter's tears, and she lay down on the bed and cuddled Amy to her chest. She pressed a soothing kiss to the top of her head and said, "He called you on the telephone and told you he had to work at the hospital. Don't you remember?"

"Uh-huh, but he always comes home," the girl said on the tail end of a sob. "He don't love me anymore."

Whitney didn't know how to respond, because how did she explain to Amy that he was staying away because he wanted to avoid her new mother?

She stroked Amy's hair as she said, "Honey, your daddy had to work today, even though he wanted to come home. It made him very sad that he missed your tea party, but I bet you and I can make him feel better about it."

"How?" Amy asked as she raised her tear-washed eyes to Whitney's face.

"Well, one night this week we'll have a special tea party with a very special treat. You can even help me make it, okay?"

" 'Kay," Amy answered, her bright smile returning.

"Good," Whitney said. "Now I don't know about you and Dolly, but I'm really sleepy. Why don't we turn out the light so the sandman can pay us a visit?"

"Sure," Amy said as she snuggled down into the covers. But long after Amy's breathing had become deep and even, Whitney was frowning into the darkness. Sean being upset with her was one thing, but when it started affecting Amy, then something had to be done. She'd have to find a way to approach him, and it had to be a way that wouldn't make the situation worse. But how?

By morning Whitney still didn't have a solution, and she sighed heavily as she put one of the carved birds back on its shelf in the living room and lifted another, carefully dusting it. She'd grown rather fond of the collection. The problem was, not only were they dust collectors, but there were far too many of them clustered together on the wooden shelves, making it difficult to distinguish one from the other. What she'd like to do was have a glass display case built that would control the dust and have enough room to show them off properly, but if Sean got upset over her moving his umbrella, heaven only knew how he'd react to a display case.

She was aware that the minor changes she'd made were bothering him. At first she thought he was simply going through a period of adjustment, and as each change took place it would become easier for him. Then Whitney learned from an elderly neighbor that Margaret had been raised in this house. She'd loved it so much that when she inherited it, she and Sean had moved in.

Whitney had enough insight into human nature to understand that, at least on a subconscious level, Sean would view any major change as a desecration of sacred ground, because this had been more than the home his wife had created for him. It had been Margaret's home from the beginning, and in his mind, it would always belong to her.

She released another sigh as she completed her task and walked to the window that faced the tree-lined street. It was Mrs. Wilkens's day to cook, and she listened to the clatter of pots and pans in the kitchen. Sean was still at the hospital and had called to say he was monitoring two women in labor and not to expect him home until after dinner. Amy was upstairs taking her nap, and suddenly Whitney felt bored and restless.

What she needed was something to help fill the hours, she decided, but outside of her rose gardens, she'd never had much interest in hobbies. She didn't want to open her greenhouse until Amy was in school, and considering her past work experience, most part-time jobs would be tedious and unchallenging. What she needed was something where she could make a contribution.

And then it came to her. Her godmother, Barbara Lass, was the founder and president of the Mile High Women's Foundation, a non-profit, volunteer organization actively involved with women's needs in the community. Barbara was forever complaining that she lacked enough help, and was constantly on the lookout for qualified volunteers. Surely she could use what Whitney had to offer, and Whitney knew she'd be able to pick and choose her hours. She'd call Barbara first thing in the morning.

"Whit-nee?" a small, tear-choked voice said, and Whitney spun around, her eyes narrowing in concern.

"What's wrong, sweetheart?" she asked as she hurried to Amy, whose eyes were brimming with crocodile tears.

"Me and Dolly fell down, and she got hurt."

"Oh, dear," Whitney said as she accepted the toy that Amy thrust at her. Even if she hadn't known that the doll was Amy's favorite, its well-worn appearance would have made that apparent. Its blond hair, which had probably once been curly, was now lank and thin. There were unidentifiable dark smudges on its body that would be there forever, and its clothes were ragged and frayed. As she examined the doll, she saw that its soft plastic arm was crushed and irreparably split. She glanced up at Amy and asked, "Did you get hurt, too?"

"No, but we have to make Dolly all better," Amy answered with a pitiful sniff.

Whitney glanced down, at a loss for what to do. She knew that there were doll repair shops, which could probably replace the arm, but it was Sunday and she was sure they'd be closed. She couldn't tell Amy that they'd just have to wait until tomorrow. Then it dawned on her that she could use Dolly's accident as a way to get Sean and Amy together.

"Well, Amy, the first thing we have to do is put some splints on Dolly's arm, because it's broken," she told the child as she took her hand and led her toward the bathroom. "When you have a broken arm, you have to make sure it doesn't get moved around, because when it does, it hurts. We also have to cover her up, because when you get hurt, you have to stay warm."

"Oh," Amy breathed softly. "I'll go get my blanket off my bed."

"I don't think we'll need a big blanket. I think a towel will keep Dolly warm enough," Whitney said, trying to control the twitching of her lips at the girl's grave expression.

Amy watched intently while Whitney retrieved a towel from the linen closet and carefully wrapped it around the doll. Then she laid the toy on the counter and searched the drawer of the vanity, looking for something she could use as a splint.

When she couldn't find anything appropriate, she told Amy, "Please go ask Mrs. Wilkens for two Popsicle sticks."

"'Kay," Amy said, racing out of the room. She returned a minute later with the housekeeper on her heels. Mrs. Wilkens's face was etched with worried concern.

"What's going on? Amy said something about a broken arm," Mrs. Wilkens asked.

Whitney nodded as she accepted the Popsicle sticks from Amy's outstretched hand. "Thank you, Amy." She looked at the housekeeper and solemnly informed her, "Dolly fell down and broke her arm. Amy and I have to take her to the hospital to get it fixed."

"Take her to the hospital?" the housekeeper repeated, her tone indicating that she thought Whitney had just lost her mind.

"That's right," Whitney said, never cracking a smile, though she was about to choke on her laughter at the housekeeper's look of incredulity. "Would you call Sean, tell him what's happened, and ask him to meet us in the emergency room in about fifteen minutes?"

"I suppose so," Mrs. Wilkens said hesitantly, her expression clearly proclaiming that she wasn't particularly pleased to be informing the man that his wife had just gone Loony Tunes. "What if he isn't available?"

Whitney hadn't thought about that. Since he was monitoring two women in labor, he could very well be tied up. Then she shrugged. She'd embarked on this plan, and she was going to carry it through to the end.

"Then we'll just have to wait for him," Whitney answered. "Now, Amy," she said, returning her attention to the child, "when you put on a splint, you have to be very careful because you might make a broken arm worse if you don't."

"'Kay," Amy murmured, catching her lower lip between her teeth as she watched Whitney put the Popsicle sticks into place and apply tape to secure them.

When Whitney was finished, she handed the doll to Amy instructing, "You must be very careful with her arm, okay?"

"Uh-huh."

"Good. I'll go get my purse, and then we'll take her to the hospital."

Mrs. Wilkens was just getting off the phone when Whitney walked into the living room in search of her purse.

"Dr. Fitzgerald said he'd meet you," the woman stated.

Whitney chuckled as she took note of the high color flagging the older woman's cheeks. "I have a feeling that wasn't a direct quote. Should I expect butterfly nets and a straightjacket when I walk in the door?"

"Well, you must admit that this is a bit strange."

Whitney shrugged dismissively as she spied her purse, picked it up and slung it over her shoulder, saying as she did so, "I don't think it's strange at all. See you later."

She couldn't help but giggle when she walked out of the room and heard the woman mutter to herself.

But she didn't feel like giggling when she parked the car in the visitors' parking lot and walked Amy around to the emergency room entrance. Sean was pacing outside, his expression stormy. She stopped at the edge of the building, trying to decide if she should turn around and leave, but Amy spotted him before she could make up her mind.

She let go of Whitney's hand and sprinted toward her father, yelling, "Daddy, Dolly broke her arm!"

Sean automatically caught Amy and lifted her into the air, even as his eyes strayed over the top of her head in search of Whitney. When Mrs. Wilkens called him he'd thought she was joking, however, the housekeeper insisted that it wasn't a joke. But why in the world would Whitney bring a broken toy to the hospital?

Amy was chattering away about splints and blankets, but her words didn't register because he'd just spotted Whitney and the lovely vision she presented made him catch his breath.

The sun was glinting off her hair, creating a golden halo around her beautiful face. Her eyes were a more sparkling blue than the clear summer sky that backlighted her, and he gulped when the wind caught the folds of her full skirt and molded it to her legs, emphasizing their length and the elegant grace of her stride as she walked toward him.

"You're mad at me," she said when she came to a stop in front of him.

Sean had to blink to make sense of her words. He sat Amy down on a low brick wall protecting a thatch of ground-cover evergreens, deciding that this was definitely one of those conversations that should be conducted out of the girl's hearing.

"You wait right here, pumpkin," he instructed. Then he took Whitney's arm and led her a short distance away. "I'm not mad. I'm confused. After all, bringing a doll to the hospital is a bit ..."

"Odd?" she provided with a chuckle.

"Definitely," he agreed.

"Actually it's not odd at all," she said, glancing over to make sure Amy hadn't wandered off. Satisfied that the child, who was cradling her doll against her chest protectively, wasn't going to move a muscle until its arm was fixed, she returned her attention to Sean. "It makes very good sense."

He arched a brow skeptically. "I see."

Whitney grinned. "Look, by bringing Amy here she not only gets to see where her daddy spends so much of his time, but it will give her a better grasp on why he has to go away so often and stay away so long. It will also give her a chance to become familiar with the routine of an emergency room, so if, heaven forbid, she ever has to go to one, she'll understand what's going on."

Sean had to admit that her explanation made perfect sense, and he smiled and shook his head wryly. "So you expect me to walk her through a broken arm experience at the hospital."

"If you have the time. If you don't, we can wait."

"As it so happens, I have the time. Also, it's one of those rare days when the ER is practically empty. The staff will probably have fun doctoring up Dolly."

Whitney's smile grew broader as she watched Sean and Amy go through the stages of hospital procedure. He sat down with her and they filled out a patient questionnaire. Dolly got wheeled to the X-ray department in a wheelchair, where the radiology staff went through an entire bogus X-ray routine. When the radiologist earnestly confirmed the break, it was back to the ER where Dolly got her arm set and put into a cast. The emergency physician explained to her that Dolly had to keep her arm dry until the cast came off, after which the nurse added the final touch by asking if she could be the first to sign Dolly's cast.

Whitney and Amy waited while Sean checked with labor and delivery. After being assured that he still wasn't needed upstairs, he walked them out to the car.

Amy crawled inside, totally immersed in crooning to Dolly, and Whitney turned toward Sean and smiled. "You done good," she said.

"You did pretty well yourself," he replied. "Not only was Dolly's trip to the hospital ingenious, but it was nice spending some time with Amy. I've missed her."

Whitney caught her hair with her hand as the wind blew it into her eyes and gazed up at him, wondering if he knew just how revealing those last three words were. It wasn't what he'd said, as much as the way he'd said it, and her mind traveled back over the past two weeks.

Suddenly she realized that when Sean had withdrawn from her, he'd also withdrawn from Amy. Not blatantly, of course. If the child demanded his attention, he gave it to her completely. But if she and Amy were involved in some activity, he didn't ask to join in. She was ashamed to realize that she hadn't thought to invite him. She'd been monopolizing the child. No wonder he hadn't been able to bring himself to communicate with her!

Her heart went out to him, and she wanted to throw her arms around him and hug him tight. She wanted to apologize and tell him she wouldn't do it again. She wanted... What? she wondered at the elusive stirring of feelings inside that made her want to reach up and brush his hair into place.

Instead she said, "Amy's missed you, too."

And what about you? Sean was startled by the question that flashed into his mind. He also wondered if he'd voiced it aloud without realizing it, because Whitney's eyes were dark with concern.

Feeling painfully self-conscious, he glanced down at his watch. "I've been out of the hospital too long. I'd better get back."

"Sure," Whitney said. "Do you think you'll make it home at a decent hour tonight?"

He shrugged and stuffed his hands into the pockets of his white coat. "That's anyone's guess."

"Well, I hope you do. You look tired."

He smiled ruefully. "Obstetricians are supposed to look tired. If they don't, then you know they aren't doing their job." When she nodded, he said, "I do have to go. I'll see you later."

Whitney nodded again, but he'd already turned away, and she gazed after him thoughtfully, knowing that it wasn't just work that had put those soft bruises beneath his eyes. They definitely needed to resolve this ridiculous dilemma or Sean was going to collapse from exhaustion.

As luck would have it, Sean did make it home before Amy's bedtime, and Whitney deliberately busied herself downstairs so that he took responsibility for reading Amy her bedtime story.

After Amy went to sleep, he had joined Whitney in the living room. Now she peered at him over the top of the newspaper from her position on the sofa. He was slumped in the matching overstuffed chair, his feet propped up on the hassock, staring at the television set. He hadn't shifted his position once in the past hour, and Whitney doubted that he even knew what he was watching. She knew they needed to talk, but what could she say that would start a conversation?

She frowned at the newspaper and decided that what she needed was a little humor to lessen the tension, so she rattled the paper until Sean glanced toward her.

When he did, she said, "Did you see this article about the woman who was arrested for premeditated decaffeination of her husband? The DA says it's such a heinous crime that she should be prosecuted to the maximum. I have to agree with the DA. It is a most heinous crime, isn't it?"

"Yes, it is," Sean murmured absently and returned his attention to the television. An instant later his head snapped back toward her. "She *decaffeinated* her husband?"

"Gotcha!" Whitney said, bursting into laughter at his dumbfounded expression. She simply couldn't stop, although she knew the joke wasn't *that* funny. It was just such a relief to see him drop the polite mask of indifference he'd been wearing.

At first, Sean experienced a surge of anger at being the brunt of her joke, but then his lips began to twitch as she continued to laugh. A chuckle emerged, and then another, and another. Before he knew it, he was laughing so hard his sides ached. Whenever he'd come close to getting himself under control, she would begin to laugh, and he'd start all over again.

"Oh, stop it!" he finally begged. "I can't take anymore."

Whitney sobered at his words, and as her eyes searched his face, she discovered that she loved the way the corners of his eyes crinkled and the laugh lines bracketed his mouth. They were the telltale marks of time that spoke of a man's past. But like her, Sean had had his laughter stolen away by fate.

"I can't take anymore, either, Sean," she said quietly, seriously.

Sean's mind shied away from the impact of her words, though he knew exactly what she meant. The tension between them had become unbearable. Involuntarily his gaze traveled over her. Her hair was in disarray. Her face was devoid of makeup. Her jeans and blouse were worn and faded. For all practical purposes, she was the perfect image of an average housewife who'd put in a long day, but he knew there was nothing average about her.

"What do you want from me?" he asked, his voice half angry, half plaintive.

"No more than you want to give," she answered, "but I can't stand you hiding from me. Yell at me, curse at me, throw something at me if that's what it takes, but please, don't hide."

Sean sighed, leaned his back against the chair, and closed his eyes. A part of him did want to yell at her, curse her, and, yes, even throw things at her. Not because she'd done anything wrong, he acknowledged, but because she simply was. Because she was a solution to all his problems when he shouldn't have needed a solution in the first place. Because, he finally admitted, she made him feel when he didn't want to feel.

The sound of the television echoed in his ears, but there was no other sound in the room. He was sure she'd left, but when he opened his eyes and shifted his gaze to the sofa he discovered that she hadn't left. She was sitting there staring at him, and he had the feeling that she was holding her breath.

His suspicion was confirmed when she exhaled as he said, "I won't hide anymore."

"Good." She rose to her feet, once more reminding him of her grace as he watched the fluid motion of her limbs. "Good night, Sean. Don't stay up too late."

Once she was gone, he discovered that he missed her, and he was stunned to realize how, in only two weeks, he'd become accustomed to her presence. Even with the tension between them, he'd found himself seeking her out just to be near her. There was a serenity to her that was soothing, and he loved listening to her voice, which was low and well modulated. If he could just control those crazy flashes of desire that hit him unexpectedly, their life together would be perfect.

It was something he'd have to work on, he decided as he turned off the television and headed for bed. But when he walked into the bathroom they shared, he knew it would be a Herculean task. Not only was the scent of her heavy in the room, but his gaze was drawn to the lacy underwear drying on the towel rack, and his mind provided him with a provocative image of what she'd look like in them.

With a muffled groan, he stripped off his clothes and stepped into a cold shower. By the time he climbed out, he'd come to the conclusion that even if he couldn't control his attraction to her, he was an adult and could ignore it. He

wanted to be a part of what Amy and Whitney were building, and if a small sacrifice was necessary to reach that goal,
then so be it. From this day forward, he was going to be the
best friend Whitney had ever had.

Chapter Eight

When Barbara Lass came on the line, Whitney's eyes misted with tears. During the past few years, she and Barbara had rarely seen each other due to their busy schedules that never seemed to mesh, and just the sound of her godmother's voice made Whitney realize how much she'd missed her.

"It's been so long since we've talked!" Barbara exclaimed, "and I've been terribly remiss. I saw that wonderful article about you in the newspaper and meant to call, but you know how time gets away from me. So tell me, what's new with Denver's Businesswoman of the Year?"

A feeling of trepidation swept through Whitney at the question. She wasn't sure how Barbara would react to the news that she'd married Sean in order to regain her daughter. For a moment she actually considered keeping the marriage a secret, but she knew she couldn't do it. Eventually Barbara would learn the truth, and she'd be terribly hurt to know that Whitney had hidden it from her.

She drew in a deep breath and said, "I'm married."

"Married?" Barbara yelped. "Why wasn't I invited to the wedding?"

Whitney blessed the fact that the telephone had a long cord, and she rose to her feet and paced to the living room window. Peering out it, she said, "We were married by a judge, so there wasn't a wedding." The silence at the other end stretched to the point that she finally asked, "Barbara, are you still there?"

"Just picking myself up off the floor," Barbara muttered. "When you break news like this, you should at least warn a person to sit down."

Whitney chuckled. "Sorry about that."

"You should be. Now tell me all about this man who's evidently swept you off your feet."

Whitney paced back to the sofa and sat down, knowing that this was the sticky part. Should she lie or tell the truth? She decided on the latter since she knew a lie would only catch her.

"He didn't sweep me off my feet. He gave me back my daughter." When Barbara didn't respond, she said, "Sean was my obstetrician. He and his wife adopted Amy. His wife died and Amy needed a mother, so here I am."

Whitney knew she'd oversimplified. She also knew that her explanation sounded absurd, but then, she reasoned, the truth often did. Again Barbara was silent, and Whitney held her breath in anticipation of her reaction. She was surprised when all Barbara said was, "I see."

Whitney responded with, "Barbara, I cut my ties with Price Manufacturing, and since you're always complaining that you need more help, I thought maybe I could volunteer some time at the Foundation."

"Well, we can always use another body. I have a free hour at ten today. Why don't you come in and we'll talk about it?"

"Great," Whitney said with a sigh of relief.

"Good. And, Whitney, be sure and bring the child with you. I can't wait to see her, and we have a free day-care facility where she can play while we get down to business."

WHITNEY HAD VISITED the Foundation only twice, and she'd forgotten that pandemonium reigned inside the building. There were several banks of ceaseless ringing telephones, staffed by volunteers around the clock who were trained to handle everything from general information questions to hot-line assistance. Women milled through the corridors and in and out of offices, but despite the frenzy of activity, everyone seemed to have a smile and laughter filled the air.

Barbara's office was empty when they arrived, and Whitney settled Amy into a chair and sat down beside her to wait. Nearly fifteen minutes had passed when Barbara came charging through the doorway, her salt-and-pepper hair in disarray and her sensible cotton dress looking as if it had been slept in. Though she barely stood five feet in height, she had so much energy that she looked like a giant.

"Whitney! I'm sorry I kept you waiting, but today is one of those days that proves Murphy's Law."

Whitney laughed when she rose to her feet and Barbara tossed her arms around her in a rambunctious hug. "Isn't that the norm around here?"

"Of course. Let me look at you," Barbara said as she stepped away and surveyed Whitney from head to toe. "You look absolutely fabulous." She stepped around Whitney and smiled down at Amy. "Hi, there, kiddo. My name is Barbara, and I'll bet you're Amy."

"Uh-huh," Amy said as she peered up at Barbara wide-eyed.

"Eloquent little devil, isn't she?" Barbara said with a chuckle.

"Actually she is quite eloquent. She's just shy around strangers," Whitney responded stiffly.

Barbara glanced toward her with one brow arched. "Already developed that killer mother instinct, huh?" Whitney blushed, and Barbara laughed. "It's okay. I'd be disappointed if you hadn't. The resemblance between you is startling."

She shifted her attention back to Amy. "We have a playroom downstairs, and there's going to be a puppet show starting in about five minutes. I bet I could talk a friend of mine into taking you to it. Would you like to do that while Whitney and I talk?''

Amy glanced toward Whitney, and Whitney said, ''You can go if you want, or you can stay with me.''

Amy frowned in indecision, and Barbara said, ''I think they're also going to have milk and cookies.''

''What kind of cookies?'' Amy asked.

Barbara grinned at Whitney. ''That's what I love. A woman with her priorities in order.'' To Amy, she said, ''I don't know what kind. I guess you'll have to go and see.''

'' 'Kay,'' Amy said as she scrambled out of the chair.

''She's adorable,'' Barbara told Whitney after she'd hailed a woman who collected Amy and headed for the day-care center. ''But I wouldn't have expected any less after knowing her mother. Sit down and tell me all about this marriage of yours.''

''There's not much to tell,'' Whitney said as she settled back into her chair while Barbara collapsed behind her desk. ''As I explained this morning, Sean and his wife adopted Amy. His wife died, and he asked me to marry him.''

''You're so good at condensing. Are you sure you wouldn't prefer part-time work at *Reader's Digest*?''

''There's no need to be sarcastic, Barbara.''

Barbara shook her head. ''You're always so damn polite. Why don't you just tell me it's none of my business?''

''All right, it's none of your business.''

''Of course it's not, but if God hadn't wanted me to meddle, he wouldn't have given me a nose. So out with it.''

''I already told you the truth. What do you want me to do? Embellish it with lies?''

''A few details would suffice. I am your godmother, Whitney, which makes me family. Do you love this man?''

Whitney released a sigh of resignation. ''You sound just like Simon.''

Barbara nodded knowingly. ''Which means you don't love him, and that explains your sudden interest in volunteering your time at this zoo. You need to fill the hours, right?''

''What I need is to feel as if I'm doing something for my fellow man, or woman, in this instance. You, of all people, should understand that. Isn't that why you opened this zoo, as you call it, in the first place?''

''As a matter of fact, it is. But I'd also raised three children and buried a husband. I was alone and had to find something productive to do or go insane.''

''Why are you making this difficult for me?'' Whitney pleaded. ''I want to volunteer my time, just like all those other women out there. Is there something wrong with that?''

''No,'' Barbara answered. ''It just bothers me that you not only just got married, but you regained the daughter that you thought you'd lost forever, and now you're feeling cornered. I can't help but wonder if you shouldn't be directing your energy into fixing your problems at home, rather than spending your time here trying to fix other people's.''

''Believe me, Barbara. There are no problems in my home life.''

Barbara looked as if she were going to say more, but then shook her head as if changing the subject. ''Let's take a tour. After you've seen the place, you can decide where you'd like to work.''

Whitney was astounded by the services being provided as Barbara led her through every part of the building, introducing her to the employees and volunteers who handled everything from mental health counseling to job testing and training.

When her tour was over, Barbara asked, ''So now that you've seen it all, where would you like to work?''

''I'd like to work with Dr. Bauer,'' Whitney answered, naming the child psychologist who ran a twenty-four hour hotline for pregnant teenagers.

Barbara arched a brow. "Are you sure? You'll be working with an issue that's pretty close to home."

"I'm sure," Whitney replied with conviction. "Who can better identify with what those girls are going through than me?"

"It's that very fact that worries me. You could be too involved."

"How can you be too involved in such an important issue?" Whitney asked fervently.

Barbara looked doubtful, but said, "We'll give it a try."

Whitney spent the remainder of her morning with Dr. Mary Beth Bauer, a small, birdlike woman in her late fifties, who delivered a passionate speech about the growing problems of teenage pregnancy. She loaded Whitney down with a bagful of reading material to familiarize her with the subject and set up a training schedule to teach her how to deal with the calls.

After putting Amy down for her nap that afternoon, Whitney dug into the bag and began reading. The national figures for teenage pregnancy shocked her, and the inherent problems that followed birth appalled her. She was still reading when Sean walked into the room, and she glanced up at him in surprise.

"Hi," she responded to his greeting. "What are you doing home so early?"

Sean shrugged as he sat down on the sofa beside her. "I only had three patients scheduled this afternoon, and one of them canceled. Since it was such a nice day, I thought I'd come home and spend it with you and Amy."

"Amy will be thrilled," she said.

He smiled at her, and Whitney's stomach performed an unexpected somersault. As she had last night, she noted the laugh lines at the corners of his eyes, and she had to fight against the urge to reach out and touch them.

Confused by the feeling, she glanced away and said, "Amy's still napping, but I expect her up at any minute."

"Mmm," Sean murmured as he lifted a Foundation pamphlet off the coffee table and began thumbing through it. "What's this?"

Whitney felt a slight pinprick of panic. How would Sean feel about her volunteering at the Foundation? After all, she'd told him that she wanted to spend concentrated time with Amy. Now, two weeks later, she was talking about volunteer work. Even to her it sounded contradictory, and she started thinking of ways to defend her decision. When she realized what she was doing, she frowned inwardly. Good heavens, she was Amy's mother, not a slave. She didn't have to defend devoting a few hours a week to a good cause.

"It's some reading material that I picked up at the Mile High Women's Foundation today. My godmother runs it, and I'm going to be doing some volunteer work there," she informed him.

"I didn't know Barbara Lass was your godmother," he said.

"You know Barbara?" Whitney questioned, involuntarily relaxing at his unconcerned response.

He chuckled wryly. "I doubt there's a physician within a fifty-mile radius that doesn't know Barbara, or isn't intimately acquainted with the Mile High Women's Foundation. In fact, my group handles a good number of her indigent cases."

"Then you're aware of the good work she's doing. By the way, I can take Amy with me," she said. "They have a day-care center on the premises. It might be good for her to be around children her own age."

"I'm sure it would. What will you do at the Foundation?"

Whitney was unaware that her eyes were blazing with zeal as she said, "Working the teen pregnancy hot line. In fact, I spent most of the afternoon reading up on teenage pregnancy in this country, and I can't believe what a major problem it is. What's even worse is what happens after birth.

Did you know that most of these girls keep their babies and never go back to school? And many times they don't go back simply because they can't afford day care. Without an education, they can't get decent jobs, which means they become a burden on their families or the system. Resentment builds up, which increases the chances of child abuse. If they did marry the father, the marriage usually breaks up within..."

Her lecture was interrupted as Sean suddenly chuckled. Whitney felt her cheeks flame with embarrassment. "I'm sorry. I guess I was getting a little carried away. You probably know all about this."

"Yes, I'm familiar with it," Sean said, "and I wish more people would become as incensed about the problem as you are. However, I have to say that I'm not sure it's an area you should be working in. It could dredge up a lot of memories for you that might be best forgotten."

Whitney bristled. "You sound just like Barbara. Good heavens, you'd think I was mentally unstable. I'm perfectly capable of handling this."

Sean looked as doubtful as Barbara had, but he nodded. Then he rose to his feet and said, "I'll go change. What would you like to do this afternoon?"

"I don't know. What do you and Amy normally do?"

"Play Frisbee."

"Frisbee?" she repeated. "Isn't Amy a little young to play Frisbee?"

Sean laughed. "No. In fact we've been playing it since she started walking. She'll give you a run for your money."

"That wouldn't be hard to do," Whitney said. "I've never played Frisbee."

"You've never played Frisbee!" Sean gasped as he brought his hand to his chest in mock-alarm. "Lady, you haven't lived, and we're certainly going to correct that this afternoon. So let's get you upstairs and into jeans."

Whitney arched a brow in skepticism. "Why do I have the feeling I've just been set up?"

Sean grinned as he caught her hand and pulled her to her feet, asking, "Now, do you really think I'd do something like that to you?"

"Of course not," she said in a tone that belied her words and let him lead her toward the stairs.

WHITNEY DIDN'T THINK she'd ever laughed so hard in her life as she raced across the backyard, her eyes centered on the golden disk that disappeared momentarily against the silhouette of the sun before reappearing against the blue sky.

For the past two hours, Sean and Amy had been trying to teach her how to play Frisbee, and she felt like a klutz next to the three-year-old, who not only never failed to catch the disk, but had a throw that, Whitney suspected, could get her into major league baseball.

"Come on, Whitney, you can do it!" Sean yelled in encouragement.

"Yeah, Whit-nee, you can do it!" Amy echoed.

"Yeah, I'm going to finally do it," Whitney muttered beneath her breath.

And there it was, flying down to her. She leaped into the air and let out a whoop of success when her fingers closed around the plastic circle. But her whoop changed into a yelp of surprise when she came back to the ground, only to have her feet knocked out from under her by a flying ball of yapping white fur. She landed flat on her back with enough force to leave her gasping for breath.

"Whitney, are you all right?" Sean questioned in concern.

Whitney cracked one eye open far enough to look at him. He was straddling her, a knee on each side of her hips, and a hand above each of her shoulders. His face was so close that all she'd have to do was raise her head to meet his lips.

She closed her eyes and scolded herself severely for the wayward thought. Good heavens, what was wrong with her? Just because the man was gorgeous, just because she'd had to spend the past two hours looking at his bare chest with the intriguing mat of hair, and admiring the provocative fit of his jeans didn't mean she was attracted to him.

Well, maybe she was a little bit, she acquiesced. After all, she was a red-blooded woman, and it was quite evident that he was a red-blooded man. It was also time that she assured him that she was fine.

In answer to his question, she folded her hands over her chest and said, "Just plant a rosebush above my head and let me rest in peace." Snowball chose that moment to test his skills at reviving his victims, and Whitney wailed, "Oh, yech! Dog germs!" when he licked her face.

Sean burst into roaring laughter, and Amy began to dance around them, chanting, "Whit-nee has dog germs! Whit-nee has dog germs!"

Whitney opened both eyes and gave Sean a mock-glare as she grumbled, "She's your daughter, you know."

He chuckled as he stood, still straddling her hips and extended his hand to help her up. "Only when she's bad. When she's good, she's yours."

"I'm glad to see that you have a complete understanding of the difference between us," Whitney said when she stood and proceeded to dust off her backside.

"Oh, believe me, I know the difference," he said in a low, husky drawl that made Whitney's head shoot up in surprise. If it had been anyone but Sean, she would have actually thought he was flirting with her. But she was sure it was nothing more than her imagination when he asked conversationally, "Are you okay?"

"My pride will probably never recover, but outside of that I'm fine. However, I am retiring from the game of Frisbee. I refuse to stand by and let a three-year-old kid and an obnoxious puppy make a monkey out of me."

Sean chuckled and tossed his arm around her shoulders, giving them a friendly squeeze. "I'll have to give you some private lessons."

That was a line that she'd love to prod with a ten-foot pole, just to see what happened. Instead she relaxed against him, enjoying the weight of his arm and the contact of his hip.

"Where does she get all of that energy?" Whitney murmured, smiling at Amy, who was running around the yard, squealing with laughter as a barking Snowball chased after her.

"That's one of those scientific wonders that will probably never be explained," Sean answered, as he, too, smiled at the child, and decided that today had been one of the most pleasant days he'd had in years. In fact, he felt so good that he chuckled.

He glanced down at Whitney when she nudged him in the ribs, saying, "It's not polite to stand around chuckling to yourself. Care to share the joke?"

"Nope," he replied with a wide grin.

"Well, golly gee whiz," she complained in a nasal Western twang. "A girl could develop a complex around here. At least you're my friend, aren't you Midnight?" she crooned as she bent and scooped up the kitten, who was rubbing against her ankles.

Sean laughed as he watched her rub her cheek against the kitten's silken fur, though inwardly he felt a spark of jealousy toward the cat. "That's because she knows who fills her milk bowl."

"Well, let that be a lesson to you," Whitney responded pertly. "If you want to eat, you have to be nice to the cook. And speaking of eating, it's time for me to start dinner. I'll let you have the honor of collecting and cleaning up Ms. Munchkin."

"Well, golly gee whiz," Sean complained mildly. "How come I always get stuck with the hard jobs?"

"Because you're the man of the house, why else?" she answered with an outrageous bat of her lashes. Then she turned and walked away with a saucy swish of her hips that caught and held Sean's total attention, causing a tightening in his stomach that was too hot to even contemplate. When the door closed behind her, he dragged in a deep breath and released it slowly. This friendship business was going to be harder than he'd realized, because what Whitney did to a pair of jeans should be outlawed. He went to collect Amy, deciding that he needed some space to cool off. Maybe he'd go to the hospital and clean up some of his paperwork before dinner.

But he didn't have to leave, because when he walked into the house, Whitney was slinging her purse over her shoulder.

"Going somewhere?" he asked.

"I just received a call from the realtor about my house and I have to go meet with her." She automatically dropped a kiss to Amy's cheek before saying, "Mrs. Wilkens said she'd start dinner."

Before Sean could respond, she was gone out the door and he stood frowning in the doorway,. Though she'd seemed cheerful enough, he sensed an underlying emotion that he couldn't quite identify. Then he convinced himself it was only his imagination. He washed up Amy and went into his small den to catch up on some medical journals.

Sean didn't become concerned until dinnertime arrived and Whitney hadn't even called. He went ahead and fed Amy, bathed her and dressed her in her pajamas. An hour later, he still hadn't heard from Whitney, and he began to panic.

Since neither he nor Mrs. Wilkens knew the name of the real estate agency handling the property, he decided to drive over to the mansion. To his relief, Whitney's car was parked in the driveway. Minutes later, he found her kneeling in one of the rose gardens, pruning the bushes.

"I've been worried about you," he said when she glanced up at him.

She pushed her hair away from her face, leaving a smudge of dirt on her cheek. "Why?"

"Because it's past dinnertime."

"It is?" She glanced down at her watch, and then gave him a guilty smile. "I guess I lost track of time."

Sean squatted so that he was at eye level with her and could search her face. There was a touch of sadness reflected in the depths of her eyes. "Is something wrong?"

"No."

Sean knew she was lying, and he found that even more disturbing. He reached out to wipe the dirt off her cheek with his thumb.

"Was your call about the house good news?"

She nodded. "I've just accepted an offer on it. If everything works out, we'll close in a month."

"How do you feel about that?"

She shrugged. "Happy and sad. I'm getting more money than I'd hoped, but I don't like to think about other people living here."

"Then maybe you should hold on to it a little longer."

"No. The longer I wait to sell it, the harder it's going to be. By the way, the people said they'll keep the piano until I have a place to put it."

"We'll call Don about the conservatory. Did you ever decide which of his designs you wanted?"

"No, but I guess I have to now."

She was too calm, and Sean could sense that she was holding her emotions in check. His first inclination was to pull her into his arms, but he sensed that wasn't what she wanted from him.

Not knowing what else to do, he glanced around the rose garden and asked, "Are there any of these roses that you'd like to dig up and bring home?"

She followed his gaze. "No. It would ruin the symmetry of the gardens. I can replace them when I finally open my greenhouse."

He hadn't thought about the greenhouse for so long, that the reminder came as a slight shock. He'd gotten used to her being home, just as Margaret had been. But Margaret had been content with her sewing and her crafts, and he knew Whitney needed more. In order to be happy, she had to be satisfied. That meant she had to open her greenhouse.

"Of course. In fact, we can start looking at property. Do you have any idea how much land you'll need?"

She shook her head. "I'll have to do some research and decide what size an operation I want."

"Then I think you should start doing that."

"I will, but there's no rush. I don't want to open it until Amy starts school."

An uncomfortable silence fell between them, and Sean coughed uneasily before asking, "Are you about ready to come home?"

She shook her head again. "If you don't mind, I'd like to be alone for a while."

Sean did mind, but he bit back his protest. If she needed time alone, he had to give it to her. But he felt responsible for her, and he didn't want her facing anything alone. "Okay, but don't be too late or I'll worry about you."

"I'll be home by ten."

After Sean was gone, Whitney resumed her pruning. Signing the contract on the mansion had been harder than she'd imagined, and it wasn't just the loss of her childhood memories that bothered her. It was the feeling that once the house was gone, she'd have no ties—no place to run to if everything suddenly went wrong between her and Sean. She'd never be able to come home again, and that scared her to death, because home was all she'd been able to hold on to when her life fell apart four long years ago.

She sat back on her heels and stared at the sprawling house. For a time this afternoon, she'd actually considered asking Sean to move here. Then she'd realized that by doing so, she'd be doing to him what he'd done to her—asking him to live with her memories—and knowing firsthand how that felt, she simply couldn't do that to him.

For the first time in longer than she could remember, she let a wave of self-pity overwhelm her, and she threw the pruning shears to the ground and buried her face in her hands. All her life, she'd been struggling to find her place in the world, but it seemed as if she was destined to fill everyone else's needs.

First, it had been her father, who despite his success on the Senate floor, had been helpless at home. Even Duncan had used her to fulfill his dreams. She'd been the perfect date, the perfect hostess, and damn him to hell, the perfect bedmate. Then it had been all the employees at Price Manufacturing, who'd depended on her to save their jobs. Now it was Sean and Amy. When was it finally going to be her turn?

"When, dammit? When?" she whispered hoarsely as she raised her eyes heavenward, dashing away the angry tears that flowed down her cheeks. "If I can't be first, can't I at least be a part of something special?"

She returned her gaze to the house, and she envisioned her mother walking across the lawn, her head tossed back in laughter as she led Whitney toward the rose gardens, clinging to her small hand as she named the different roses and explained what made each of them unique.

Whitney knew it was a dream—a mirage—but in her mind it was real. It also made her realize that what she was seeking was within the palm of her hand. She could—in fact already had—recaptured that pure and holy love with Amy. She was a part of something special, but she also knew that Sean could destroy it on a whim, and what would she do then?

She'd be cast adrift. She'd have to start rebuilding her life from the ground up. But what choice did she have? If she didn't sell the mansion, she'd be financially dependent on Sean, and she could never let that happen.

With a sigh, she picked up the pruning shears and worked in the rose garden until it was so dark she couldn't see. Then, as she'd done on the day she'd decided to accept Sean's marriage proposal, she made a journey through the house. But this time it wasn't to relive all her memories; it was to tell them goodbye. Her chest ached, and her eyes burned when she finally closed the front door behind her, but for once, the tears wouldn't come.

When she returned home the house was quiet, and she went into Amy's room. Sitting in the rocking chair, she stared at her daughter, knowing that her future was here with an adorable little girl, who would be a young woman much too soon. She rose from the chair, brushed Amy's hair away from her face and pressed a loving kiss against her cheek.

Only when she turned toward the door did she become aware of Sean. He was standing in the room, leaning against the wall, and Whitney knew instinctively that he'd been there for a long time.

She smiled at him hesitantly, and he smiled back. Then he opened his arms, and she walked across the room and into them. As she rested her head against his chest and listened to his steady heartbeat, she admitted it was dangerous to accept his comfort. It was just another form of dependence that could be snatched away as quickly as it was given. But she needed to hold on to someone, and Sean was all she had. The significance of that thought made her sigh, for she wondered if there was anyone in the world who felt more alone than she did.

Chapter Nine

t was one of those too rare occasions when Sean could have lept in, but he was awake at the crack of dawn. Every time e'd closed his eyes the night before, his mind conjured up he image of Whitney kneeling in the rose garden and then itting beside Amy's bed. She looked so sad, and the guilt e'd managed to hold at bay for weeks had begun to resurace.

No matter how much he argued with himself, he kept aving to face the same question. By marrying her, what ys had he stolen from her? Though he knew she adored my, he couldn't help but wonder if it was going to be nough. Would there come a day when she'd resent him and ransfer that resentment to Amy?

The questions drove him out of bed, and deciding to rown them in coffee he pulled on a pair of jeans and padled barefoot to the kitchen. To his surprise, Whitney was lready there, and he paused in the doorway to study her.

She was sitting at the table, her feet propped up on the hair next to her, and the kitten on her lap. Even from that listance he could hear its rumbling purr of satisfaction, and ean experienced another twinge of jealousy as he watched er pet the cat in long sensuous strokes.

His eyes flowed down her, taking an inventory of her high ounded breasts that swelled against her T-shirt and her hapely legs revealed beneath a pair of cotton shorts.

Though she still needed to gain weight, she had put on a good five pounds, and he liked the softness it had added to her curves.

When the cat leaped off her lap, he returned his attention to her face and discovered that she was watching him. The yearning look in her eyes caused an unexpected surge of desire, which hit him with enough force to make him reach out and grasp the doorjamb. But by the time he'd steadied himself the look was gone, and he wondered if he'd imagined it.

"What are you doing up so early?" he asked.

Whitney shrugged and glanced down at her hands, unable to answer as she struggled to find her voice. When she'd glanced up and saw him standing there in nothing but denims, his hair mussed and his beard heavy, yearning passion had flared through her. She told herself it was only because of the ordeal she'd been through the previous day, and the tender hug he'd given her when she came home. The excuse didn't lessen the feeling.

"I had a sudden craving for steak and eggs for breakfast, and I got up to take steaks out of the freezer," she told him.

"Now who's hiding?" he asked softly as he strolled into the kitchen, pulled a chair from the table and spun it around so he could straddle it. As he rested his arms across the back, he quoted her with, "Yell at me, curse at me, throw something at me if that's what it takes, but please don't hide."

"Touché." She sighed and shook her head. "It suddenly dawned on me that if everything goes as it should, I'll be signing closing papers on the house and the business within the same week. I have this strange feeling of excitement and melancholy that I had when I graduated from high school. You know the one where you can't wait to get on with your life, but as you sit through the ceremony and watch your classmates, you get a really sad feeling inside, because you know that this part of your life is over. That nothing will ever be just like this again."

"Oh, Whitney," Sean murmured huskily as she gave him one of the most heart-wrenching smiles he'd ever seen and bravely blinked back her tears. He rose off the chair and knelt beside her, pulling her into his arms. As he stroked her back soothingly, he said, "It's okay to cry about it."

"I know, but I can't," she whispered miserably as she rested her forehead against his bare shoulder, which was soft and cool against the emotion-heated warmth of her own flesh. "All night long I tried to cry, but the tears just won't come."

Sean caught her chin and raised her head. As he peered down into her eyes, he felt as if he were peering into a kaleidoscope of blue. There were so many emotions swirling in their depths, and he found himself struggling with his own conflicting feelings for her. They were a mixture of warmth and tenderness, much like the feelings he bore for Amy. Yet he knew those feelings were deepening, shifting. He wasn't convinced he wanted to analyze them, because he sensed that they were also laced with desire, which he was determined to avoid at all costs.

But despite his firm resolve to offer Whitney no more than friendship, a part of him was urging him to pursue that feeling, find out where it was going. Another more insistent part told him the idea was crazy. What they had was working. It would be ridiculous to screw it up over a bunch of giddy hormones.

Unfortunately the assertion didn't stop him from touching her. He wrapped his hand around the side of her neck, caught his thumb beneath her chin and tilted her head a notch higher. He wanted to kiss her so badly his lips burned with the need, but he couldn't do it. No matter how much he wanted to, he simply couldn't do it!

He'd almost convinced himself to pull away when Whitney placed her hand against his chest. Her eyes widened with a look of wonder as her fingers curled in the mat of dark hair, and his chest heaved beneath her touch as he watched her lips part invitingly.

His heart rate increased, matching itself to the rapid cadence of the pulse in her neck, which was fluttering beneath his palm, and he drew in a deep shuddering breath when her lips parted even farther. He lowered his head slowly, watching her eyes dilate in anticipation, and then her lashes fluttered down and fanned across her cheeks, a silent declaration of her surrender.

With a groan, Sean kissed her. Her lips were everything he'd imagined—soft and sweet and complaisant. His tongue traced the full curve of her lower lip, and then the perfect bow of her upper one. He tested each corner, and the fullness in between.

Whitney was trembling so badly from his gentle onslaught, that she wondered why her teeth weren't chattering, and she wound her arms around his neck, needing an anchor in the sensual storm he was stirring up inside her. She buried her fingers in the thickness of his hair as he deepened the kiss, and she flexed them against his scalp when his tongue swept into her mouth and parried with hers.

Her senses were spinning. Her nerves were tingling. She'd never felt more alive, and she refused to acknowledge the little warning voice crying out in alarm inside her, warning her that this was wrong. She couldn't listen, because, heaven help her, she needed this, and if it was so wrong, why did it feel so right?

"What's you doing?"

Whitney and Sean jerked apart like guilty children as Amy's question resounded from the doorway. They both turned stricken eyes on their daughter.

"Kissing Whitney," Sean said hoarsely as he rose to his feet and swept Amy into his arms when she ran to him.

She peered at both of them with wide-eyed curiosity. "Why?"

Sean cleared his throat uncomfortably. Why indeed? he wondered. "Because that's what mamas and daddies do," he answered as he gazed over her head at Whitney. "Right?"

Whitney had to clear her own throat to find her voice. "Right." She reached up and caught one of Amy's bare feet. "I bet you're starving, so while you run upstairs and put on your slippers, I'll start breakfast."

"'Kay," Amy said.

Sean dropped her to her feet and fondly swatted her bottom to send her on her way. Then he stuffed his hands into his pockets as he glanced around the room, too self-conscious to look directly at Whitney. There were so many things that needed to be said, but he didn't know where to begin.

"Whitney, about what just happened between us . . ."

Whitney was studying her hands, still trying to cope with the remnants of their kiss, and her head shot up. He sounded so grim and looked even grimmer. When he didn't continue, but shifted from one foot to the other as his eyes roamed the room, looking at everything but her, she knew he regretted kissing her. She lifted her chin proudly. She wasn't about to sit there and let him expound on what had happened and give her a list of reasons why it shouldn't have.

"You don't have to explain, Sean," she said, forcing herself to give him what she hoped was a cheerful smile. "I was upset, and you were trying to comfort me. Things got a little out of hand, and I'm sure it won't happen again." Without waiting for him to respond, she rose to her feet and walked to the refrigerator.

Sean frowned at her back in confusion. She'd taken the words right out of his mouth, but suddenly he didn't like the taste of them. She was right. Their kiss had just happened, but it was that very spontaneity that had made it special; too special for his peace of mind.

"I'll go supervise Amy," he told her, hating the gruff sound of his voice, but unable to control it.

"Great," Whitney responded as she removed a carton of eggs from the refrigerator and turned toward him, only to discover he was gone.

She placed the egg carton on the counter, and then braced her hands against its edge, gripping it until she could feel the hard edges digging into her palms. But the physical pain was inconsequential when compared to the ache inside her. For every step she took forward with Sean, she seemed to take two backward, and she was beginning to feel like a wisp of straw caught in a tornado.

For Amy, she had to find a balance in her life, and the first way to do that, she decided, was to stay away from Sean.

THE TELEPHONES WERE QUIET, and Whitney peered out the second-story window of the Mile High Women's Foundation. Though her gaze was centered on the lofty peaks of the Rocky Mountains that filled the western horizon, her thoughts were turned inward.

During the past month she'd been trying to keep her distance from Sean, but he was making it impossible. Whenever he had an afternoon or weekend off, he insisted on some kind of family outing. So far they'd hit the Denver Zoo, the Denver Museum of Natural History, and the Denver Children's Museum, whose exhibits were designed to teach children through participation and had been as much fun for her and Sean as it had been for Amy.

This past weekend they'd gone to Elitch Gardens, a major amusement park, where Sean and Amy had coaxed a cowardly Whitney onto every hair-raising ride on the grounds. And yesterday he'd announced that it was adults' night out, and taken Whitney out to dinner and then to the Denver Center for Performing Arts for a Mozart concert.

Whitney had felt self-conscious that night when she came down the stairs and Sean gave her a rakish smile as his eyes glided over the turquoise silk dress that draped over one shoulder Grecian fashion leaving the other bared.

He let out a low wolf whistle and said, "I think we're going to play dress up more often. You look positively stunning."

Whitney blushed under the compliment, finding herself too tongue-tied to speak.

But her shyness had been obliterated when Sean stuffed his hands into his pockets and said, "I just realized what Amy is going to look like when she grows up. Do you think I should buy a shotgun?"

His sober expression, more than his question, sent Whitney into gales of laughter, and that gaiety set the tone for the evening.

When they'd returned home and she slipped her shoes from her feet to carry upstairs, she turned and found Sean staring at her. She tried to tell herself that it wasn't desire she saw flaring in his eyes, but her body had refused to listen.

"Thanks for the night out," she'd stated huskily.

"Sure," he responded. She climbed three steps before he said, "Whitney?"

She'd turned back to find that he'd come to the bottom of the stairs and they were on direct eye level. She knew then that it hadn't been her imagination. His eyes were filled with desire, and her mind began clamoring with the memory of that kiss they'd shared, urging her to relive it.

Her body began to sway toward him of its own volition, but just as she raised her hand to put it on his shoulder, he took a step backward and said, "I haven't told you how much you've come to mean to us. You're a wonderful mother, and I consider you a cherished friend. I just wanted you to know that."

And then he walked away, leaving her feeling light-headed and confused.

"Whitney, is everything all right?"

Whitney blinked away her introspection and turned her head from the window. Dr. Bauer was standing a short distance away and watching her.

"Yes, Mary Beth, everything's fine," Whitney responded quickly, while reaching for the messages she'd taken for the woman. "In fact, it's been so quiet today that

I've been indulging myself in a little daydreaming. It's so gorgeous outside that it seems a shame to be indoors.''

"Yes," Mary Beth agreed. "I'm also glad it's quiet, because I'd like to talk to you. Why don't you come into my office?''

Whitney followed after her, feeling like a child being led into the principal's office, though she couldn't think of anything she'd done wrong.

"Please sit," Mary Beth instructed, absently waving toward one of the chairs in front of her desk as she finished perusing her messages. Then she laid them aside, sat, and folded her hands on the top of her desk. Whitney had to fight to keep from squirming in her chair beneath the woman's piercing gaze.

"How do you like what you're doing, Whitney?''

"I love it," Whitney answered. "Of course, I haven't taken many calls, but those I have I think I handled fairly well.''

"Actually, you handled them beautifully. I've watched you, and you're good. Very passionate. Very effective.''

"Thank you," Whitney murmured helplessly at the unexpected compliment.

Mary Beth leaned forward, her expression earnest. "I want to make a special request of you, but I want you to know right up front that if you say no, I won't be offended.''

Whitney was becoming more baffled by the minute. "Okay.''

"I've been working with a runaway teenager, who, I suspect, is pregnant," Mary Beth said. "She's been at one of our shelters for a few weeks, but I haven't been able to reach her, nor have any of the other counselors who've tried to work with her. All we've managed to get out of her is that her name is Debbie and that she's sixteen years old. We can't get her to see a doctor, nor can we get her to discuss the possibility of pregnancy. She's also stopped eating, which we both know is dangerous if she is pregnant.''

"And you want me to talk to her," Whitney said, having already reached the logical conclusion to Mary Beth's speech.

"Only if you want to, and I have to honestly say that I'm not completely comfortable even asking you. However, I don't have much choice, because I'm afraid that if we push Debbie too hard, she'll just run away again."

"I'm not completely comfortable with your asking me, either," Whitney told the woman honestly. "I'm not sure I'd know how to talk to someone face-to-face, but I suppose it wouldn't hurt to give it a try."

"Great. I'll be at the shelter all day Wednesday, if you'd like to come by then." When Whitney nodded, Mary Beth jotted down the directions and handed them to her. "See you, Wednesday, Whitney. Good night."

IT WASN'T UNTIL Whitney had settled Amy down for the night that she let her mind mull over her conversation with Mary Beth. Since Sean had left a message on the answering machine that he was tied up with an emergency and didn't have any idea when he'd be home, she had plenty of time to ponder the situation.

She wanted to help the girl if she could because she knew how terrifying it was to be all alone and pregnant. But could she handle the problem on a face-to-face basis? Dealing with the girls over the telephone was hard enough at times. What Mary Beth had described as "very passionate," when referring to Whitney's conversations with them was, in actuality, outright panic. She wasn't just talking to them, she was talking to herself four years ago, convincing herself that she had to go on. Was she strong enough to confront someone who was a reflection of her past?

She prowled the living room and grabbed a hand-stitched pillow from the sofa, resisting the urge to throw it at the wall. What she needed was her piano. A few hours at the keyboard, and she'd find her answers. The mansion was still unoccupied, but she knew she couldn't go back there. When she walked away, she'd said goodbye forever.

She tossed the pillow back onto the sofa and walked through the kitchen and out the back door, where she drew in great gulps of air. Then her eyes shifted to the spot where the conservatory was to be built, and she wondered why she still couldn't choose a design, especially since the mansion was sold. She couldn't ask the new owners to keep her piano indefinitely, and by now, the contractor should already be hard at work.

With a purposeful stride she walked to what she supposed would be the center of the building and stood there, trying to absorb something from it, something that would say it was right to build. When nothing happened, she turned back toward the house and gazed up at the second-story, seeking Amy's room, but latching on to the window of the master bedroom instead, and suddenly, she knew what was wrong.

This was Margaret's home and Margaret's land, and even if Whitney razed the entire house and built a new one, it would still be Margaret's in her mind. It was the reason why she'd stopped making even minor changes inside the house. It was why she couldn't commit herself to the conservatory. It simply wasn't home to her, and never would be.

She wondered if she should tell Sean about her feelings, but she decided that they sounded silly to her, so they would most likely sound insane to him. A house was a house was a house, and if Margaret hadn't spent her entire life here, Whitney supposed she could have accepted it. But Margaret had, and Whitney didn't want the conservatory, because once it was built, she'd always feel obligated to remain here.

"Oh, damn," she whispered miserably as she went back inside. "How am I going to tell Sean that I've changed my mind?"

SEAN COULD ONLY GAPE in disbelief when he walked into his living room and found a tepee sitting in the middle of it.

"What the hell?" he muttered.

Amy promptly stuck her head out the opening. "That's a bad word, Daddy, and Whit-nee says when you say bad words, you get your mouth washed out with soap."

"Yeah, Daddy," Whitney agreed as her head appeared above her daughter's. "You get your mouth washed out with soap."

"Is that right?" Sean said with a laugh as he looked at them. Their faces were covered with what he supposed was meant to represent war paint, but looked suspiciously like lipstick, and they had feathers in their hair. "Well, I guess I'll have to watch what I say. What's this all about?" he asked, gesturing toward the tepee.

"We're learning about the American Indian," Whitney answered.

Sean chuckled. "And you needed props?"

Whitney grinned. "Sure. Want to join us?"

"Why not." He walked across the room and ducked inside the tent, surprised to find so much space inside. "Nice," he said as he dropped onto the blankets spread around the floor.

"Yeah," Amy said as she thrust a book at him. "See, they put a fire in the middle. I wanted to do that, but Whit-nee said no, because we'd burn the house down."

"Isn't that something," Sean automatically responded, though he wasn't looking at the book. He was gazing at Whitney, who was gazing at Amy. The look of love on her face was so poignant that it brought tears to his eyes. He reached out and caught her hand. When she looked at him, he asked, "Everything all right?"

"Perfect," Whitney answered, giving his hand a squeeze and returning her attention to Amy, who was thumbing through the book and expounding on each picture on each page.

But Sean knew that everything wasn't perfect. In the past few days Whitney had become more and more quiet, as if turning inward to worry at some internal problem. He hadn't been able to get her to talk about it, and it worried him, because she was usually so quick to express what was on her mind.

As he continued to watch her, he found himself wanting to reach out and trace the contour of her cheek, the delicate point of her chin. Whitney, as if sensing his scrutiny, turned her gaze toward him, and Sean felt as if he were drowning in the blue of her eyes.

His heart began to pound in his chest, his stomach twisted into a hard knot of need, and he felt as if his lungs were going to burst as he caught his breath and held it. His world narrowed until there was nothing in it but her. He could hear her tinkling laughter, though she hadn't uttered a sound. He could see the mesmerizing fluidity of her body, though she hadn't moved a muscle. He lowered his eyes to her mouth, and he could taste the sweetness of her lips. Feel the warmth of them. And when her tongue nervously flicked over her bottom lip, he nearly groaned aloud.

When he returned his gaze to hers, he discovered that she was eyeing him warily, almost fearfully. He wanted to reach out and draw her into his arms to reassure her. To...

"Daddy, is it 'kay?" Amy asked as her small face popped into his line of vision.

He had to shake his head to clear it. "Uh, is what okay, pumpkin?"

"Whit-nee said I could sleep in here tonight if it was 'kay with you. Is it?"

"Sure," he said, letting his gaze move over the top of her head to Whitney. "But from now on, if Whitney says it's okay with her, then it's okay with me. Okay?"

Whitney's lips lifted into a smile. "Okay."

"Yeah!" Amy screamed and tore out of the tepee.

"You are spoiling her," Sean said, though his words hadn't come out as a chastisement. "A tepee for a history lesson?"

Whitney shrugged and stretched her legs out in front of her. Leaning back on her hands, she said, "I found it up in the attic, and it looked so forlorn lying there all dusty and torn apart, that I decided, what the heck."

"You found it in the attic?" Sean questioned. "What in the world was a tepee doing in the attic?"

"Keeping the stuffed buffalo company?" she suggested.

Sean's mouth dropped open in shock. "There's a stuffed buffalo in the attic?"

Whitney grinned. "I don't really know. There's so much junk up there that an entire herd of buffalo could be hiding out, and we'd never know it. How long has it been since you've been up there?"

"I don't know. Seven, eight years, I suppose. Why?"

She grinned again. "I just wanted to make sure that those gigantic footprints didn't belong to Big Foot."

Sean pointed to his size eleven foot. "Does this look familiar?"

She made a show of studying his stockinged foot. "Vaguely."

Sean stretched his leg out and pressed his foot against hers. "If you had to compare, just whose footprints are up there?"

Whitney stared down at their touching feet, feeling oddly off kilter. It was crazy that just the touch of his foot could send her senses spinning, but it was happening. She pulled her foot away and tucked it beneath her leg.

"We definitely need to call in a big game hunter," she stated.

When he didn't answer, she raised her eyes to his face. He was regarding her intently as he said, "You don't have to be afraid of me, Whitney."

"I'm not," she replied, and it wasn't a lie. It wasn't him she was afraid of, it was herself. With each passing day, she was growing more aware of him. The most frightening part was that it wasn't strictly on a physical level, for if it had been, she knew she could have dealt with it. She was being drawn in by the inner man. The man who'd opened his arms to her when she'd sold her home. The man who'd told her it was okay to cry when she'd wanted to cry. The man who'd let her spoil Amy, because he loved her as if she were his own.

And it was that last part that was drawing her in deeper and deeper, she realized. Not every man could love a child who hadn't come from his loins, and rarer still was one so devoted to even his own child that he'd marry a woman he didn't love to make sure his child was happy. So why couldn't she find satisfaction here? Why did every day in this house make her feel more and more isolated?

"What is it?" Sean asked when she glanced up at him, her brow furrowed.

"Nothing. It's just that when I was up in the attic, I remembered someone telling me that people should move every five years so they'd get rid of all their junk. Have you ever thought of moving?"

"No," Sean said. "I like it here. The house is close to work and the hospital. It's in a good neighborhood. It's close to excellent schools. It's also paid for. Why should I give it up?"

"I see your point," Whitney said, and she did, though she didn't want to.

"Whitney, if the junk in the attic is bothering you, we'll clean it up."

"Yeah, we probably should," she said. "I'd better go check on dinner."

Sean frowned at her back as she climbed out of the tent. He felt as if there'd been some hidden meaning beneath their conversation, but he had no idea what it was.

EVEN IF MARY BETH hadn't pointed her out, Whitney would have recognized Debbie. The girl was sitting beneath a tree in the small neighborhood park across from the shelter. Her knees were drawn up to her chest, her arms linked around them, and her face buried against them.

Her pain was so acute that Whitney could feel it across the hundred yards separating them, and she took an involuntary step backward in recognition. Every self-protective instinct she had told her to turn and run, but some greater urge drew her forward.

Debbie didn't look up when Whitney came to a stop in front of her. Whitney knew the girl had to be aware of her presence, but Whitney didn't speak. She just stood there, twirling a pink rosebud between her fingers.

Finally Debbie raised her head, and Whitney's heart lurched. The girl wasn't particularly pretty, but her vibrant green eyes were spectacular. They were also as old as time.

Debbie's lips quirked in a demeaning half smile. "Don't tell me you're another shrink come to probe my mind."

Whitney laughed softly at the macabre intonation the girl had put on the words. "Sorry to disappoint you, but I'm not a shrink. My name is Whitney, and I'm a homemaker with a husband and a very active three-year-old."

Debbie regarded her with distrust. "Yeah, and I'm the Queen of England."

"I'm glad to meet you, Your Grace," Whitney said, giving a royal bow before rising and extending the rosebud.

Debbie glowered at the flower, but reluctantly accepted it. "What's this for?"

"For no reason." Whitney sat down in front of the girl and folded her legs Indian fashion. She rested her elbows on her knees and pulled up a piece of grass. As she slid it between her fingers, she said, "You know, I envy you."

The girl released a harsh bark of disbelieving laughter. "You're crazy."

"No," Whitney said with a shake of her head.

Debbie's eyes glided over Whitney disparagingly. "You're sitting here in your designer jeans without a care in the world, and you envy me? Lady, believe me, you are crazy."

"My husband calls me that."

"Crazy?" Debbie said with another harsh laugh.

"No, lady."

Debbie's brow wrinkled in distrust. "What do you want?"

"Nothing," Whitney answered. "I have everything I want. What do you want?"

"For you to go away."

"No, I don't think so," Whitney murmured. "And even if you do, I want to stay, so I guess we're at a standoff."

Debbie glowered. Whitney smiled.

Finally the girl said, "Why do you envy me?"

"Because you have so many people who care about you."

"Sure."

"It's true, and four years ago I would have given anything to have people around me who cared."

Debbie's lips tightened and she regarded Whitney with a combination of anger and curiosity. Finally she said, "Okay, why?"

Whitney shrugged and raised her eyes to the sky. "Because my father and fiancé had been killed and I found out I was pregnant. I was all alone in the world, and I was so scared."

"I never said I was pregnant," Debbie stated quickly.

Whitney lowered her eyes. "I never said you were, either. I said I was. Do you know what I did?"

"No, what?" the girl asked reluctantly.

"I refused to believe it, because I didn't want it to be happening. I stopped eating. I stopped thinking. I stopped living. I went home and shut myself inside and didn't come out for a month."

"So why did you come out?" Debbie finally questioned when Whitney's silence made it apparent that she wasn't going to continue.

Whitney shrugged. "I came to the conclusion that hiding away wasn't going to change anything. All it was going to do was make me sick, and maybe the baby. I didn't care about me, but I did care about the baby, because it didn't seem fair. After all, it couldn't take care of itself. It had to depend on me. I had the power to let it live or let it die. That's a pretty heavy responsibility, isn't it?''

When Debbie didn't respond, Whitney pushed herself to her feet. ''Well, I'd better go. Next time I'm in the neighborhood, I'll stop by and say hi. You take care of yourself, and thanks for listening.''

Whitney had just reached the edge of the park when Debbie yelled, ''Hey, lady.''

Whitney turned around and placed her hand over her eyes to shield them from the sun. ''Yes?''

The girl shrugged uncomfortably. ''Anytime you want to talk, well, I'm here, okay?''

''Thanks,'' Whitney yelled back. ''I really appreciate it.''

And as Whitney walked away, she knew she'd be back. Maybe not tomorrow, or the next day, or even the day after. But she'd be back, because she'd seen a part of herself in Debbie. A part that she knew had never been resolved and had to be put to rest, because if it wasn't, she knew that she'd never be able to find happiness.

Chapter Ten

Whitney grumbled to herself as she studied her checkbook, which according to her bank statement, was five dollars off. She knew five dollars wouldn't make or break her, but she couldn't stand not having it balance to the penny.

She cursed beneath her breath when the phone rang, interrupting her in the middle of her figuring. The call was for Mrs. Wilkens, and she tossed the checkbook aside, grabbed her coffee cup and headed for the kitchen in search of the housekeeper.

While the woman took the call on the kitchen extension, Whitney refilled her coffee cup, and she frowned in concern when Mrs. Wilkens let out a cry of distress. Listening to one side of the conversation, Whitney couldn't determine what had happened, but she knew it was something serious. When Mrs. Wilkens hung up, she asked, "What's wrong?"

"It's my daughter, Susan," the housekeeper informed her. "She took a girl scout troop to the ice skating rink and fell and broke her leg. It's a spiral fracture, and her husband says she'll be in the hospital for a few days, and then confined to a wheelchair. They have six children, and he wondered if I could come to Atlanta for a few weeks to help out."

"Well, of course, you can," Whitney said.

Mrs. Wilkens nervously adjusted her apron. "No offense, Whitney, but maybe I should check with Dr. Fitzgerald first."

Whitney's first response was a surge of anger, but she quickly capped it as she surveyed the woman's worried face. And, she thought ruefully, she couldn't really blame Mrs. Wilkens for feeling as if she should check with Sean. As Whitney had determined on her first day here, the housekeeper had been working for him for more than a year, and her first loyalty would lie with him.

"Sean said he'd be in surgery all afternoon and part of the evening," she informed the woman. "You probably won't be able to talk to him until late tonight, which means you wouldn't be able to catch a flight until morning. I don't think you should have to wait that long. Just pack your bags. I'll take full responsibility."

Mrs. Wilkens looked as if she'd object, but then she gave Whitney a grateful smile. "I really do appreciate this."

Whitney returned her smile. "No appreciation needed. I know how I'd feel if it was Amy. I couldn't stand not knowing for sure that she was all right."

"Only another mother would understand," Mrs. Wilkens said as she stepped forward and wrapped her arms around Whitney.

The woman's professed alliance in motherhood caused a strange little ache in the middle of Whitney's chest, and she returned her hug with more force than was normal.

When they parted, she said, "You go pack your bags. I'll call the airport and make reservations for you."

It was only after Whitney hung up the phone that she realized how much responsibility she'd taken upon herself. She felt she knew Sean well enough to know he'd let the housekeeper go; however, she wasn't sure that he wouldn't feel that he should have at least been consulted. Then she shrugged, deciding that if he didn't like it, she'd just have to deal with the consequences.

SEAN STOOD IN THE KITCHEN doorway as he watched Whitney put the finishing touches on a plate of food before sliding it into the microwave oven. Since it was nearly midnight, he'd been startled to find her up when he came home. While he changed his clothes he wondered if this late night vigil had something to do with whatever had been bothering her for the past week.

Though he was exhausted and not in the best frame of mind for heavy discussions, he hoped that she was ready to open up. Each day that passed made him more nervous, and he'd begun to take stock of life before Whitney and life after Whitney. He didn't think he'd be able to stand it if she weren't around.

After she closed the door and set the timer, he asked, "Having trouble sleeping?"

Whitney spun around in startled surprise, and Sean watched in mesmerized fascination as her lips lifted into a beautiful smile.

"You're going to have to stop sneaking up on me," she told him with a soft laugh. "Someday you might catch me doing something embarrassing."

Sean couldn't help but return her smile. "Somehow, I doubt that. You're much too well-bred to do anything embarrassing. Now back to my question. Are you having trouble sleeping?"

Her smile faded and she glanced toward the kitchen table. "No. I need to talk to you about Mrs. Wilkens."

"What about her?" Sean questioned cautiously. So far, she and the housekeeper had been getting along, and he hadn't been aware of any underlying problems.

"We'll talk while you eat," Whitney answered as the timer went off.

Sean frowned at her response, but instead of insisting that she give him the details right then and there, he walked into the kitchen and helped her carry his plate and coffee for both of them into the dining room.

After they were seated at the table, he said, "What about Mrs. Wilkens?"

"Her daughter—the one that lives in Atlanta—broke her leg. She's going to be confined to a wheelchair for a few weeks and has six kids, so Mrs. Wilkens went to help out," Whitney explained. She eyed Sean nervously before continuing with, "She didn't want to leave without consulting you first, but I told her it wasn't necessary. It is all right, isn't it?"

"Of course, it's all right," Sean said. He leaned back in his chair and stared at her for a long moment. "Have I really made you feel you have to ask permission before making a decision?"

"No," Whitney whispered as she gazed down into her coffee cup self-consciously. "But until now I've never had to make a decision of any magnitude, either. I didn't know how you'd feel about letting Mrs. Wilkens go, but I didn't want her to have to wait until morning. I know how I'd feel if it was Amy."

"I agree, and you don't have to defend your position."

"I'm not defending it," she stated. "I'm just . . . well, maybe I am defending."

Sean smiled at the soft flood of color that flowed into her cheeks at the confession, and he reached for his coffee cup to control his itching fingers, which were begging to stroke the remembered softness of her skin—to test the warmth of the becoming blush.

After he took a sip of coffee, he said, "You're the mistress of this house, Whitney. What goes on inside of it is your prerogative."

He'd meant the words to be reassuring, and he frowned in concern at the way her eyes darkened and dropped to her hands. His gaze automatically followed hers, and his frown deepened when he noted that her fingers were linked together tightly enough to whiten her knuckles. He raised his eyes back to her face and willed her to look at him. When she didn't, panic fluttered in the pit of his stomach.

"Whitney, what's wrong?"

"Nothing," she said, though she couldn't look at him directly. How could she ever tell him that she'd never feel like the mistress in Margaret's house? The house he didn't want to sell. The house she'd begun to hate more with each passing day. But he'd given her so darn much, and complaining about the house seemed so petty.

Sean, determined to get to the bottom of whatever was bothering her, rose to his feet and rounded the table. He dragged a chair from the end and positioned it beside Whitney. To his surprise, she immediately leaped to her feet the moment he sat down beside her.

"I don't know about you, but it's been a long day for me, and tomorrow I'm going to be a full-time mother without Mrs. Wilkens to run interference. I'd better do the dishes and get to bed," she said.

She jumped when Sean grasped her wrist and urged her back into her chair. "Talk, Whitney," he ordered quietly, but firmly. "You have to talk to me. Tell me what's wrong."

Everything! she wanted to yell, but then he'd want her to define everything, and she really didn't know how to do so, because in the end, he was what was wrong. He was too nice, too compassionate, too considerate, and too darn sexy. He also didn't want a wife, and she wanted to be a wife in every sense of the word. She wanted to be wanted. To be loved. To be cherished. She wanted it all!

She rose back to her feet, even though Sean still had a hold on her wrist. "There's nothing wrong, Sean. I'm just tired."

At first Sean looked as if he wouldn't let her go, but then he released her hand. "I'll help you clean up, and we'll both call it a night."

The last thing Whitney wanted was for the man to be in the kitchen with her when she was feeling so darned morose. "It'll only take me a minute. You don't need to help."

Sean started to object, but thought better of it as his gaze slid down her robe, which had parted at her neck and thigh, revealing a lacy white nightshirt and far too much skin. They were friends, he reminded himself. Just friends. He suddenly found he didn't like that distinction. He didn't like it at all.

"I'll check on Amy and go to bed. Are you going to be all right without Mrs. Wilkens, or would you like to hire some temporary help?"

"Amy and I will be fine," Whitney stated firmly. "The house might get a little more dusty than usual, but I think we'll all survive."

WHITNEY WAS AGHAST when she opened her eyes the next morning and saw the time on her alarm clock. She knew she'd set it, but she must have rolled over and hit the alarm switch rather than the snooze button when it had gone off.

With a yawn, she climbed out of bed, pulled on her robe and crossed over to Amy's room. When she found the child gone she panicked, knowing that a three-year-old on the loose could get into trouble faster than a person could blink. She rushed down the stairs and gasped as her stunned gaze locked on the kitchen floor. What looked like an entire box of cereal and half gallon of milk was strewn from the refrigerator door to the table.

"Amy, what are you doing?" she asked in disbelief as her gaze followed the soggy trail to the table where the toddler sat.

"Eating breakfast," Amy answered.

Whitney groaned as she once again eyed the mess. But it was her own fault, she acknowledged. If she'd gotten up with the alarm, this would have never happened. Gingerly she tiptoed to Amy's side, relieved to see that the toddler had managed to provide herself with an adequate breakfast, even if the top of the table closely resembled the aftereffects of a bombing.

"Amy, please don't feed yourself anymore," Whitney said as she wrapped her robe around her legs to keep the hem dry and sat down beside her daughter. "Come wake me up, and I'll get your breakfast, okay?"

"'Kay," Amy agreed as she stuffed another spoonful of cereal into her mouth.

Whitney crept back through the mess and fixed herself a cup of instant coffee, needing the caffeine to restore her sense of balance. She rejoined Amy at the table and sipped the coffee as she waited for the child to finish eating.

When Amy was done, Whitney stripped off her robe. Then, clad only in her nightshirt, she retrieved the mop bucket and broom from the utility room. She swept up the majority of the soggy cereal, rinsed the broom in the sink and then got down on her hands and knees to begin sopping up the milk.

Vaguely she heard water running, but she was so intent on her chore that she didn't pay attention until Amy yelled, "Whit-nee!"

Whitney leaped to her feet and ran to the bathroom where Amy was standing beside the bathtub.

"Amy!" she screeched as she watched water cascade over the edge of the tub. "What are you doing?"

"My ducky wanted to go for a swim, and the water wasn't deep enough," Amy explained with a childish giggle.

Whitney almost burst into tears as she sloshed through the bathroom, turned off the water and lifted Amy into her arms. She sloshed back out of the bathroom and took the child upstairs, dried her and dressed her. Then she went to her own room and changed into denim cutoffs and an old T-shirt, after strictly ordering Amy to remain in her room.

When she returned, she found that Amy had complied, but she'd strewn every toy she owned across the floor and was having a tug of war with her puppy over her pillow, whose stuffing suddenly decided to take a test flight. It wasn't the nice polyester kind, either. It was the clingy, rubbery kind that was almost impossible to clean up, and it blanketed the room.

Whitney couldn't believe that so much stuffing could have been inside such a small square. She gazed at her daughter incredulously. In all the time she'd known her, Amy had been a model child. Whitney wondered if she'd been replaced by a changeling during the night.

"Come on," Whitney said as she lifted Amy in one arm and the puppy in the other. "The two of you are going outside where you can't possibly get into any trouble."

After she'd placed the two mischief-makers in the fenced-in backyard, Whitney walked back into the kitchen and groaned. The milk was starting to dry, and the water from the bathroom was flowing out at an alarming rate. She dropped back down to her knees, finished cleaning the kitchen floor and then began working her way toward the bathroom.

She'd made it halfway into the room when the abject howling of a dog filled her consciousness. At first Whitney ignored it, knowing that the moaning animal didn't belong to the Fitzgeralds. But when the howling became more insistent, Whitney sat back on her heels and blanched. It sounded like the German shepherd next door, and she knew that the neighbors had left it in the dog run while they were away on a long weekend, because they'd asked her to feed and exercise it.

She once again leaped to her feet and ran out the back door. Amy had turned on the hose full blast and was drowning the neighbor's dog.

"Amy, what are you doing?" Whitney bellowed.

"Giving the doggy a bath."

"Well, stop it, and stop it right this minute!"

"'Kay," Amy said, and blithely turned the hose on Whitney, who was instantly drenched from head to foot.

Whitney fought her way through the waterfall to the spigot and turned off the water. Then she surveyed herself, and thought about the milk-soaked kitchen, Amy's stuffing-filled bedroom and the flooded bathroom. It would take her all day to clean up the mess. It was suddenly more than she could handle, and she sat down in the flower bed, crushing a dozen petunias. The tears that had eluded her since she'd signed the contract on her house arrived in full force, and she began to sob.

"It's 'kay, Mama," Amy said as she walked up to Whitney and cradled her mother's tear-washed cheeks in her small hands.

Whitney sniffed and raised hopeful eyes to her daughter's face. Her heart was dancing in her chest, but she refused to believe what her ears had heard—what her heart wanted to believe she'd heard. She was trembling so badly that she had to take several deep breaths before she could speak.

"What did you say?" she finally managed to say. Amy's brow furrowed in confusion. "Did you call me Mama?" Whitney asked as she hooked her hands beneath Amy's armpits and drew her between her thighs. She realized her tone had been too harsh when Amy's bottom lip thrust out and she burst into tears. Whitney buried her hand in the little girl's hair and caught the back of her head, drawing her face close.

"It's all right, Amy. You didn't do anything wrong. Did you call me Mama?"

Amy nodded, and Whitney swept her to her chest, her tears returning as Amy threw her arms around her neck and sobbed, "Don't go away. I love you. I don't want you to go away."

And Whitney understood that Mrs. Wilkens's departure had terrified the child. In that terror, Amy had christened Whitney with the most holy of titles. She'd called her Mama.

"I love you, too, and I'm never going to leave you," she whispered hoarsely. "I promise you, Amy, I'm never going to leave you."

But how could she make that vow? Hadn't her own mother left her? Hadn't she, Whitney, walked away from Amy three years ago and never looked back?

No, she'd looked back, but she was forever telling herself that she made the right decision. And maybe she had, but it never felt right, would never feel right because no matter how sensible it all seemed, Amy was still a part of her and would always be a part of her. From the moment she walked away from her, a piece of her heart had died. Her tears became a torrent as the anguish from the past engulfed her.

She had no idea how long she'd been crying when she felt he tug on her arm and heard Sean's murmured, "Come on, you two. Let's go into the house."

She rose to her feet with the consciousness of a zombie, unable to stop sobbing, even when Sean wrapped his arm around her and cradled her against his side. She burrowed against him, wanting him to take away the pain, but even his strength wasn't enough, and when he urged her down into a kitchen chair, his withdrawal made her feel even more bereft. She folded her arms on the table, heedless of the milk and cereal that clung to them, and let herself go with her grief.

Sean felt torn between Whitney, who was crying so hard her entire body was shaking, and Amy, who was sobbing and clinging to him so desperately that he could barely breathe.

It only took a glance around the room to tell him what was wrong. Amy was an angel, but every couple of months he got the urge to trade her halo in for a pitchfork. It looked as if she'd just initiated Whitney, and with a hose path to boot. He would have laughed if Whitney hadn't been so upset, and he reached out to stroke her wet hair.

"You wait right here," he told her. "I'll be back in a few minutes." Then he took Amy to the upstairs bathroom, stripped off her dirty clothes, washed the mud off her, and dried her.

"Are you okay?" he asked his daughter when he finished the chore.

She nodded and hung her head. "I'm a bad girl."

"I can't disagree with that," Sean stated solemnly, though his lips were twitching at her comically woebegone expression. "What kind of punishment do bad girls get?" he asked as he carried her to her room.

"Have to stay in my room till you say I can come out," she said forlornly as she laid her head on his shoulder.

"That's right." Sean rested his chin on the top of her head to hide his smile, but the smile died when he pushed open her door and saw the destruction. "Oh, Amy," he groaned, deciding that she'd just taken the forays into misbehavior to a new dimension. Whitney really had been initiated by fire.

"I'm sorry," she said on a hiccup that was a forewarning of a new bout of tears.

Sean swung her down to her feet and squatted down in front of her. He brushed his thumb across her cheek to catch a tear as it tumbled off her lashes. "Remember what I've told you before? When you've done something bad, you don't cry about it. You apologize, and then you do what you can to make it better. In this case, you're going to have to clean up your room."

He found her a change of clothes and helped her into them. Then he sent her to the bathroom to get a paper bag. When she returned, he popped the bag open and instructed, "You pick up every piece of your pillow's inside and put them into the bag. After that's done, you put all your toys into your toy box. I'll be back in a little while to check on you, and I expect to find your room clean. Understand?"

Amy sighed disconsolately. "Uh-huh."

"Good. When your room is clean, you can apologize to Whitney."

With that, he headed back to the kitchen, but Whitney wasn't at the table where he'd left her. She was on her hands and knees in the bathroom, attempting to mop up the water on the floor, though Sean had a feeling that her dripping hair and clothes were defeating her efforts.

She sat back on her heels and peered up at him when he said, "Should I be building an ark?"

Raking a hand through her wet hair, she said with a sniff, "I'm sorry about the mess. I should have kept a better watch on Amy."

"Oh, Whitney, what am I going to do with you?" Sean asked as he marched into the room and pulled her to her feet. "This certainly isn't the first time Amy's gone on a rampage. In fact, I've lost count of the number of times she's flooded this bathroom, and if anyone's at fault here, it's me. I should have warned you about her fascination with water and her proclivity for flooding."

He opened the linen closet, pulled out a towel and handed it to her. "I saw your robe in the kitchen. I'll get it for you. Then I want you to get out of those wet clothes. While you're doing that, I'm going to fix you a cup of tea."

"But I have to finish the floor."

"I'll finish it while you have your tea." She nodded, and Sean felt a tug at his heart. She looked as woebegone as Amy had only minutes before, and he impulsively pulled her into his arms. He cradled her head against his shoulder and soothingly stroked her back. "It's going to be all right, Whitney."

No it's not, and it never will be! Whitney wanted to scream, but how could she explain to him that the past had just slammed into her? That she'd been forced into choices she hadn't wanted to make, but had made nonetheless? Nothing he said was going to change anything. The guilt was there and always would be, because she'd never be able to forget Amy begging her not to go away. Never be able to forget that she'd already committed that sin.

She was so sick of spirit that she was tempted to collapse against him and indulge in the comfort he was offering. Instead she pushed away, whispering, "I'm getting your suit wet." She then frowned at him as the significance of that statement hit her. "What are you doing home at this time of day?"

"My surgical case was canceled, so I made rounds cleaned up some paperwork at the hospital and found tha I had a few free hours before I had to go to the office. Since this was your first day alone with Amy, I thought I'd come home and find out how things were going."

Her laugh was brittle as she turned away from him and braced both hands against the marble countertop. "I sup pose I should be glad you did. Right now you must be thinking that I'm a pretty irresponsible mother."

"I don't think anything of the kind," he stated, and when she didn't respond, he had a feeling that there was more going on here than some toddler mischief.

"What happened this morning?" he asked, placing his hand on her shoulder.

Whitney jerked away from his touch and began to towe dry her hair. "I overslept. Amy made her own breakfast which resulted in a major redecoration of the kitchen. While I was cleaning it up, her rubber duck decided he wanted to go for a swim. Unfortunately he preferred the Atlantic Ocean to Lake Michigan. Then Amy and Snowball decided to redecorate her room with early pillow stuffing. By tha time, I knew I was in dire need of a cleaning crew and I pu her outside where she couldn't do any more remodeling. A that point she decided the neighbor's dog needed a bath. He and I both got hosed down."

"And?" Sean prodded when she finished, knowing there was more and that she wasn't going to offer it unless he pushed.

She drew in a deep breath. "And I couldn't handle it and started crying. It upset Amy, and she started crying. That's when you arrived."

"I see." She was still drying her hair, and Sean caught an end of the towel, tugging until she was forced to turn around and face him. When she did, he said, "Now how about telling me the truth?"

"That is the truth," she said, inwardly cursing those damn tears that once again crept to the surface. Was she

oing to spend the rest of her life suffering from watery-eyed
nyopia?

Sean caught the other end of the towel and pulled a cap-
ured Whitney toward him. She knew that all she had to do
vas duck her head to escape, but his eyes had locked with
ters, and she couldn't have been more of a prisoner if she'd
been shackled.

Sean was feeling his own form of imprisonment as he
tared down at her. Under the worst of conditions, Whit-
tey could never be described as anything less than beauti-
ul. But right now, drenched to the skin, her hair framing
er face in a sleek cap, and her eyes wide and tear washed,
he was exquisite. She'd also never looked more fragile to
im, and it brought every protective instinct he had to the
urface.

He dropped his hold on the towel and caught her shoul-
ers to pull her into his arms. He wanted to hold her, to
omfort her, to shield her from whatever anguish was tor-
tenting her, but she began to back away from him, and he
eluctantly let her go. He wanted to ask her why she
rouldn't let him help her, but he couldn't bring himself to
o it. He could only stand there with his hands hanging at
is sides, feeling helpless and confused.

Whitney saw the tumult in his eyes and knew he didn't
nderstand why she was pulling away. She longed for what
e was offering—needed it far more than she could ever ex-
ress—but she knew this was something she was going to
ave to face alone. Only she knew of the demon that had
een haunting her for the past four years. Only she knew the
ruth behind Amy's conception. And only she could carry
he burden of the guilt.

"Amy called me Mama," she told him on a half sob.
"She called me Mama."

Sean's confusion increased. Why should she be upset
bout Amy calling her Mama? If anything, he would have
hought she'd be thrilled.

"It was bound to happen sooner or later, Whitney," he stated, though a part of him was saddened by the fact that it had. He could remember the first time Amy had said the word and how thrilled Margaret had been about it. She, too, had cried, but he knew it was somehow different today.

Whitney drew in a shuddering breath. "I know. It's just that..."

He took a cautious step toward her. "It's just that what?"

"I don't deserve it!" she exclaimed miserably. "Oh, God, I don't deserve it."

Despite her earlier withdrawal, Sean caught her in his arms when her tears returned and she began to sob so hard he feared she was going to collapse. He refused to release his hold, even when she struggled against it.

"Whitney, don't cry," he commanded hoarsely. "Please, don't cry."

"But I can't help it," she rasped. "I don't deserve to be called Mama. I walked away from Amy! I gave her to you and your wife to love, and..."

"And we did," he interrupted as he pulled her head tight against his shoulder. "We did, Whitney. We gave her everything you wanted her to have. Now you and I are going to give it to her. Don't do this to yourself."

Whitney knew it was wrong. She knew she couldn't trust him. But she had to hang on to someone, and she wrapped her hands around his neck, buried her head against his shoulder, and cried brokenly.

Sean tried everything he could think of to get her to calm down, but his efforts only seemed to make her worse. Finally he swung her up into his arms, carried her through the house and up the stairs. When he settled her into her bed, wet clothes and all, and tucked the covers around her, she curled into a fetal position and hugged her pillow to her chest as she continued to wail.

Sean felt as if he'd aged ten years by the time he walked out of her room. He knew he had to get back to Amy, but he went into his room and reached for the telephone. His

rst call was to the office, informing them that he had an
nergency and couldn't make it in that afternoon. Then he
lled Bill Hughes.

When the psychiatrist came on the line, he said, "Bill, I
:ed your help, and I need it right now."

Chapter Eleven

"How are they?" Bill asked when Sean walked into the living room after checking on Whitney, who'd cried herself to sleep, and Amy, whose body had acknowledged it was nap time and had simply crawled into bed.

"They're both asleep." He raked his hand through his hair. "I'm sorry I dragged you over here for nothing, but I didn't know what else to do. Whitney was hysterical."

Bill smiled his understanding. "I'd rather arrive and find out it's a false alarm than have you ignore a true crisis situation."

Sean nodded as he dropped wearily into the chair. "I don't understand why she fell apart like that. Why would Amy calling her Mama send her over the edge?"

"Guilt," Bill answered. "Whitney never wanted to give Amy up, but she'd rationalized her decision in minute detail. With Amy back in her life all her reasons are being challenged, and I'm sure many of them seem very unreasonable to her right now."

"But her reasons for adoption were very valid ones," Sean insisted.

"Sure, but choosing adoption and living with that choice are two different matters."

"But Whitney adores Amy, and she has her back. She shouldn't be upset. She should be ecstatic," Sean stated in confusion.

"Oh, I'm sure she is," Bill replied. "The problem is, whenever you mix the pleasure of the present with the pain of the past, you're walking a very fine edge. You're bound to slip a time or two. Today Whitney slipped." He hesitated for a moment before he continued with, "I may be crossing over the line on patient confidentiality here, but I think you should know that when I talked with Whitney in the hospital, I had a feeling that there was something about her pregnancy that she wasn't telling. Something that she felt was so horrible that she couldn't confess it."

Sean's head shot up and he could feel the color draining from his face. "You aren't saying that you think Amy's a product of . . . violence."

"No," Bill stated quickly. "Her feelings for the child were too intense for me to believe that there was any form of rape involved, but there was still something there. Since my job was to only make sure that she knew what she was doing in regard to the adoption, I didn't pursue it. I did suggest that she go into counseling, but we both know how that goes."

Sean nodded. "So what should I do?"

Bill shrugged. "Be patient and supportive. Talk to her about it if she wants to talk, but don't force her into it. When she's ready to discuss her feelings, she'll let you know. You also need to make her feel as if she belongs here."

Sean stared at Bill in surprise. "I do make her feel that way."

Bill arched a brow. "Look around you, Sean. There must be a hundred photographs in this room. You and Whitney have been married almost two months, and there isn't a single picture of her in here. If I was a betting man, I'd wager that you haven't even taken a snapshot of her."

Sean didn't bother to answer, because he knew his guilty blush was doing it for him.

Bill rose to his feet. "I have to get back to the office. If you need me later, just call."

"Thanks, Bill," Sean stated as he also rose and walked the man to the door. "I owe you one."

Bill chuckled. "I know, and believe me, someday I'll collect."

When Sean returned to the living room, he surveyed it critically, realizing that there was an almost morbid display of his life with Margaret. This wasn't really surprising. Hardly a week had passed without their taking at least a half dozen photographs, particularly after Amy came into their lives. He felt another rush of guilt as he realized that not only had he not taken any pictures of Whitney, but he hadn't even thought of doing so. Why?

Because he would have had to admit that she was more important in his life than he wanted her to be. Because he'd come to rely on her as much as Amy had. Because...

"Daddy, can I come out of my room?" Amy asked, stopping his thoughts in midflight.

He glanced up and saw her standing at the top of the stairs, one bare foot on top of the other and her expression tentative.

He smiled. "Well, let's check out your room. If it's clean, you can come out."

Upstairs, he made a cursory inspection of Amy's room, since he'd already been in it several times during her nap and knew she'd put all of her toys away and had made a valiant effort to collect all the stuffing. He picked half a dozen pieces of the foam rubber off the bedspread and dropped it into the paper bag before he sat down on the edge of her bed.

"You've done a good job," he told her. "I'm proud of you."

"Thank you," she responded very properly, and Sean couldn't help but smile.

He reached out and tousled her hair. "I love you, did you know that?"

"Uh-huh," Amy said. Then she giggled and threw herself at him.

He caught her to him and held her tight. Why couldn't everything in his life be as simple as this? He rested his cheek against her hair and marveled at the miracle of her. Right now her life was telescoped and centered around this house and the people in it. But in just a couple of years, the range would start widening, and he'd be sharing her with her friends and school activities. Then there'd be boyfriends, eventually a husband, and most likely a family of her own. When examined in that light, his future looked terribly lonely. What was he going to use as a buffer against that loneliness?

A year ago, he would have said Margaret, but Margaret was gone. In Amy's life, Whitney had become her substitute. Was it possible that she could become his, too?

A part of him shied away from that line of thought, wouldn't let him follow it to its conclusion, because he knew where it would lead him, and he simply wasn't ready to face the answer.

"Is Mama still mad at me?" Amy asked.

He smiled down into her small, solemn face. "Of course not. I don't think she was ever mad at you. She just isn't used to little girls suddenly deciding that they're wild Indians. She's very new at this job, and you have to cut her some slack."

"What's that mean?" Amy asked with a confused frown.

"That means that you have to be the best little girl you can possibly be. Think you can do that?"

"Uh-huh."

"Good." He tossed her down onto the mattress and tickled her until she was roaring with laughter.

When she was breathless and begging him to stop, he hugged her again, while wondering how in the world he was going to cheer up Whitney. He also couldn't help but wonder about her secret surrounding this marvelous bundle of joy.

WHITNEY STOOD at her bedroom window and watched Sean and Amy as they played Frisbee. A yapping Snowball raced back and forth between the two of them, leaping high into the air as he tried to catch the disk. She was pleased to see that every few throws Sean would toss it low enough for the puppy to succeed. Then he and Amy would spend several minutes trying to get the toy back, since the dog preferred the game of chase to fetch.

With a sigh she leaned her head against the window frame, knowing that she was going to have to go downstairs and face them. To say she was embarrassed would be like saying that sunshine was warm. What in the world was she going to say to Sean? Not only had she made a fool of herself, but the man had had to cancel his office appointments. Why couldn't this breakdown of hers have happened while Mrs. Wilkens was still here?

Because it was the woman's departure that had set off the chain of events in the first place. Whitney turned away from the window and walked into the bathroom.

She gave a disgusted shake of her head as she eyed her image in the mirror. Her hair was tangled and matted. Her eyes were nearly swollen shut from crying. Her clothes were still damp and felt clammy against her skin.

"Good heavens, even Midnight wouldn't drag you in," she muttered to herself as she grabbed a brush and went to work on her hair.

When she felt she'd pulled herself together enough to go downstairs, she drew in a deep breath and tilted her chin upward, determined to issue her apologies with as much decorum as possible.

But the back door had barely closed behind her when Sean yelled, "Heads up, Whitney!" and the Frisbee came sailing toward her with Snowball hot on its trail. The dog caught the disk before Whitney could grab it, and he growled playfully while shaking his head and backing up, encouraging her to chase him.

"Give me that," she ordered the animal and reached for him, which was his cue for a take off. She glanced toward Sean, who was standing with his legs braced apart and his hands on his hips.

"You let him catch it," he told her. "Now you have to get it back."

"Yeah, Mama, you have to get it back," Amy echoed.

Whitney's gaze flew to Amy, and she had to bite her lip to hold back another flood of tears. She'd convinced herself that the endearment had been a fluke, that Amy would never say it again. She wanted to race across the yard and hug the child until she couldn't breathe. But she knew that such a reaction would only upset Amy.

Instead she drew in a shaky breath and said, "Won't you at least help me?"

"Well, I don't know," Sean drawled. "What do you think, Amy? Should we help her?"

"Don't know," Amy said, picking up on the game.

"Please?" Whitney cajoled.

"Well, since you hate dog germs, I suppose we should help," Sean said. Then he added, "Whoever catches the mutt first and retrieves the Frisbee gets treated to pizza."

"Yeah!" Amy squealed and took off after the dog.

Sean sauntered toward Whitney, his hands stuffed into his back pockets. When he came to a stop in front of her, he asked, "Feeling better?"

"Yes," she murmured and glanced toward the ground in acute embarrassment. "I'm sorry about what happened."

Sean remembered how she'd backed away from his touch earlier in the day, and he knew he shouldn't take a chance on touching her now, but she looked so sweet and vulnerable that he couldn't resist. "You don't have anything to be sorry about, Whitney."

"But I made a fool of myself."

"Oh, I see, and Whitney Price Fitzgerald, Mother Extraordinaire, isn't allowed to make a fool of herself?"

Whitney's lips curved upward. "I don't think I like you throwing my words back at me."

Sean returned the smile as he touched a fingertip to one uplifted corner of her lips. "That's what I like to see. A happy face."

Whitney didn't think she'd ever be able to frown again.
His finger was feather light against her skin, but she could
feel its warmth right down to the tips of her toes. She was
also aware of his closeness and the solid strength of his body
as it shielded her from the sun. The unique scent of him
teased her nostrils, but as she stared up into his liquid brown
eyes she felt something much deeper than mere physical attraction. She tried to tell herself that it was only gratitude
because he was treating an awkward situation lightly, but
some inner voice nagged that gratitude was far too tame a
word.

Sean, too, was very cognizant of Whitney, and he shivered as he peered down into her beautiful face. He wanted
to reach out and sweep her into his arms. It wasn't the first
time that he'd experienced the urge. It was, however, the
first time that he'd wanted to do so for no other reason than
to hold her close because, oddly enough, his body wasn't
responding to the overwhelming emotion. He found that
conflict both exhilarating and a little frightening, particularly when Whitney began to sway toward him.

He'd just started to raise his arms to reach for her when
Amy raced between them, waving the Frisbee and excitedly
proclaiming, "I got it, so I get pizza!"

Sean peered down at the dancing toddler with a sense of
disappointment. Her timing was sure off, or maybe it was
just right, he decided as he glanced back up at Whitney.

She'd caught her bottom lip between her teeth and was
regarding him with uncertainty. He released an inward sigh,
wanting to say something prophetic, but unable to think of
anything but a curse.

"Come on, Mama," he said as he tossed an arm around
Whitney's shoulder and pulled her to his side. "Let's get the
kid cleaned up so we can take her out for pizza."

Whitney smiled up at him gratefully and blinked back
another mist of tears. The casual way he'd called her Mama
told her that he wasn't upset about Amy's change of allegiance from Margaret to her. She wanted to tell him how

much she appreciated the sensitive way he'd let her know that it was all right, but she knew if she tried to speak her voice would crack. So instead of saying the words, she wrapped her arm around his waist and gave it a squeeze.

As they went into the house, she realized that for the first time she felt as if they were really becoming a family. She wanted—no, she was determined—to do everything she could to make that dream come true.

DEBBIE WAS SITTING beneath her tree again when Whitney approached her, but this time the pain wasn't so intense, and the girl was looking across the park instead of hiding her head. When Whitney was a few feet away, Debbie shifted her gaze toward her and smiled wryly.

"Well, the lady's back in the neighborhood, huh?"

"Yep," Whitney said as she extended the yellow rosebud.

Debbie took it and brought it to her nose before asking, "What's the gig with the flowers?"

"I like roses."

"Why?"

Whitney settled down on the ground in front of her and shrugged. "I could say I like them because they're pretty and they smell good, but I wouldn't be telling you the truth."

Debbie leaned her head back against the trunk of the tree and twirled the flower between her fingers. "So what's the truth?"

Whitney drew her knees up to her chest and linked her arms around her knees in a mimicry of Debbie's posture. "The truth is, my mother loved them, and she used to tell me all about them. I didn't understand what she was telling me, but I loved listening to her voice." She paused and rested her chin against her knees before continuing with, "She died when I was seven. Whenever I'd miss her terribly, I'd go out to the rose gardens. I could hear her talking and I wouldn't be so afraid. You know, I still do that to this day. Weird, huh?"

"Yeah," Debbie replied. Then she sighed and said, "My mom split when I was five. I used to stand at the window and think that if I prayed hard enough she'd come back, but she never did. My old man is still waiting for her to come back. You'd think he'd finally get the picture, wouldn't you?"

Whitney shrugged. "People have different ways of dealing with their problems."

Debbie nodded her agreement. Then she ducked her head and asked, "How did you feel when you were..."

"Pregnant?" Whitney supplied.

"Yeah."

"I was scared. Really scared. I was also ashamed until one day I asked myself what exactly I'd done wrong. I hadn't killed anyone. I hadn't stolen anything. I finally decided that if it wasn't something bad enough to send me to jail, why was I making such a big deal out of it? After that, it was a lot easier."

"You didn't have an... you know."

"Abortion?" Whitney said. When Debbie nodded, Whitney said, "I could have, but it just didn't feel right for me. That doesn't mean I think abortion's wrong. It's just a personal preference."

"So you kept the kid?"

"No. I gave it up for adoption."

When Debbie didn't respond, Whitney knew it was time to leave, and she levered herself to her feet. "Well, my meter's running out, so I'll see you around, okay?"

"Sure," Debbie said. "Thanks for the flower."

"You're welcome."

When Whitney reached the edge of the park, the girl yelled. "Hey, lady! Do you know the name of a good baby doctor?"

"Sure do," Whitney answered. "Dr. Sean Fitzgerald. He's the best."

WHITNEY WAS FIT TO BE TIED. During the past two weeks, Sean had taken up photography. At first, she'd felt self-conscious about finding herself the constant object of his viewfinder, but Amy loved hamming it up, so she indulged him. But indulgence was turning into impatience.

"Sean, would you please put that camera away?" she snapped when he invaded her kitchen for at least the dozenth time in an hour.

"Aw, come on, Whitney," he cajoled. "Be a good sport."

But Whitney didn't feel like being a good sport. She'd soon discovered that the afternoons she spent at the Foundation left her rushing to prepare dinner before Sean got home. It wouldn't have been such a chore if not for Amy. The girl, always excited about the afternoon she spent with her new friends, remained underfoot, determined to regale Whitney with every little detail, and even outright bribery wouldn't keep her out of the way.

Whitney concluded that the only way to maintain her sanity was to spend a day cooking and freezing meals that could be popped into the microwave on the days she came home late. Thus, she had spent all day in the kitchen. She was hot, disheveled and irritable, and Sean's photography bug wasn't improving her temper.

She waved her ladle at him, stating, "Either you and your camera cease and desist, or I won't be responsible for my actions."

Sean laughed. "Going to bop me with that big spoon of yours?"

"If I do, just remember it was your idea," she muttered ominously.

He grinned at Amy mischievously. "If she comes after me, you're my linebacker."

"'Kay," Amy responded with a conspiratorial giggle, even though Whitney knew that the girl had no idea what a linebacker was.

Whitney scowled at them, but she was having a difficult time not returning their grins. "You two may be in cahoots, but the cook rules the kitchen, and this cook says that if you want to eat dinner any time soon, you'd better get out.''

Sean walked toward her with a bowlegged swagger and, in the worst John Wayne imitation Whitney had ever heard, drawled, ''Well, ma'am, me and my partner would sure like to oblige you, but we've got this here problem. We have one shot left on the roll. So if you'll just oblige us, we'll finish it off and be out of the kitchen by sunset.''

Sean had been funny enough, but when Amy tried to mimic his swagger as she approached Whitney, saying, ''Yeah, out of the kitchen by sunset,'' Whitney's impatience turned to laughter.

''All right, I give up,'' she said, raising her hands in defeat. ''You want a picture, I'll give you a picture.'' To which, she promptly stuck the handle of the ladle between her teeth, hitched up the hem of her apron with one hand and tossed the other high above her head, assuming the position of a flamenco dancer.

Sean barely managed to snap the picture before he was roaring with laughter. His mirth was contagious, and Whitney laughed so hard she could barely stand. He caught her around the waist and pulled her against him, where they leaned on each other for support.

When they were finally down to chuckles and giggles, he smiled at her. ''Lady, I like your style.''

''Well,'' she replied grinning up at him, ''I will admit that I'm different.''

''Yes,'' he agreed as he tenderly smoothed her tangled hair away from her face, ''you're definitely that.''

And then their eyes caught and held. The sudden current of desire arcing between them was so strong that she was certain it had to be visible. When he began to lower his head, she placed her hand against his chest to hold him back.

''Amy,'' she reminded him, instinctively knowing that any kiss they shared at this moment would not have a G rating.

Sean closed his eyes and nodded wryly. "Yes, Amy." Then he drew in a deep breath and released her. "Come on, pumpkin," he said, turning immediately to the child. "We've got our picture, so we have to get out of here."

Whitney collapsed against the counter, her heart fluttering wildly, her pulse beating madly, and her stomach twisted into a knot of half desire and half fear, because she wondered if he'd try to pick up where they left off after Amy had been put down for the night.

Unfortunately she never found out, because an hour later Sean was called away on an emergency.

IT WAS A FEW MINUTES after midnight when Whitney heard Sean enter the house, but ten minutes later, he still hadn't come upstairs. Concerned, Whitney got up, pulled on her robe and went looking for him. To her surprise, he was lying on the living room sofa with a glass of Scotch in his hand.

Since Sean rarely drank more than a glass of wine with dinner, she knew he was upset. She stepped into the room, asking, "Sean, what's wrong?"

He glanced toward her in startled surprise, and Whitney widened her eyes in alarm. He looked exhausted and in physical pain.

"I'm sorry. I didn't mean to wake you," he said gruffly before taking a healthy gulp of the alcohol.

"You didn't wake me. I was reading."

He nodded and glanced away from her. Whitney moved farther into the room and rounded the sofa. She sat down on the edge beside him.

"What's wrong?" she repeated.

His brown eyes deepened in color until they were almost black, and he shook his head in frustration. "Nothing, really. I've just had one hell of a night." He tried to smile at her, but failed miserably. "Why don't you go back to bed?"

"I'd rather stay and keep you company."

His laugh was harsh. "I'm afraid I won't be very good company."

Whitney took the glass from his hand and set it on the table. "Why don't you tell me why you're so upset?"

He didn't answer for several seconds, and at first she didn't think he was going to reply. But he finally released a sigh and said, "I have a patient who's been trying to have a baby for three years but has never been able to carry one past the first trimester. When she got pregnant this time, we put her to bed. She's just spent the past five months flat on her back, and today she lost the baby."

After a long silence, he continued with, "I had to perform a D & C on her. I'm waiting for the lab results on the tissue, but I think she needs a hysterectomy. How do I tell a woman, who wants a child so badly she spent five months in bed, that she'll never have another chance?"

"I don't know," Whitney whispered as tears welled in her eyes.

He rolled to his back so he could look up at her. "I don't know, either, and it's killing me."

Whitney knew that the first rule of the medical profession was that you had to maintain your objectivity, but it was apparent that, in this instance, Sean had not only lost it, but was hurting terribly over the situation. Her tears began to roll down her cheeks.

"Hey, what's this all about?" Sean asked hoarsely as he sat up and pulled her into his arms, his fingers stroking away her tears.

"I can't stand to see you hurting like this," she answered.

"Oh, Whitney, don't. I can't stand to see you cry."

He began to stroke her cheeks again, and when she leaned into his hand, Sean impulsively caught her lips with his. He'd meant the kiss to be soothing, but when she parted her mouth and touched her tongue to his lower lip, need hit him with such force that he shuddered. In response, she trailed her fingers over his beard-stubbled cheeks, and then wound her arms around his neck leaning into him until her body was pressed against him. Softness against hardness, and

Sean needed to lose himself in that softness. To soothe himself with the sweet, gentle essence of her, and he let his hand trail down her side to give him tactile veracity of her curves.

He groaned and burrowed his fingers into her hair, raining kisses from her forehead to her chin as he lowered her to the sofa and levered himself over her. This time she groaned, but it was more of a sexy mew, and Sean caught her lips, trying to coax another one out of her so that he could capture it and take it inside him, make it a part of him. And he had to make it a part of him. When she not only complied, but arched her hips into the cradle of his thighs, Sean thought he'd explode.

"Whitney. Oh, God, Whitney," he gasped as he tugged her robe open, and when his hand encountered silk, his eyes flew open. He lifted his head and gazed down at her yellow nightshirt, the line of provocative pearl buttons lacing from the neck to midthigh stealing the breath from his lungs. His fingers itched to unbutton them one by one. His lips ached to explore her silken flesh inch by inch as he released them. He raised his head and what he saw in her eyes sent his head spinning, and he reached for the first button, frowning in confusion when Whitney caught his hand.

She gave him a trembling smile as she whispered huskily, "We have a three-year-old in the house. Perhaps we should move this upstairs?"

Whitney was completely bewildered by the look of shock that settled on his face, and when he tried to pull away, she held on to him tightly, refusing to let him go. A moment ago he'd been out of his mind with desire, but now he looked as if he'd been drenched in cold water.

She searched his face for several seconds before finally asking, "What is it, Sean?"

He cleared his throat, but his voice was still no more than a rasp when he said, "I think you'd better go to bed."

"Or what?" Whitney whispered. She was a wife consoling her husband, and it felt so right to be in his arms, to be using the physical as a balm to his emotional turmoil. "What is it you want?"

Sean closed his eyes reluctantly. "What I want doesn't matter, because it isn't for the right reasons."

"And what are the right reasons?" Whitney challenged, her temper flaring. "For that matter, why do we have to have reasons? We're married. Would a physical relationship be so bad?"

"Yes," he hissed between his teeth as he broke her hold on him and sat up on the sofa. "It would be bad, because we'd only be..."

"Satisfying our baser needs?" she provided when his voice trailed off and he reached for the Scotch. She gave a weary shake of her head and her temper waned as she watched him take a gulp. "I never realized it before, but you're just like my father."

"I'm not anything like your father," he snapped.

"Oh, yes you are." She sat up beside him and belted her robe closed as she said, "It took me a long time to figure it out, but I finally realized that I'd spent my life being my mother's stand-in because he was too much of a coward to go out and look for a woman to replace her, and do you know why?"

When Sean didn't answer, but merely drained his glass, she said sadly, "He was afraid of losing again, and he didn't want to go through the pain. Unfortunately, even when I finally realized what was happening, I didn't try to change it, and that was wrong."

Her voice was soft but firm as she concluded with, "I'm not going to be your escape from the world, Sean. I'm not going to fall back into the roll of being the pretty little doll in the background who keeps everything well oiled and running smoothly, so you can sit around and indulge yourself in self-pity. And I'm most certainly not going to spend the rest of my life letting you take me on an emotional roller coaster."

Sean slammed his glass down on the coffee table and turned a furious glare at her. "What does that mean?"

She rose to her feet and returned his glare. "If you want a baby-sitter for Amy, put me on the payroll, and I mean that literally. If you want a wife, then invest a little time in me and see what happens. It might not work out, but then again it might. The question is, do you want to spend the rest of your life living with a stranger, or as a member of a family with all the privileges that come with it? And I'm not just talking about sex, Sean. I'm talking about sharing and caring. Think about it and let me know what you decide."

With that, she turned on her heel and walked regally out of the room.

"Well, hell," Sean muttered irritably as he leaned back against the sofa, needing another drink but too tired to cross over to the portable bar to get it.

As he continued to sit, his eyes strayed around the room with a curious sense of dispassion. Was Whitney right? Did he fear that he would get too close only to be left alone again? He pushed both hands through his hair, as if doing so would help him find his answers.

When it didn't, he closed his eyes and rested his head against the cushions. When he lost Margaret, he'd been blinded by the pain. If it hadn't been for Amy, he wasn't certain he would have been able to survive it. He'd spent months walking through life on remote control. Everyone had kept telling him that as the days passed, it would get easier, but it never got easier. It got harder. His life mate had been stolen from him, and with her went all the sharing and caring that Whitney had alluded to.

For weeks he'd been fighting his attraction to Whitney, and he reluctantly admitted, it was because what he felt for her went beyond the physical. That scared the living hell out of him because if he went with the feelings, he'd be taking a chance again, and he didn't know if he was strong enough to take another chance.

So what was he going to do about her ultimatum? Sleep on it, he decided as he forced himself off the sofa and headed for the stairs.

Chapter Twelve

Sean took his time as he showered and shaved. After he rinsed off his face, he regarded his image in the mirror. He was thirty-six, nearly nine years Whitney's senior. What did she see when she looked at him?

Age had treated him well, he decided, pivoting his face from profile to profile. His flesh was firm. The character lines only added to his looks. His hair was laced with a few strands of gray, but not enough to be obvious. He stripped the towel from his hips, turned toward the mirrored shower doors and eyed his body, front and back. It was lean and a notch above average muscularity, though he'd never be considered muscle bound.

Suddenly he chuckled wryly. He'd never been particularly conscious of his body, so why was he absorbed with it now? Because he wanted a wife. He wanted the sharing and caring Whitney had talked about. He wanted to be part of a family again. But in order for him and Whitney to begin to build, they had to have some time together. He wrapped the towel back around his hips, strode purposefully into his bedroom and picked up the phone.

WHITNEY FELT as if she were forever in the kitchen but, she decided with chagrin, it was the one room in the house where she felt totally comfortable. Because of that it had become her retreat—her hideout—and this morning she definitely wanted to hide out. She just wished Amy hadn't chosen today to sleep in because she needed some time to figure out how to deal with Sean, and he certainly wouldn't confront her in front of the child.

She couldn't believe she'd given him an ultimatum the night before. Normally she weighed her words before speaking, but last night her temper had gotten the best of her. She'd spoken in haste, and in all probability had destroyed the friendship they'd managed to build. She didn't think she could live with that, and when she heard the shower turn off, she was sorely tempted to race back to her room, crawl into bed and pull the covers over her head until Sean had left for work.

But, she decided, that would be too obvious since she routinely fixed Sean's breakfast unless he had an early surgery. With a resigned sigh she poured pancake batter onto the griddle.

Though he hadn't made a sound, she sensed Sean's presence and she reluctantly glanced over her shoulder, searching his face for some sign of his thoughts. But his expression was as neutral as white on white.

"Good morning," she said, grimacing inwardly at the tremor in her voice. She coughed delicately before saying, "Your timing is perfect. I just took your pancakes off the griddle. While you eat, I'll check on Amy. I've never known her to sleep this late."

She knew she was babbling but she couldn't help herself, and she nervously lifted the plate of pancakes to carry it into the dining room. She let out a yelp of surprise when Sean grasped her arm with one hand and removed the plate of pancakes with the other. He set it on the counter and led her to the kitchen table. After seating her, he walked to the coffeepot, filled two mugs and brought them back to the table. It was only then that he said, "We need to talk."

Whitney latched on to the mug as if it were a lifeline, and, indeed, it was. He didn't take his usual place across from her, but instead swung a chair around so that he was next to her. Having him so close was playing havoc with what little control she had left. What in the world was she going to do if he said he was putting her on the payroll as a baby-sitter?

"Did you know that I'm nearly nine years older than you?" he asked.

Whitney glanced toward him in disbelief. That was definitely the very last opening she had anticipated. "Yes. Why?"

He shrugged, blew on his coffee and took a sip. "That age difference could be considered a generation gap."

Whitney resisted the urge to release a nervous giggle. "I suppose it could."

"Does that bother you?"

"No. Does it bother you?"

"I haven't decided." He took another sip of coffee before saying, "I know you've been putting a lot of time in at the Foundation, but can you clear next week?"

"I suppose so. Why?"

He leaned forward so that his nose brushed against hers. "Because I want to take you on a honeymoon."

Whitney jerked her face away from his and gazed at him wide-eyed. "You what?" she asked hoarsely.

He caught her head in his hand and tangled his fingers in her hair. Drawing her back to him, he repeated, "I want to take you on a honeymoon. We'll have separate rooms. I just want us to have some time together. Some top quality, uninterrupted time where we can look at our relationship and decide where we want it to go. I called my parents a few minutes ago, and not only have they offered to come and baby-sit Amy, but they've given us the use of their cabin."

Whitney didn't know what to say. *A honeymoon?* Even with separate rooms, the word carried connotations that she wasn't certain she wanted to deal with. She knew they needed time together, but she'd prefer to have it right here with Amy acting as a buffer. She suddenly realized she was as cowardly as she'd accused him of being.

"What about Snowball and Midnight?" she questioned in an effort to gain some time. "We're still in the training stages. We shouldn't saddle your parents with that kind of responsibility."

Sean knew a delay tactic when he saw one. "My mother's raised enough dogs and cats to write a book. She can handle it."

"But Amy..."

"Is in seventh heaven when Granny and Gramps come to visit," he interrupted. "Again, what do you say?"

Whitney wrapped her arms around her middle and resisted the urge to rock back and forth in her chair. She wanted to try to build a life with him, so why was she so scared? Because, she suddenly realized, she was desperately in love with him. When had it happened? *Why* had it happened? And what was she going to do if she never saw even a glimmer of the love on his face that she'd seen in the labor room when he told her about Margaret? Die one piece at a time.

"I'll clear out next week," she told him, deciding that it was best to learn the truth now. Then, if it couldn't be worked out, she'd still be strong enough to insulate herself against the pain. Strong enough to build herself a satisfying life around him. "When will your parents be here?"

"Sunday."

"That's only four days away!" She glanced around her in horror. "The house is in a shambles, and with my work at the Foundation, I'll never be able to get it cleaned up in four days."

Sean followed her gaze around the room. "The house looks fine to me."

"But there's dust everywhere! And..."

Sean kissed her. It wasn't a kiss meant to excite her, but quiet her. It worked almost too well, because the desire that had been stirring in him for weeks began fighting him for domination as her lips became complaisant beneath his. He released her and placed some distance between them, knowing that if he let himself flow with his feelings he'd be tempted to carry her off to the closest bed. He was determined that if they made love, it wasn't going to be impulsively. It would be because they'd reached a mutual decision that it was the right direction for their relationship to go.

"My mother doesn't worry about dust, Whitney."

Whitney nodded mutely, still reeling from his kiss. It had been sensuous yet undemanding, which had made it even more mind-boggling.

He glanced down at his watch. "I have to leave for work now. Sorry about breakfast, but I'm sure Amy will make good inroads on that stack of pancakes."

With that he rose to his feet, dropped a kiss on her forehead, and walked out of the room. After he'd gone, Whitney folded her arms on the kitchen table and rested her forehead on them. Come Sunday a new chapter in her life would begin, and she shivered as she wondered what destiny had in store for her.

"WHITNEY, WAKE UP. Come on, honey, wake up."

Whitney rolled away from the hand that was shaking her shoulder. She didn't want to wake up. She wanted to go back to that wonderful dream where Sean was kissing her, and loving her, and . . . Oh, my God, it was Sean talking to her!

"What's wrong?" she asked when she rolled to her back and saw his grim expression.

"Nothing." Then he thrust his finger through his hair. "That's not exactly true."

"Amy?" she said in alarm as she sat up.

"Amy's fine," he assured as he reached out to massage her shoulder. "It's just that...well, my parents called from the airport, and they're on their way over."

Whitney tried to blink herself awake. "I'll get up."

"Uh, yeah." He thrust his fingers through his hair again. "Whitney, after I hung up the phone, I realized that my family doesn't know about the circumstances of our marriage. I figured it was best for all concerned if they thought that we got married under normal conditions. That we were..."

"In love?" Whitney offered when his voice trailed off. It was her turn to look grim when he nodded.

"I understand." She reached for her robe at the foot of the bed. "I wouldn't want to upset your parents, either."

"It's not my parents I'm worried about," he objected as he listened to the dry tone of her voice. "It's you. I don't want you to have to face uncomfortable questions."

She couldn't help the angry tears that flooded her eyes as she jammed her arms into her robe. "Sure. We don't want your family to know that you're married to a woman who gave birth to an illegimate child and was crass enough to give it up for adoption."

"Whitney, stop it!" he exclaimed impatiently. He grasped her upper arms and gave her a gentle shake. "That isn't how I feel about you, and you know it. You do know that, don't you?" he asked as his eyes searched her face.

She closed her eyes and gave a forlorn shake of her head. "I don't know what to think, but don't worry about my performance. After living with my father in Washington for all those years, I learned how to act with the best of them. You know, smile at your enemies. Engage in polite conversation with someone you'd rather kick in the shin. Your parents will never know that anything is wrong."

This conversation wasn't going the way Sean wanted it to go. He'd hurt her, and he'd done it with the best intentions in mind. He hadn't told his parents the truth because he wanted to protect Whitney, who he knew was sensitive about her past. He instinctively reached out and drew her into his arms, tightening his hold when she tried to push away from him.

Gently, soothingly, he stroked her hair as he cradled her head against his chest, searching for the words to convince her that he didn't care if his family knew about her past. How they felt, or what they thought, wasn't going to change his feelings for her. He admired her. He respected her. He wanted to try to make a life with her, but how did he convince her of that?

"I don't want you to act," he murmured against her hair. "I want you to be yourself. I want my parents to get to know the woman I've grown so fond of and am proud to have as my wife. I've never cared about your past, and I never will. If it bothers them, then they don't need to come back."

Whitney slowly raised her head and stared at him in disbelief. "But they're your family!"

"And you're my wife, and my daughter's mother," he stated firmly. "My allegiance lies with the two of you, and it always will. No one else matters, Whitney, and I want you to believe that."

"You really mean it," she murmured in awe.

His lips curved into a slow devastating smile, and she knew he was sincere. She also knew at that moment that it would never matter if he loved her, because she was filled with enough love for both of them. She'd do anything to please him, to make him happy, and she wasn't about to take him away from his family.

"I think I can be myself and still make them think we're newlyweds," she told him. "Why don't we try it and see what happens?"

Sean started to object, but the look in her eyes stopped him. There was an emotion in their depths that he couldn't quite interpret, but it arrowed its way straight to his heart. He nodded, and leaned forward to kiss her, his pulse pounding in his ears as her lips moved beneath his, warm and welcoming.

The sound of the doorbell penetrated through the fog in his brain, and he forced himself away from her. "I think the Huns have arrived," he rasped. "I'll go keep them occupied. You take your time getting dressed."

Whitney nodded, unable to speak as she watched him leave the room. In just a few hours they'd be leaving on a honeymoon, and if she had her way, it would be a real one—

not just a time to get to know each other, but a consummation of their marriage.

WHEN WHITNEY WENT downstairs, she stepped hesitantly into the kitchen. It was empty except for a small, silver-haired woman, who was standing at the sink and peering out the window with a fond smile curving her lips. From the laughter and barking wafting in from outside, Whitney knew that Sean and Amy were in the backyard playing with her pets.

She cleared her throat and said, "Hello."

The woman turned toward her, her smile widening in welcome. "Well, hello. You must be Whitney."

"Yes, and you must be Mrs. Fitzgerald."

The woman laughed as she stepped forward and took Whitney's hands. "Please, call me Mom, or if you're uncomfortable with that, Bonnie." Her eyes, the same shape and color as Sean's, traveled over Whitney with interest. Whitney panicked when the woman said, "It's amazing. Do you have any idea how much you resemble Amy?"

"It is amazing, isn't it," Sean stated as he entered the back door. He walked to Whitney and wrapped an arm around her shoulders, tucking her against his side protectively while sending a prayer of thanks heavenward for his perfect timing. "Now you can understand why I married her."

"Absolutely," Bonnie agreed.

Whitney relaxed beneath Sean's comforting arm, but she felt another pinprick of panic when the woman gave her another assessing look. *She knows the truth!* a part of her cried, but she gave an imperceptible shake of her head in denial. It was impossible for the woman to know anything.

She forced herself to say, "It's very kind of you to do this for us, Mrs.... Uh, Bonnie."

Bonnie chuckled. "There isn't anything kind about it. I don't get to spend enough time with Amy, and I'll drop anything and come running if someone can drag my son away from work. He works much too hard, don't you agree?''

"Yes, he does," Whitney said.

At that moment, Amy came bursting through the back door with Snowball, Midnight and an older version of Sean on her heels. The man caught Amy around the waist and swung her up into his arms, tickling her until she was giggling hysterically.

"Mama, help!" she squealed.

Whitney, laughing, went to her daughter's aid. The man handed her over and then sobered so suddenly that Whitney worried that he was ill.

"My word, Bonnie, they look . . ."

"Amazing, isn't it?" Bonnie interrupted as she crossed quickly to the man and linked her arm with his. "Whitney, I'd like you to meet my husband, Patrick. Patrick, it's obvious who Whitney is."

"Yes," the man said, and Whitney had a feeling that he wasn't referring to her marital status.

Sean quickly joined the group, and once again protectively tucked Whitney against his side, while inwardly railing at himself. He should have known that his parents were far too perceptive to miss the obvious. Through their eyes, he'd been reminded of the startling resemblance between mother and daughter. He forced a jovial tone into his voice, determined to save Whitney from embarrassing questions.

"Whitney, why don't you go upstairs and finish packing? By the time you're done, Mom will have whipped us up some breakfast."

"Don't be silly," Whitney demurred. "I'll cook breakfast, and . . ."

"No, you won't," Bonnie stated firmly. "It's a four-hour drive to the cabin, and I want to see the two of you out of here before noon. You'll have to do a lot of work to get the place habitable, so you need to get there while you still have enough light to do it. Besides," she continued as she leaned forward and kissed Amy's cheek, "I can't wait to start spoiling this little angel. That's what grannies are for, huh, toots."

Amy giggled and went into her grandmother's arms. "Uh-huh."

Left with no other option, Whitney went upstairs to her room, but her hands were shaking so badly she couldn't finish her packing. She sat on the bed, caught her hands between her knees and kept telling herself that she was being silly. After all, this was what she wanted, wasn't it? Her eyes strayed to her unmade bed and her cheeks flushed crimson.

"Oh, my," she whispered and bolted off the bed in search of her toothbrush.

Downstairs, Sean sat at the kitchen table and eyed his parents warily. He felt like an errant schoolboy beneath their prying eyes. When Amy went back outside to play with her pets, he prepared himself for the onslaught of questions. He didn't have to wait long, though he was surprised it was his father who spoke first.

"Why didn't you tell us Whitney was Amy's mother?" his father asked.

Sean shrugged. "I didn't think it was important."

"Not important?" Bonnie repeated in disbelief. "Sean, it was cruel not to prepare us! Do you have any idea how that poor girl must have felt when she realized that we knew the truth?"

"Uncomfortable," Sean answered irritably.

"Amen to that," his father muttered. Then he frowned at Sean. "Does Amy know?"

"Of course not. She's too young to understand any of this."

"I'm not sure I'm old enough to understand what's going on," Bonnie said in exasperation. "Are you in love with the woman?"

"I don't know," Sean answered honestly as he transferred a steady gaze between his parents. "But in order to find out, we need some time alone. That's why I asked you to come."

His parents exchanged glances, and then his mother nodded and walked over to him. As she hugged him, she said, "We love you, and we'll stand by you. Just promise me that you'll come to us if you need help."

"I asked you here today, didn't I?" Sean said as he dropped a kiss to his mother's head and then regarded his father. "Thanks."

His father nodded. "I think you'd better go finish packing."

"Yeah," Sean said, but when he reached the bottom of the stairs, he found his knees were shaking. This was the first time in his life he'd ever taken a step forward without knowing exactly what lay ahead and for one brief moment, he actually considered canceling the honeymoon. But then he remembered how much life and laughter Whitney had brought into this house, and he knew he had to follow this trip through to the end.

SEAN GLANCED OVER at Whitney in concern. Her hands were folded loosely in her lap. Her head was resting against the window as she stared straight ahead. She didn't look upset, but he sensed that she was.

Had she changed her mind about their trip to the cabin and was afraid to tell him? he wondered as he eyed her delicate profile, a worried frown creasing his brow. Surely if that was the case, she wouldn't look so... blank, and that's exactly how she looked. Blank. Like a pretty little lifeless doll.

When she remained quiet for another fifteen miles, Sean decided to take matters into his own hands. He pulled into the next small rest area on the side of the road and switched off the ignition.

When Whitney glanced toward him in question, he said, "What's wrong?"

"Nothing's wrong. Why?" she responded.

He shook his head, climbed out of the car and rounded it. After opening the door, he took her hand and pulled her out to stand beside him. She was peering up at him warily, and he smiled, laced his fingers with hers, and began leading her into the woods.

"Where are we going?" Whitney asked in confusion.

"For a walk. We both need some fresh air."

"If you're tired of driving, I'll be glad to take over."

"I'm not tired."

Whitney fell into a muddled silence, letting him lead her, and wondering what this was all about. They ascended a rolling foothill and she couldn't help but gasp as she found herself staring down into a pine and aspen covered valley with a narrow stream winding its way through the center, the water a shimmering crystalline in the late afternoon sunlight.

"How beautiful," she whispered. It seemed irreverent to speak aloud when facing such a spectacular view.

"Yes, how beautiful," Sean murmured, and she glanced toward him, surprised to find him staring at her and not the valley. "Now tell me what's wrong."

Whitney shrugged self-consciously and reached up to tug on an evergreen branch that was mere inches above her head as she returned her gaze to the valley. How could she tell him that everything was so right that it had to be wrong? With a sigh, she turned back toward Sean, knowing she had to answer his question.

He was leaning against the narrow white trunk of a quaking aspen, his arms folded loosely over his chest and his ankles crossed as he patiently waited for her answer. The green leaves rustled over his head, creating the mesmerizing quaking sound that gave the tree its name, and she heard the shrill call of a bird, and the chattering scolding of a nearby squirrel.

As she stared at his handsome face her mind started pulling the scattered pieces of her thoughts together into a coherent answer.

"When my father and Duncan died, and I found out what Duncan had done, I thought I'd die myself. Then when I gave you Amy, I felt as lost as Dorothy in the land of Oz or Alice in Wonderland. My life was a nightmare and I was so lost and afraid.

Closing her eyes tightly and gritting her teeth, she fought against the tears she could feel surfacing. It seemed that all she'd done since Sean had reappeared in her life was cry, and she wasn't going to cry anymore. The past was gone, and it couldn't hurt her unless she let it. She drew in a deep cleansing breath of air, and opened her eyes. They were clear.

She bent to capture a pinecone lying at her feet, and she tossed it from one hand to the other, unaware that Sean's eyes had darkened with the pain he could feel radiating from her.

Finally she continued with, "Now I feel as if I've finally found my way home. I haven't felt this . . . safe since before my mother died. It's all so wonderful, but instead of being happy, I'm still afraid. I feel as if this is the dream, and if I pinch myself, I'm going to wake up and find I'm still living the nightmare."

When she stopped speaking, Sean didn't respond. He continued to lean against the tree, his eyes dark with unidentifiable emotion, and his brow creased with a frown. The sounds of nature seemed amplified as the silence stretched, until it grated against Whitney's nerves and she wanted to scream. Had she been wrong to tell him what she was thinking? Did he think she was being foolish?

He pushed away from the tree abruptly and walked toward her. When he reached her, he ordered, "Close your eyes."

Whitney blinked at him in confusion, but he looked so determined that she obeyed. A moment later, she yelped with pain and her eyes flew open to stare at him accusingly as she rubbed at the spot on her arm where he'd pinched her hard.

Before she could say anything, his lips curved into a grin, and he pulled her gently into his arms. "I just pinched you, and you're still here. Is that enough to prove to you that it's not a dream?''

Whitney parted her lips, but she couldn't make any words come out. Instead she burrowed against his chest and clung to him, loving the solid feel of him, the warmth that radiated from him, the reassuring beat of his heart.

They stood there for a long time, Whitney hugging him tightly and Sean hugging her back while his cheek rested against her hair. Finally he released a sigh of regret and reached down to tilt her head up.

"Do you know what time it is?"

Whitney shook her head. "I forgot my watch."

He smiled as he caught her hand and brought it to his lips. "You don't need a watch because, my dear, it's time that we got on with our lives, and I'll have you know that I'm looking forward to every minute."

Again Whitney found herself at a loss for words because she didn't think she'd ever heard words more precious in her entire life, and she knew that she, too, was looking forward to every minute he would share with her.

Chapter Thirteen

Whitney could only gape at the huge redwood A-frame as Sean pulled to a stop. When he and his family had talked about a cabin, she envisioned a little log cabin tucked beneath a few pine trees, not a Taj Mahal. But she should have expected it, she realized. Not only was Sean one of seven children, who would have required space, but he and his family were notoriously wealthy.

She shot him a curious glance. It was funny, but she never thought of him as a man of means, and she couldn't help but compare him to Simon Prescott. Though Simon was her closest and dearest friend, she knew he wore his wealth like a badge. Sean, on the other hand, seemed oblivious to his station. It was the first time she'd understood the old saying that money was not the measure of a man.

"Come on, I'll give you a tour," Sean stated as he leaped out of the car and rounded it, pulling open her door.

Whitney was amused by his obvious excitement as he hurried her up the steps and unlocked the front door.

"Oh, I love it," she said in delight when he led her inside.

The living room was spacious and flowed into a modern kitchen that opened onto a gigantic redwood deck. The furnishings were a conglomeration of mismatched pieces that showed heavy use, but instead of appearing shabby, the furniture gave the cabin a comfortable, homey feeling.

"There are four bedrooms and a bath down here," he told her. "But it's the master bedroom I love. Wait until you see the view."

Whitney's lips lifted in a smile of chagrin as he led her up the stairs. Considering the reason they were up here, she found his reference to the master bedroom and its view in the same breath rather ironic.

But she could understand his reasoning when they reached the top of the stairs. The master bedroom and bath encompassed the entire second floor, and Whitney could only shake her head in awe when she stepped onto the small balcony that provided a view of woods and mountain peaks, many of which were already capped with snow and framed against the purple-hued sky of approaching sunset.

Sean leaned against the railing beside her and said, "It's beautiful, isn't it?"

"Yes, it's beautiful," she agreed, but her eyes weren't locked on the scenery. They were locked on him. She'd never seen him look so carefree and relaxed. It was as if he'd shed his skin and become an entirely different man.

He glanced toward her and smiled. "You can sleep up here."

"No," she responded with a gentle shake of her head. "I'll be more comfortable down by the kitchen."

"Don't be silly. I didn't bring you up here to cook."

Something inside her vibrated at his words, but she knew it wasn't time for that. She reached out and brushed the hair the wind had tossed onto his forehead back into place.

"I know you didn't, but I'd still feel more comfortable downstairs."

He caught her hand and held it as he studied her. For a moment he looked as if he'd continue to object, but then he seemed to change his mind. "Okay. I'll take up. You can take down." He glanced toward the sky. "It's getting late. I guess we'd better get settled in."

While Sean went to start the generator, Whitney unloaded the groceries they'd bought in Breckenridge. With those chores out of the way, Sean suggested they take a walk, and they hiked through the woods, hand in hand. When they entered a small meadow filled with wildflowers, Sean picked a yellow black-eyed Susan, and tucked it into Whitney's hair. Then he pulled her into his arms for a slow, warm kiss that was sexually undemanding, but filled with sensual promise.

Back at the cabin, Sean offered to cook his specialty—steak and salad—for dinner, and Whitney unpacked and made up their beds. Upstairs, her hands lingered on the sheets where Sean would sleep as she smoothed them into place, and her cheeks warmed with the thought that before the week was over, she might be able to join him there.

In the kitchen, she walked to Sean's side and stole a bite of carrot out of the salad he was making. He laughed as he swatted ineffectually at her hand when she swiped a piece of tomato.

"No snacking before dinner. You'll spoil your appetite."

"Impossible," Whitney said, taking a slice of cucumber he offered her. "I guess it's true what they say about mountain air building up your appetite. I'm positively starving."

"In that case, we'd better hurry up and feed you. How do you like your steak?"

"Well done."

"Well done!" he cried in mock-horror. "How can you do that to a perfectly good piece of beef?"

She grinned. "I want to make sure that it can't moo when I stab it."

He chuckled. "Fine. I'll take the moo out of it if you'll set the table."

By the time she'd set the table, the steaks were done. They ate in companionable silence for several minutes before she said, "How long have your parents had this cabin?"

Sean wrinkled his forehead while he did some mental arithmetic. Then he let out a low whistle. "I was seventeen, so almost twenty years. It doesn't seem that long."

"Well, you know what they say about how time flies."

He nodded. "I remember when my parents decided to build. We'd all skied for years, and half of us preferred the slopes in Breckenridge, while the other half preferred the slopes in Vail. Every Christmas and spring vacation we drove my dad crazy arguing over which place had the best skiing, and telling him why he should stay in one town as opposed to the other. Even when he alternated, we still argued. He finally decided to save himself the hassle and built this place. It's halfway between both and we all went in the direction we preferred."

"A sensible solution."

Sean chuckled. "It's called protecting one's sanity. Do you ski?"

Whitney shook her head. "My father felt that any sport synonymous with broken bones should be avoided at all costs."

Sean braced his elbows on the table and cradled his folded hands beneath his chin. "So what did you do for fun?"

Whitney frowned at the question. "I really don't know."

"Oh, come on, Whitney. You had to do something. What about vacations? Where did you go?"

"To every one-horse town in Colorado. When we weren't in Washington, we were on the campaign trail, though my father always referred to it as, 'Getting out to see to the needs of his constituents.'"

"You mean you never went to Hawaii or the Caribbean or Europe?" he questioned in disbelief.

"No. In fact, I've only been in two states outside of Colorado."

"You're kidding me!"

She laughed. "I'm not kidding. Since D.C. is bordered by Maryland and Virginia, I did do a little exploring there. But that's it. The rest of the time we were in Colorado."

"Lady, you have lived a very sheltered life."

She shook her head. "Not sheltered, Sean. Limited."

Sean eyed her curiously. "And you hated it."

"I've never really thought about it, but I guess I did hate parts of it. Politics is a very commendable profession. Unfortunately it's also a very phony life."

"Like smiling at your enemies and engaging in polite conversation with people you'd rather kick in the shins," he said, repeating her words from that morning.

"Yes," she agreed. "It means that you're always on center stage. If you sneeze, everyone knows it." She circled her finger around the rim of her wineglass. "I guess that's why I'm still so amazed that I managed to cover up the scandal. My father's been gone a long time, but it would still make front-page headlines."

"And that would bother you?"

"Yes, it would bother me, because, despite his faults, my father really was trying to make a difference. If he'd ever learned the truth about Duncan, it would have killed him. It may sound awful, but I'm glad he never had to face that."

"I don't think it sounds awful at all," Sean murmured as he reached across the table and caught her hand. "You loved him."

"I loved him," she confirmed, unconsciously squeezing his hand in an effort to shut out the painful memories of the past.

Sean didn't even flinch when her nails bit into his flesh. Instead he studied her face, wanting to take her even farther down the trail of memories so he could find out why she'd fallen apart when Amy called her Mama. He knew it was important that he understand it. But she looked so saddened by the past, that he didn't have the heart to push her onward.

"I think it's time I cleaned up," he said.

"You cooked. I'll do the dishes."

"Why don't we make it a team effort."

She grinned. "Great. You can wash and I can dry. I hate dishpan hands."

Sean rolled his eyes heavenward. "Why do I get the feeling I asked for that?"

Whitney laughed gaily and rose to her feet. While she gathered the dishes, Sean switched on the radio. As they did the dishes, they discussed the golden oldies that echoed through the small speaker, bringing special memories back from their pasts. Then Sean wrapped his arms around her shoulders and led her out to the deck.

They stood side by side, leaning against the railing, and Whitney asked, "Why do the stars always seem so much brighter in the mountains?"

"Because they aren't competing with city lights," Sean answered as he slipped his hand beneath her hair and settled it around her neck. He urged her closer to him as he pointed at the distant horizon. "There's the Big Dipper, and the Little Dipper, and Orion, and..."

"And what?" Whitney whispered throatily when he turned his head and they were no more than a pursing of the lips away.

"And that's my favorite Lionel Ritchie tune."

The music from the radio drifted out the open sliding glass doors. He opened his arms and Whitney stepped into them. Her eyes shut as he pulled her close and they moved in time with the music. When he urged her head to his chest, she gratefully rested it against him, reveling in the sensation of his muscled hardness, which was pressed against her softness from shoulder to knee.

When the song ended and was replaced with a primitive rock beat, Whitney released a disappointed sigh and tilted her head back to peer up at him. Sean lowered his head, and Whitney released another sigh, but this one was of pleasure as his lips swept over hers briefly and then settled firmly into place. He deepened the kiss and groaned softly when her lips parted. Whitney groaned back when he slipped his hands beneath her shirt and caught at her waist as his tongue dipped inside her mouth in a gentle exploration.

His fingers climbed up her spine, stopping at the edge of her bra, while his other hand swept down to her hip and he drew her closer to him. Whitney went willingly, her body languorous as it molded itself to his.

"Sean?" she whispered again when he pulled away from the kiss and rested his forehead against hers.

"We should stop now," he murmured halfheartedly. "If we don't, I'm going to make love to you."

"Would that be so bad?"

"No. It would be damn good," he answered as he tightened his hold around her and drew her deeper into his thighs, giving her proof of his desire. "But all good things come to those who wait, and I think we need to wait."

A part of Whitney objected to his declaration. Another part agreed, and she smiled to herself as he walked her off the deck and through the woods. When they arrived at the meadow they'd visited earlier, he drew her to a stop.

"You're even more beautiful in moonlight," he murmured huskily as he caught her lips in a kiss so potent that he felt as heady as the wine they'd had with dinner.

She murmured softly in disapproval when he ended the kiss and led her back to the cabin. He left her at the door to her room with a smile and a kiss to the back of her hand, as he whispered, "See you tomorrow."

SEAN DIDN'T KNOW whether to groan or to cry as Whitney leaned across him to peer out the window of the gondola so she could get a better look at the herd of deer grazing far below them. One of her hands was pressed against the edge of the window, the other high on his thigh. He drew in a deep breath against the desire raging through him, but all he succeeded in doing was getting an overdose of the fragrant scent of her, and he cursed inwardly.

He'd come far too close to carrying her off to bed last night, so he decided that the best way to ensure he'd keep his hands off her would be to spend the day sight-seeing in Vail. But as they explored the Alpine-style town he was aware of her every movement, her every nuance. The way she laughed curled his toes. The way her eyes glistened with excitement did crazy things to his pulse. And the way she was constantly touching him to point out something that had caught her attention, or to make a point as she talked, had the hair on the back of his neck standing on end, not to mention what it was doing to a more intimate part of his body.

He had to curl his hands in to fists to keep from hauling her onto his lap and ravishing her right then and there when she turned her head and her breath fanned softly across his lips as she said, "I think deer are some of the most beautiful creatures in the world."

As far as Sean was concerned she was the most beautiful creature on the face of the earth and he murmured, "I guess beauty is in the eye of the beholder."

Whitney's heart gave a funny little jerk at his words, and she gulped at the raw desire glowing in his eyes. Every nerve in her body jumped to attention, and she had to force herself to pull away from him because she wanted to wind her arms around his neck and kiss him until her lips were numb.

She sat back abruptly, but withdrawing from him didn't help. In fact it made her more conscious of the muscled length of his body. Of the heat that radiated from him. Of the scent of him, that was a mixture of man, soap and sunshine. She had to bite her lip to keep from groaning. Thank heavens, they were on their way down from the top of the mountain and would be heading back to the cabin, because her sudden awareness of him had sapped her strength.

They didn't speak another word and the tension between them increased in the car. Whitney began to take short, shallow breaths to counteract his scent. She kept her eyes glued to the road to refrain from staring at the play of muscles in his thighs, at the way his long fingers gripped the steering wheel in a light, almost caressing manner as he drove.

When he finally stopped in front of the cabin, Whitney was torn between leaping from the car or throwing herself into his arms. Slowly she pivoted her head toward him, and began to tremble when she met his gaze. He didn't move a muscle, but as she met his eyes she felt as if he'd touched every inch of her body. The sensation was intoxicating, and she knew that she had to know the reality of his touch and she had to know it now.

She reached out and stroked his jaw, thrilled by the way his chest rose and fell heavily, as she said, "Make love to me."

Sean closed his eyes and forced himself to count to ten. It was the only way he could refrain from dragging her into his arms, and he feared if he did he'd end up taking her right here and now.

But what little measure of control the count had given him was nearly shattered when he opened his eyes and saw her face. No one had ever looked at him so yearningly, so hungrily. He could barely find the strength to open the car door and climb out.

When he rounded the car and opened her door, she held out her hand, and something inside him recognized that it was more than a gesture for assistance, but a symbol of trust, and his heart expanded and contracted with the upheaval of emotions that flowed through him.

Silently he took her hand and led her into the cabin and up the stairs to the master bedroom. Only when they reached the top did he stop, and he turned toward her, his expression serious, as he said, "Make sure this is what you want, Whitney, because once we've made love, there'll be no turning back."

Whitney knew what an effort it had taken for him to say those words, and her heart swelled with her love for him, because she knew that no matter how much he wanted her right now, he would let her walk away. She stepped forward and drew his head down for a kiss in answer.

Sean groaned as he caught her lips, and he swung her up into his arms. He carried her to the bed and came down beside her as he lowered her to the mattress.

Whitney shifted restlessly as he undressed her slowly, gently touching her in the most erotic manner, which was even more devastating because he never touched her in an erotic place. By the time she was disrobed, her senses were humming, her nerves tingling, and her body burning. She tried to help Sean undress, but her hands were trembling so badly that he chuckled softly, pushed them away and stood by the bed to complete the task.

Sean couldn't remember ever feeling so aroused as he stripped off his clothes. Whitney's eyes were wide with hungry curiosity as she watched him, and he began to throb with desire as he watched feminine approval spark to life in their depths. His jeans had barely hit the floor before he was on the bed beside her.

Whitney shifted eagerly toward him. She didn't know who closed the distance between their lips. She only knew that he was kissing her, his tongue probing and seeking, and she wanted all he had to offer—wanted to give all she had to give. He gathered her against him, his legs tangling with hers.

"So soft," he whispered hoarsely as he swept his hand up and down her thigh, and then over the gentle slope of her hip to rest in the valley of her waist.

Then he kissed her deeply, passionately, forcing his hands to remain still. He had to have her, but he didn't want to rush her. He was determined to let her set the pace. It took all of his control to remain passive when she pressed her hips against him, and he groaned deep in his throat when her hands caressed his chest.

She teased and tormented, but he forced his hands to remain still. Only when she caught one and brought it up to her breast did he give free rein to his own desires. He palmed her until her nipple was hard, and then he moved to the other breast until she was whimpering against his lips. Leaning her back against the pillow, he replaced his hand with his mouth, and she arched to meet him.

He ached with the hardness of need, but he didn't want to take her yet. He needed to explore her—to discover the secrets that made her Whitney. He slid his fingers through the curls between her thighs and swallowed the small passionate cry that escaped from her lips.

"Sean, please," she whispered frantically as she clung to him. She'd never felt like this, had never experienced such need. She raked her fingernails over his back, his buttocks, his thighs and chest. "Please."

"In a minute," he soothed as he retrieved a foil packet from the nightstand.

His preparation was quick, and then he was back against her, his lips traveling over her face, her breasts, her abdomen, and then lower. She bit back her cries of pleasure as his lips and tongue tasted and probed. By the time he levered himself over her, she was so aroused that the first touch of him sent her over the edge. He slid his hand beneath her and cradled her against him until her world began to right itself.

Then he slowly began to enter her, and he paused when he met resistance. "Tell me if I'm hurting you," he rasped.

She nodded, not bothering to explain that he couldn't possibly hurt her as much as the need to have him inside her hurt. She cried out softly as he thrust deeper.

Sean paused again, waiting for her to adjust to him. His arms began to shake as he held his weight above her, afraid of crushing her, and sweat broke out on his body as he tried to hold back. He gasped when she began to move beneath him, taking more of him inside her with every tentative thrust of her hips.

And then he was buried inside her, and he began to move against her urgently. It was better than he'd imagined. Better than he could have ever dreamed. She was sweetness and light, passion and fire, and she was his. He came down over her, his lips claiming her, his tongue entwining with hers, and when she shuddered in release, he followed her.

Whitney had no idea how much time had passed when Sean rolled to his side and drew her against him. He stroked his hand along the length of her spine, and she cuddled against him, glad that he wasn't speaking. What they'd shared had been so wonderful, so utterly fantastic, that words would have only diminished it. She yawned, closed her eyes, and drifted into blissful slumber.

Sean lay beside Whitney, his hand continuing to stroke her as he listened to her breathing slow to the rhythm of deep sleep. He wanted to join her, but the wonder—the miracle—of what had just happened between them had shaken him to the core. They hadn't just made love, they'd shared a spiritual experience, and he'd believed that nothing like that could ever happen to him again.

He peered down at Whitney's sleeping face, touched by the delicate vulnerability of her features, and he gently stroked her tangled hair away from her face. He wanted to shake her awake, talk to her about how he felt, try to define the indefinable that had taken place between them. But she was sleeping so peacefully that he didn't have the heart to disturb her, and he curled protectively around her and joined her in her sleep.

NEAR DAWN, Sean stirred and reached across the bed for Whitney. The sheets were still warm where she'd lain beside him, but she was gone. He forced his eyes open, and glanced around the room, shivering as he sat up in bed and a breeze from the open sliding glass doors hit him. It was early September and, though it was Indian summer in Colorado's high mountains, the nights and mornings were cold. He shivered again as he crawled out of bed, and pulled on his jeans, but he couldn't find his shirt.

With a frown, he padded barefoot to the sliding glass doors. Whitney was wearing his shirt and leaning against the balcony railing, her elbows braced against it, and her chin cradled in her hands as she stared off into the distance.

"What are you doing?" he asked.

She glanced over her shoulder at him with a satisfied smile. "Contemplating the universe."

"And catching your death of cold," he muttered as he walked up behind her and drew her back against him. He wrapped his arms around her to share body heat. "So what conclusions have you reached about the universe?"

"It's vast and completely unfathomable."

"I couldn't have said it better myself." He rested his chin on the top of her head and swayed them from side to side. "It's freezing out here."

"Not freezing. Bracing."

"Well, it's bracing enough to give you pneumonia. Let's go back inside."

"In a minute." She rested her head against him and said, "You know, if anyone had told me a week ago that I'd be this happy, I'd have called them a liar."

He smiled, inwardly satisfied with her words. "Well, it's just the beginning. We've got the entire future ahead of us, and every day is going to get better and better."

"Is it?" she asked turning in his arms and staring up at him, unknowingly communicating her need for reassurance.

He gazed down at her fondly. "Do I need to pinch you again?"

"No."

"Good." He swept her up into his arms. "I've had enough bracing to last me for the entire day. Let's go back to bed."

"Don't you want to see the sunrise?"

He grinned. "Sure, but we'll do it from beneath the covers."

"We'd have a better view from out here."

"True." He carried her back into the bedroom and dropped her onto the bed. As he stripped off his jeans, he said, "But out there, I can't put my cold feet on you."

"Oh! That's cruel!" she exclaimed when he dropped into bed beside her and put his chilled feet on her leg.

"It's just punishment for waking me up so early," he said huskily as he reached for the buttons of his shirt. "I think I like this."

"Like what?" she asked throatily as he released the first button and pressed a kiss to her exposed flesh.

"Taking my shirt off you. All these buttons are positively enticing."

By the time he undid the last button, his lips were hovering over her womanhood. Whitney gulped as his warm breath stirred the silver-blond curls that protected her most feminine secrets.

"The sun!" she gasped when he gave her an intimate kiss.

"Don't worry," he murmured. "It'll rise again tomorrow."

WHITNEY STRETCHED luxuriously against the fur throw rug beneath her naked body and smiled at Sean's strong back and taut buttocks as he put another log on the fire. She reached out and trailed her fingers down his spine.

He shivered and glanced over his shoulder, one brow arching as he eyed the wanton look on her face. "My word, woman, you're insatiable," he grumbled halfheartedly.

"Are you complaining?" she asked huskily as he turned and lay down beside her, propping his head up with his hand.

"*Moi?*" he murmured as he caught a handful of her hair and let it trail through his fingers, thinking that this had been the most perfect week of his life, and he hated the thought that they'd be leaving tomorrow. They'd created a poetic idyll here, and he didn't like the thought of the real world intruding into their happiness.

"Penny for your thoughts," Whitney whispered as she reached up to stroke the frown lines that had suddenly wrinkled his brow.

"Only a penny?" he teased, finding himself oddly reluctant to share his feelings. "After what I paid for my education, I think my thoughts should be worth at least two cents."

"Ah, what the heck," she said with a laugh, "considering inflation, I'll give you a nickel."

"Mmm," he hummed in satisfaction as he leaned forward to press a tender kiss to her brow. Then he dropped another one to her lips before saying, "I was thinking how soft your skin is, how sweet your lips taste, how you make those sexy little mews when you're turned on."

He swept his hand over her flat stomach, the curve of her hip, down her thigh to her knee. "I was thinking of the way you tremble when I touch you. The way you cling to me when I make love to you." He raised his eyes to her face. "How much I'm going to hate leaving here, because this had been one of the most wonderful weeks of my life."

His words thrummed through Whitney, echoing her feelings. The only thing she would have added was how much she loved him. But she could never make that avowal until she knew that he returned her love—that he was willing to make her the most cherished woman in his life.

She sensed that he was close to that point. What they shared was too perfect—too extraordinary—for him not to be falling in love with her. He just needed time to figure it all out, and until he did, she was going to shower him with every ounce of love inside her.

"It has been *the* most wonderful week of my life," she said as she threw herself into his arms.

Sean rolled to his back, catching her in a crushing embrace, and buried his face in her hair. They lay there for a long while, and when she finally raised her head, her heavenly smile arrowed its way right to the center of Sean's soul. He caught the back of her head and pulled her toward him, so impatient to kiss her that he raised his head to meet her halfway.

Whitney clung to him, desperately needing to tell him with her body what she couldn't yet tell him in words. She pulled away and began loving him. Kissing him as he'd kissed her a thousand times during the week. Touching him as he'd touched her. When he tried to return her favors, she stopped him, and continued to torment him until he groaned harshly, lifted her over him, and surged into her urgently.

Where before they'd made love together, they now cleaved, and when it was over, Whitney collapsed atop him, unable to move, barely able to breathe.

She smiled as Sean wound his arms around her, whispering hoarsely, "I didn't know it could be this good."

"I didn't know, either," she whispered back.

But even as she said the words, a little voice began to nag inside her, insisting that there was something terribly wrong with what had just been the most wonderful loving of her life.

Chapter Fourteen

As she prepared a tray of cookies, milk and coffee, Whitney decided that if happiness could be rated on a scale of one to ten, hers was registering at a glorious twenty-five. Never in her most wild imaginings had she ever thought that she could feel this way.

When she and Sean had returned from their magical week at the cabin, she waited in nervous anticipation for the enchantment to end, but it never did. In fact, if anything, the past three weeks had made her feel bewitched. Even the long hours that Sean spent away from home hadn't dampened her spirits, for when he returned, he seemed determined to make up for each minute they'd been apart.

"Mama, I drew you a picture!" Amy exclaimed as she ran into the kitchen, interrupting Whitney's reverie.

"Oh, it's so beautiful," Whitney told her as she knelt on the floor and accepted the crayon drawing the child was holding out to her.

"Uh-huh," Amy said, excitedly pointing to it as she explained. "That's me and that's you. You're holding my hand."

"I sure am. Do you know why I'm holding it?"

Amy looked at her and nodded. " 'Cause you love me."

Whitney had to catch her bottom lip to control its sudden trembling. She smoothed the child's hair, touched her cheek and her chin, wondering how she could have been blessed with such a miracle—and Amy truly was a miracle.

"Yes, that's exactly why I'm holding your hand," she said huskily as she drew the child into her arms and hugged her tight. "And I'm never going to stop holding it. Not ever."

Whitney knew Amy didn't understand the significance of her words, but she seemed to sense the profundity of the moment, and she wound her arms around Whitney's neck and pressed a wet kiss to her cheek.

Then she pulled away and announced, "I'll draw you another picture."

Whitney's eyes dampened and she smiled a sappy smile as Amy raced out of the room.

"Something wrong?" Sean asked as he appeared in front of her and extended his hand to help her to her feet.

"Everything's wonderful," she murmured as she rose and went into his arms. "I just keep thinking that it has to be a sin to be this happy."

Sean tightened his arms around her at her words and buried his face in her fragrant hair as tears flooded his eyes. He had to agree with her sentiment, because he was happy—far happier than he could have ever imagined.

Feeling embarrassed by his mushy emotions, he pressed a kiss to her temple and said, "I came in here to find out what happened to those cookies you promised me."

"They're all ready to go," Whitney said, pulling away and reaching for the tray.

But Sean beat her to it, and she followed him into the living room where Amy was sprawled on the floor in her pajamas, so intent on pursuing her burgeoning artistic bent that she actually passed up the offer of cookies.

Whitney settled onto the sofa, pulling her legs beneath her as Sean handed her her coffee. She sat cuddled up next to him, loving the feeling of his arm draped around her shoulders. His soft, teasing kisses. His whispered promises of later passion.

When Amy fell asleep on the floor, Sean carried her upstairs, and Whitney went into the kitchen to finish loading the dishwasher. Sean joined her a few minutes later, wrapping his arms around her waist and pulling her back against him.

As he pressed a kiss against the side of her neck, he murmured, "By the way, I ran into Don this afternoon, and he wanted to know what you've decided about the conservatory."

Whitney stiffened at his words, but Sean was so intent on nibbling on her ear that he didn't notice.

He chuckled softly as he said, "I told him that we'd been too busy to think about it, but sweetheart, you need to make up your mind soon. Your house closes next week doesn't it?"

Whitney nodded and leaned her head back against his chest as her eyes traveled around the room, the sheen on her happiness dulling. She kept telling herself that she was being silly, that a house couldn't have any effect on what they were building, but no matter how hard she tried to ignore the feeling it was still there.

She didn't want to build her life with Sean in Margaret's home; she wanted a place that was new to both of them, a place where each memory was one that only they shared. She wanted to know that if they made love in front of the fireplace, he wouldn't experience a sense of déjà vu, that she'd be the only woman in his thoughts.

She turned in Sean's arms and looked up at him, warmed by the tender glow in his eyes, trembling beneath the sensuous stroke of his hands. She loved him so desperately, and she felt that he'd never be able to return that love if they remained here, if he was always under Margaret's aegis—always linked to his past with her.

"Sean, I want to move," she told him before she could lose her courage.

Sean blinked, certain he'd heard wrong. "Move? Why?"

"Because this house just isn't me."

Frowning, Sean lifted his head and glanced around the room, noting how few changes had been made. Lulled by the familiar, he'd never really noticed, or maybe he had and just hadn't been ready to face the fact that changes were necessary. He had no idea what Whitney's decorating taste was like because her mansion had been stripped, but he knew instinctively that it wasn't this.

An elemental part of him rebelled at change, but it was quickly overridden when he glanced down into Whitney's worried face. Tenderly he smoothed her hair away from her face.

"Honey, I've already explained the advantages of this house. I think redecorating would be a bit more reasonable, and definitely less of a hassle, don't you?" When she didn't respond, he gave her an encouraging smile. "Do whatever you want to the house, and while you're at it, pick out a design for the conservatory. You can't expect your buyers to hold on to your piano indefinitely."

Whitney didn't know whether to scream or cry at his response. He'd reminded her of the advantages of living here, which she knew were all valid. He'd also given her carte blanche to make changes. He'd offered her what he considered a pragmatic solution. How could she explain her feelings without sounding like a jealous child?

Not trusting her voice, she nodded and rested her head against his shoulder. But even as he rocked her reassuringly, she couldn't hold back the wave of desolation that washed over her.

When he whispered huskily, "Let's go to bed," she went with him, hoping that their lovemaking would restore her happy feelings.

As they stood beside their bed, Sean kissed her passionately, and she responded eagerly, and when he swept his hands down her body, passion flared through her so brightly she felt blinded.

"You're so soft," he murmured as he stripped her clothes from her and urged her down to the mattress, his own clothes disappearing magically.

She thought she'd die from need as his hands and lips honored her, cherished her, but she shivered from a sudden chill when he rolled away from her and reached for the foil packet. As she had during their last night at the cabin, she felt something was wrong—terribly wrong—but she couldn't put her finger on it. She switched on the bedside lamp, needing to see his face, needing to reassure herself that she was the one he was making love with.

When she turned back, Sean was regarding her with a questioning expression, and she smiled as she went into his arms.

"I want to see you make love to me," she said as she rained kisses over his face. His chest. His abdomen.

"Oh, Whitney!" he rasped harshly when her hands touched him intimately, delicately. He rolled, dragging her beneath him, and entered her urgently.

She couldn't have stopped her response to his lovemaking if she'd wanted to, but even as he brought her to the brink and pushed her over the edge, her gaze was still centered on his face. It was her image she saw in his eyes, her name vibrating on his lips. So why wouldn't the chill go away?

When Sean had fallen asleep, she crept into Amy's room and sat beside the child's bed, seeking solace. But when even Amy's sleeping countenance didn't comfort her, Whitney felt true panic, for she finally understood: she was building a fantasy out of dreams, and she knew far too well the fragility of dreams.

SEAN HUNCHED his shoulders against the cool October wind as he walked across the lawns of Whitney's mansion. She was standing out in the center of the rose gardens and staring at the house.

Knowing instinctively that she'd be upset after signing the closing papers, he'd taken the day off. When she didn't return home within a reasonable time, he left Amy with the neighbors and went looking for her.

"Everything okay?" he asked when he reached her side, linked an arm around her shoulders, and drew her against his side.

"Everything's fine," Whitney answered as she continued to stare at the house.

Sean had expected tears, and he was both confused by and distrustful of her dry eyes and resolute expression. He followed her gaze, hoping it would explain what she was feeling, what she was thinking. But all he saw was a large, sprawling house.

"Want to go inside one last time?" he asked her.

Whitney shook her head. Not knowing what else to do, Sean simply stood there holding her.

Several minutes passed before she said, "It's funny how you can twist your life around so it will be what you want it to be, isn't it?" Before Sean could respond, she continued with, "For years I considered this home because it was the place where I'd been the happiest. But today, when I was signing those papers, I realized that it wasn't home. It was just a house where I could relive twenty-year-old memories."

"But memories are what makes a house a home," Sean said as he pulled her closer, telling himself that he was protecting her from the wind, but knowing deep inside that he was trying to protect himself. Her words were prodding him, demanding to be analyzed.

She looked up at him, her smile pensive, even a little chastising. "No, Sean. It's creating those memories that turn a house into a home."

Sean felt something foreboding touch him, causing him to shudder inwardly. He tried to shrug off the sensation, but when he couldn't, he said, "How about if we go home and create some of those memories?"

Her hesitation was so slight that if he hadn't been attuned to her at that moment, he was sure he would never have picked up on it. But he had, and suddenly he had a feeling that everything was about to come apart.

Then he shook his head, telling himself that he was simply identifying with her mood. She was upset, therefore, he was upset. It was as simple as that. By the time he settled her into her car and climbed into his to follow her home, he'd convinced himself that all was well.

WHITNEY DIDN'T KNOW WHY she'd come to see Debbie. All she knew was that she needed to see her.

"Ah, it's the lady who's obsessed with roses," Debbie said, accepting the red rosebud Whitney extended.

Whitney didn't say anything as she sat down. Instead she tugged the grass at her feet.

"Something wrong?" the girl finally inquired.

Whitney glanced up at her with a frown. "No. Yes. It's one of those nagging little things that you can't quite put your finger on."

Debbie nodded with understanding. She reached out and brushed the rosebud against Whitney's cheek. "It'll come when it's time."

"You're so young," Whitney said with an indulgent smile. "How can you be so wise?"

Debbie smiled back as she leaned her head back against the tree trunk, and Whitney stared at her in awe. The smile transformed the average girl into a beauty.

"Life," she answered simply. Then she lowered her eyes to Whitney's, catching them in a mesmerizing gaze. "That's what it's all about, isn't it?"

"Yes, I suppose it is," Whitney murmured.

Debbie sighed heavily and announced, "I'm pregnant."

Whitney's eyes darkened with empathy. "How do you feel about that?"

"Scared," Debbie said as tears welled in her eyes. "I'm really scared. There are so many choices, and I don't know which one's right. Do you know what I want right now?"

"No," Whitney whispered, blinking against her own tears.

"I want my mother, but I don't even know where she is."

When the girl began to sob, Whitney came to her knees and drew her into her arms. As she stroked Debbie's hair, her own tears rolled down her cheeks.

"I'm here. I'll help," she told the girl hoarsely. "I'll help you, Debbie. I promise."

By the time Debbie had calmed to sniffles, Whitney had formed a plan in her mind. Now all she had to do was convince Sean, and she was sure he'd go along with her. If he didn't... But he would. He'd understand how much this meant to her.

SEAN COULDN'T FIND his wrench, and he was so frustrated he was ready to scream. For ten years it had been in the top, left-hand drawer of the kitchen cabinets. Now he couldn't find it, and of course, Whitney wasn't here to tell him where the damn thing was.

"Dammit, where did she put it?" he growled as he jerked open one drawer after the other.

"Put what?" Whitney asked from the doorway.

Sean's head shot up, and he glowered at her. "My wrench."

"It's in the toolbox under the kitchen sink."

Sean closed his eyes and counted to ten. Of course, that's where she'd put the tool—in the most logical place. But why in hell did she have to move it in the first place?

"Whitney, I know you think everything has its place and it should be in it, but stop moving my things. I can't stand it when I'm looking for something and can't find it. That wrench has been in this drawer for ten years and..."

His voice trailed off as his gaze finally centered on her face. It was evident that she'd been crying, and he immediately moved toward her.

"Honey, what's wrong?" he asked as he walked to her and drew her into his arms.

Whitney sighed heavily and rested her head against his chest. "I just left a pregnant runaway." She raised her face, tears glistening in her eyes. "She's so alone, Sean. Just like I was, and my heart went out to her."

He stroked her cheek. "Of course it did."

"I'm glad you understand," Whitney told him, "because there's something I'd like to ask you."

Sean tensed, sensing that what was coming was something he wasn't going to like. "What's that?"

"Can we take her in?" Whitney saw his frown and quickly continued before he could object. "She's all alone, Sean. She needs a feeling of home, a sense of belonging while she decides what to do about the baby. If we . . ."

Sean shook his head. "No, Whitney."

"But . . ."

"No," he repeated firmly. When she tried to pull away from him, he caught her and held her in place, determined that she hear his explanation for his refusal. "We'd be doing her a disservice by bringing her here. She has choices to make—hard choices—and being in our home will only make them harder. I also don't think you can distance yourself enough to let her make her own decisions."

"That's not true!" Whitney exclaimed fervently.

"It's not?" Sean arched a disbelieving brow. "Did you plan on telling her your story? Did you plan on telling her how you regained Amy? Are you willing to sit back, keep quiet and let her opt for abortion if that's what she wants?"

Before she could answer, he said, "And what if she decides to keep the baby, Whitney? Are you going to want to keep her here until she does? And when she has it and walks out the door, are you going to be able to let go? Or are you going to constantly be in touch, offering help and money and anything else she needs to make her life easier?''

"Would that be so wrong?" she questioned miserably.

"In ordinary circumstances, it wouldn't be wrong. But where does it stop, and when? First it's this girl, and then it's another, and another, and another. Before you know it, we'll be supporting half the unwed mothers in the city.''

"In other words, you don't want to dip into your fortune,'' she said as she pushed herself out of his arms and turned her back on him, more angry than she'd ever been in her life. Up to this point, Sean had always been compassionate. Where was that compassion now? "You don't want to help because it might lower your bank balance. Well, I'll use my money, and...''

"I don't give a damn about the money!" Sean exploded. Gripping her shoulder he spun her around to face him. "I'd gladly give every penny I have to help any girl in trouble, but I won't do it at the expense of my family. And that's what you'd be asking me to do, Whitney. Because of your own past, you'd want to help every suffering waif who came along, and you wouldn't be able to say no when some of them began to use you, and you know as well as I do that some of them would use you.''

"Stop lecturing me as if you're my father!" she yelled in frustration, not wanting to acknowledge his words but knowing that he was partially right.

"Right now you need a father, Whitney. You're asking Amy and me to take a trip down memory lane with you, and I can't let you do that to us. I have to protect our home.''

"Our home?" Whitney repeated sarcastically. "*Our* home, Sean? This is not my home. It's your home. It's your home that I'm not supposed to move anything in. It's your home that...''

"That what?" Sean asked when her voice trailed off.

"That you shared with Margaret! It'll never be my home because I hate every damn square inch of it!''

Sean shook his head. "You don't mean that, Whitney. You're overreacting because you're angry with me."

"I'm not overreacting, Sean," she stated, suddenly calm. "I'm just tired of living other people's lives and other people's dreams. I want my own life and my own dreams, and if I can't find them with you, I guess I'll have to find them without you."

"Just what in hell does that mean?" Sean demanded, his temper now flaring.

"That I'm tired of being a pawn, Sean," she said, tears welling in her eyes. Desperately she blinked them back; it was finally time for the truth. "I spent most of my life living for my father. I did everything he wanted. Everything that would make him happy. I felt I owed him because I was all he had. But after a time I began to hate him, Sean. I began to hate him, because I never mattered. It always had to be him. What he wanted. What he needed. I kept saying, when is it my turn?"

Sean took a step toward her, feeling the anger and the pain vibrating from her in waves. Wanting—needing—to protect her from them. "Whitney, don't do this to yourself."

She laughed shrilly and shook her head ruefully. "It's time I do this to myself. It's time that I face exactly what I am and who I am. Do you know how I got pregnant with Amy?"

Sean closed his eyes and shook his head, not wanting to hear the confession, but knowing that she wasn't giving him a choice. "No, how?"

"By plan. You see, Duncan was my escape. By marrying him, I could run away from my father. I could build my own life, but I wouldn't have to feel guilty about it, because I could still meet my father's social needs. I could still be his hostess, but I'd no longer be his chattel."

She drew in a deep breath before saying, "When Duncan wouldn't set a date for the wedding, I decided to shotgun him. Of course I didn't know then that he was only using me so he could rob my father blind. In a way my pregnancy was just punishment, because when it came right down to it, I was using him.

"Well, I'm tired of it, Sean. I'm tired of using, and I'm tired of being used. I'm tired of feeling guilty. I'm tired of being scared. I'm just tired, period."

"So what is it you want from me?" he questioned plaintively.

She shook her head sadly, knowing that it was over between them because she couldn't—wouldn't—live any more dreams. She wanted reality, and if she couldn't have it, she didn't want anything.

"If I have to tell you that, then it isn't worth having. I'll have my things moved into the guest room by evening."

With that she turned and walked out of the room, leaving a stunned Sean staring at the empty doorway. When she came back downstairs to fix dinner, he was gone. She fed Amy and put her to bed, then she went into the guest room and climbed into bed, feeling lonely and bereft, but finally cleansed. She'd faced the past, and now she could put it to rest forever. She was asleep almost the instant her head hit the pillow.

But two days later, Whitney discovered that not all of the past had been resolved. She stared at the calendar, counting the days and then recounting them, as that nagging feeling that something terribly wrong had happened at the cabin came into focus. The last time they'd made love there—the time when she'd been so eager to show Sean with her body what she couldn't say in words—he hadn't used protection.

She sat on the kitchen floor, buried her face in her hands, and cried. She couldn't believe her luck was so bad. One time. One lousy time, and she was pregnant. What in the world was she going to do?

Chapter Fifteen

ean had had to beg, borrow and promise a year's worth of
ndigent care to get Mary Beth Bauer to tell him the loca-
on and the name of the girl Whitney had been seeing. He
ecognized the girl before he even reached her. She'd been
a his office two weeks before, where he'd confirmed her
regnancy. When he came to a stop in front of her, she
lanced up, her eyes widening in recognition.

"Dr. Fitzgerald! Is . . . is something wrong?"

Sean smiled his reassurance. "Nothing's wrong, Debbie,
ut you shouldn't be sitting out here in the cold."

She looked confused. "If nothing's wrong then why are
ou here?"

"Because I'd like to talk to you." He extended his hand
nd helped her to her feet. Then he shoved his hands into his
ockets and shivered. "Is there someplace that we can go
'here it's warm?"

"The shelter."

Sean transferred his gaze to the building across the street
nd shook his head. "No, let's go out for a hamburger."

"Sure," the girl said in confusion.

Sean took her elbow and led her to his car. After he'd
limbed in beside her, he said, "I don't know the neighbor-
ood. You tell me where to go."

Debbie gave him directions to the closest fast-food res-
aurant, and he turned the ignition. They didn't speak until

after they were sitting at a table with their meals in front c
them.

Sean smiled as he watched the girl eagerly bite into he
hamburger and then stuff her mouth with French fries. Sh
glanced up at him, as if sensing his observation, an
blushed.

"I'm not supposed to eat this junk, huh?" she said guil
ily.

"A little splurging every now and then won't hurt you
Just don't make a habit of it."

She nodded and leaned back in the booth. Then she eye
him warily. "If nothing's wrong, then why are you here?"

He placed his elbows on the table and cradled his chin i
his hands. "You know my wife, Whitney, and she's wo
ried about you."

Debbie's mouth dropped open. "You're married to th
rose lady?"

The rose lady? Sean repeated silently. "Yeah," he sai
aloud.

"Well, isn't that something," the girl murmured. The
she eyed him suspiciously. "She said you were the best bab
doctor around. Are you?"

"I try to be," Sean said.

She seemed to mull over his response and then nodded, "
like that answer."

Sean grinned. "I'm glad. Now let's get back to Whi
ney."

"Sure. What about her?"

"She wants you to come live with us for a while, but I'
a little shaky about it. I'd like to help you out, but I'm als
a father. I know that when my little girl grows up, I'd like t
think that she'd at least give me a chance to mend th
fences."

"So you think I should call my old man, huh?"

"I think you should call your father," Sean answered.

"I don't know," Debbie said as she shifted uncomfor
ably in the booth. "If he finds out I'm pregnant, he's goin

o go through the ceiling. I'm supposed to be his little prin-
ess, and little princesses don't get knocked...pregnant, you
now?''

"If they didn't, there wouldn't be any little princes, you
now?'' Sean stated drolly.

Debbie laughed. "I like that."

Sean grinned again. "Well, what do you say?"

"I don't know." She gnawed on her bottom lip. "He gets
ally mad."

"Maybe that's because he really loves you."

"That's pretty corny."

"The truth usually is."

"Would the lady be there to..."

"Give moral support?" Sean provided.

"Yeah."

"If you want her to be with you, I'll make sure she is."

Debbie munched on her French fries, again seeming to
aull over his words. Then she nodded, "Yeah, if the lady'll
e there, I'll call him."

"Good. When would you like to make the call?"

"Oh, I don't know. I suppose I should do it right away so
won't get too nervous. When could you get your wife over
ere?"

"Well, we could save all of us some time if you just came
ome with me. You could use my phone."

"It's long-distance."

"I'll send you the bill."

The girl giggled and took another bite of her hamburger.
fter she swallowed it, she said, "You must really love the
dy, huh?"

"Yes," Sean answered. "I really love the lady."

He had to glance down to hide his misty eyes when Deb-
ie said, "I'm glad, because she's something special."

"You took the words right out of my mouth," Sean said
uskily.

"MAMA, I FELL DOWN," Amy whined as she entered th
back door and held up her elbow.

"Oh, that's terrible," Whitney crooned as she squatte
so she could eye the child's wound. The scratch was so smal
she wouldn't have seen it if it hadn't been pointed out. "
definitely think a bandage is in order, don't you?"

"A big one," Amy replied.

"Great big," Whitney agreed as she lifted Amy, carrie
her to the kitchen counter and sat her on it. "Now hold sti
while I get what we need."

She rummaged through the top cabinet and pulled dow
some antiseptic cream and sheer bandages. Carefully sh
washed Amy's elbow. Then she pressed a kiss against it.

"Feel better?"

"Yeah."

"Good," Whitney said as she smoothed cream over th
girl's skin and then applied a bandage. She pressed anothe
kiss against the tape. "Now it should feel as good as new."

"Brand-new," Amy said.

"Yes, brand-new," Whitney agreed as she placed he
back on the floor. Squatting in front of her daughter, sh
hugged her tight. "I love you, did you know that?"

Amy wrapped her arms around Whitney's neck an
hugged her back. "Uh-huh."

Whitney knew she was holding the girl too tightly, but sh
couldn't help herself. Outside of polite, one-syllable re
sponses, she and Sean hadn't spoken a word to each othe
in a week. The rift between them was tearing her in two. No
only did she love Amy to distraction, but now she was car
rying Sean's child. Somehow she had to find a way to mak
peace with him, but how? And how would he feel about th
baby? And . . .

"Whitney, we have a visitor."

Whitney jerked her head toward the sound of Sean'
voice. "Debbie!" she exclaimed in disbelief.

"Hi, lady," the girl said. Then she eyed Amy. "Cut
kid."

"Who's that?" Amy asked as she peered around Whitney, half curious and half cautious.

"This is my friend, Debbie," Whitney said as she rose to her feet and took Amy's hand. "Debbie, this is my daughter, Amy."

"Nice to meet you, kid," Debbie said as she extended her hand.

When Amy caught Whitney's leg and held back, Whitney said, "Amy, remember your manners and shake Debbie's hand."

Amy leaned her head back and peered up at Whitney. "Don't want to."

"Tough. Do it anyway," Whitney muttered.

When Sean snickered, she glared at him. He simply grinned and winked at her, his expression clearly stating: *You spoiled her.*

She put a hand against Amy's back and pushed until the child was forced to take a step forward. Amy reluctantly shook Debbie's hand, and then rushed back to hug Whitney's leg.

"So, Debbie, what are you doing here?" Whitney inquired curiously.

"Your old man...uh, husband, talked me into calling my old...uh, father. He thought I should give my...father a chance to mend the fences, and he said you'd give me..."

"Moral support," Sean said.

"Yeah," Debbie agreed on a nervous intake of breath. "So will you?"

"Of course," Whitney said quickly.

"The call's long-distance," Debbie offered.

Whitney cast a glance toward Sean, who merely stuffed his hands into his pockets and smiled at her. "That's okay."

"You're sure?"

Whitney knew that the girl was trying to delay the inevitable, and she nodded. "I'm sure. Let's use the phone in the living room."

"I'll take Amy into the backyard," Sean said as he caught the toddler and swung her up into his arms.

"But I want to go with Mama," Amy complained.

"Tough," Sean muttered and tickled her stomach. When she giggled, he said lowly to Whitney, "You and I are going to have a very serious talk about child rearing."

Whitney wrinkled her nose at him as she caught Debbie's arm and led her into the living room.

When Debbie was seated on the sofa with the telephone resting in her lap, she glanced up at Whitney and asked, "What do I say?"

"How about, 'Hi, it's Debbie.'"

Debbie drew in a deep breath, released it and lifted the receiver. Then she dialed the number. A few moments later she said, "Daddy, it's Debbie."

Tears began to spill down Whitney's cheeks as she watched the girl begin to cry. Soon it was apparent that she wasn't needed any longer, and she walked through the kitchen and into the backyard.

Amy was sitting on the front porch of her playhouse, and Sean was leaning against the side of the house watching her. When he heard the door close, he glanced toward Whitney.

"How's it going?"

"I think the reunion is going to be spectacular." She tugged self-consciously on the hem of her sweater as she said, "How did you find her?"

His gaze drifted back to Amy. "Let's just say that you really owe me, lady."

Whitney nodded and glanced away from him. "Thank you, Sean. You didn't have to do this."

"Au contraire," he murmured as he stepped forward, pulled her into his arms and tilted her chin upward. "I had to do it for the woman I love because she was hurting, and I was hurting with her."

Whitney's breath froze in her lungs as his words tap-danced through her head, but she couldn't—wouldn't—let herself believe what he'd said.

Sean, as if knowing her reluctance, smiled. "We need to talk."

"Yes," Whitney agreed. "We need to talk."

Sean wrapped his arm around her and tucked her against his side. "I told Debbie she could stay here until either her father comes to get her, or until she decides what to do about her pregnancy."

"Thank you," Whitney said again.

Sean hugged her tight as he said, "You don't have to thank me, Whitney. In fact, I should be thanking Debbie. Without her coming between us, I don't think I would have acknowledged what was staring me in the face. I was in love, but I was afraid to take a chance."

"And now?" Whitney asked hesitantly.

Sean's gaze drifted from Amy to her. "And now, lady, you're stuck with me for better or for worse."

"You don't know how much I love the threat of those words."

"SEAN, GET YOUR COLD FEET off me!" Whitney complained when he climbed into bed and immediately pressed his feet against her legs.

"Shh," he whispered as he kissed her once, twice, and then thrice. "We have a guest in the next room, remember?"

"Which is exactly why we're going to behave ourselves tonight, right?"

"Right," he agreed as he snuggled up to her. "All I need to do is hold you, anyway."

Whitney's eyes dampened. "I missed you."

"I missed you, too. Don't ever leave my bed again, Whitney. Yell at me. Scream at me. Throw something at me, but please don't ever leave my bed. I died a thousand deaths without you by my side."

"I died twice that many times," she whispered tearfully.

He caught her chin and raised her face so that it was framed in moonlight. "I love you."

"And I love you."

"You were right about the house. We need to move. We need a place where we can make a new start. Create new memories that are ours and only ours."

"You're sure? This house has so many advantages and..."

"To hell with the advantages."

His lips closed over hers, and though he coaxed, even pleaded, Whitney knew she couldn't make love to him with Debbie in the next room, even if there was a bath separating them.

She pushed away from his kiss reluctantly, vowing, "Tomorrow night."

"And every night thereafter. Swear that to me, Whitney. Every night thereafter."

"Every night thereafter. I promise."

Satisfied with her response, he tucked her head beneath his chin. He'd nearly drifted off to sleep when she said, "Sean?"

"Mmm-hmm."

"Do you remember our last night at the cabin?"

He eased his head back and gave her the evil eye. "I thought you wanted me to keep my distance tonight."

"I do. But..."

"But what?" he asked when she began to worry her bottom lip.

"Well, do you remember that last time we made love? In front of the fireplace?"

"Do dogs have fleas?"

"Sean, that isn't romantic," she groaned.

"Okay. Do roses have petals?"

"That's better."

"Good. Now where is this conversation leading?"

"Well, if you remember that last time—and really think about it—we, uh, did something wrong."

He raised his head off his pillow. "Are you complaining about my technique?"

"Of course not," she said impatiently. "It's just that..."

"That what, Whitney? The night isn't getting any younger, and Debbie's father is going to be here early."

"We forgot to use..."

"Protection!" Sean gasped as he sat straight up in bed. "Oh, my God, are you?"

Whitney nodded as she pulled the covers up to her chin in a protective gesture.

Sean stared at her in shock for several moments, and then he began to laugh so loudly that Whitney scolded, "Sean, you're going to wake everyone in the house!"

"I don't care!" he exclaimed. "In fact, I'm going to throw open the windows and shout it to the world. I'm going to..."

"Go to sleep," Whitney ordered as she gripped his shoulders and pushed him forcefully back against the mattress.

"Our baby?" he whispered huskily as his hand slipped between them and caressed her abdomen. "You're going to have our baby?"

Whitney nodded, and then hesitantly asked, "It's not going to make a difference about your feelings toward Amy, is it?"

His expression was immediately wounded. "How can you even think such a thing, let alone ask it?"

"Because I'm scared."

"Oh, Whitney," he murmured as he touched his lips to hers.

Epilogue

"Everything's all right, isn't it, Sean?" Whitney questioned worriedly after he'd attached the fetal monitor and studied the tape.

"Everything's fine," he murmured as he reached out and caught her hand, his eyes still glued to the strip. "Everything's just fine."

"You aren't saying that just to make me feel better?"

He turned toward her and smiled. "No, I'm not. Everything is A-OK."

"But I'm three weeks early!"

"That's not uncommon for twins, Whitney."

"But—" Her words were cut off as a contraction hit her.

Sean coaxed her through it, telling her when to pant, when it was okay to breathe again. His hand never left her abdomen.

"I wish you were going to deliver them," she told him when the contraction had ended and she'd managed to catch her breath.

"Sorry, but it's against the rules to treat a member of your family. Besides, I'd rather be holding my wife's hand."

"Your wife," she repeated, savoring the words. "Do you know how I feel?"

"Pretty uncomfortable?" he surmised.

"Wonderful," she corrected with a smile. "In fact, we've come full circle, haven't we?"

"Yes," Sean agreed as he brought her hand to his lips. "We've come full circle."

Seven hours later, Thomas Patrick and Anna Elizabeth were born, and as Whitney gazed at Sean, who was holding them in his arms, she knew that she'd never been happier in her life. She'd finally found reality, and it was far better than any dream could ever be.

Have You Ever Wondered If You Could Write A Harlequin Novel?

Here's great news—Harlequin is offering a series of cassette tapes to help you do just that. Written by Harlequin editors, these tapes give practical advice on how to make your characters—and your story—come alive. There's a tape for each contemporary romance series Harlequin publishes.

Mail order only

All sales final
